HER WICKED ROGUE

ROGUE'S GUILD
BOOK THREE

SCARLETT SCOTT

Her Wicked Rogue

Rogue's Guild Book Three

All rights reserved.

Copyright © 2023 by Scarlett Scott

Published by Happily Ever After Books, LLC

Edited by Grace Bradley and Lisa Hollett, Silently Correcting Your Grammar

Cover Design by EDH Professionals

This book or any portion thereof may not be reproduced or used in any manner whatsoever without the express written permission of the publisher except for the use of brief quotations in a book review.

The unauthorized reproduction or distribution of this copyrighted work is illegal. No part of this book may be scanned, uploaded, or distributed via the Internet or any other means, electronic or print, without the publisher's permission. Criminal copyright infringement, including infringement without monetary gain, is punishable by law.

This book is a work of fiction and any resemblance to persons, living or dead, or places, events, or locales, is purely coincidental. The characters are productions of the author's imagination and used fictitiously.

For more information, contact author Scarlett Scott.

https://scarlettscottauthor.com

For Aunt Julia a second time around. Thank you for amethysts, cinnamon sticks, applesauce, laughter, and for being a magical aunt to my girls the same way you've always been for me.
XO

PROLOGUE

*P*rincess Anastasia Augustina St. George wanted her uncle dead.

She had many excellent reasons for that wish. Chief amongst them, three: her mother and both of her brothers. Two were dead, and the third was missing.

Her uncle? Responsible for it all.

And that was why Stasia was walking on a terra-cotta path in the new August Palace gardens with a man who was as heartless and cold and cruel as could be. A man with a reputation to rival her evil uncle's. A man who was also a king, albeit a rightful one.

A man who would make her his queen, whether she wanted it or not.

She very much did not want it.

"We have a mutual objective, Princess," King Maximilian of Varros told her in flawless Boritanian, the language of her homeland.

Stasia supposed some would call him handsome, but to her, King Maximilian was merely massive and terrifying. He was imposingly tall of stature with thick muscles that strained beneath his traditional court garments, as if the shot silk could scarcely contain his strength. His countenance was perpetually grim and etched in stone, and he was fifteen years her senior. The stories about him were terrifying, and she had no doubt they were true. He was ruthless, his power as a ruler having grown to overshadow even the House of St. George in recent years. King Maximilian's island nation, situated east of Boritania, was incredibly wealthy, thanks to its massive trade.

Beneath the intense scrutiny of her uncle, who watched their progression from a dais across the gardens, Stasia pinned a polite smile to her lips. "Oh, Your Royal Highness?"

She had learned long ago to feign ignorance amongst enemies and to speak as little as possible. She wasn't yet certain she could trust King Maximilian, but he was her last hope if she wanted to leave Boritania alive and continue the search for her exiled brother. If she ever wanted to bring Gustavson the justice he so richly deserved.

"Your mother was executed," King Maximilian said.

Hardly the subject for a courtship promenade. The reminder of her mother's imprisonment and death made bile rise in her throat, but Stasia swallowed it down. To her dying day, she would regret not being strong enough to do something to save Mama from the unimaginable fate that had awaited her.

"It is forbidden to speak of," she managed past numb lips.

"By decree of the king," Maximilian said somberly. "I'm aware."

"And yet you dare to defy His Majesty." The title was bitter on her tongue, for it belonged to another.

Her beloved brother Theodoric, formerly known as His Royal Highness, Prince Theodoric Augustus St. George.

"You needn't defend him to me, Your Royal Highness." King Maximilian turned them cleverly so that their faces were averted, all whilst preventing them from committing the crime of presenting their backs to the king of Boritania. "I see the hatred in your eyes when you look upon him."

Had she been so obvious, so careless? Her mouth went dry at the thought that others could sense her true feelings where Gustavson was concerned.

"I do not know of what you speak. I love my uncle. He is the right and true king of Boritania." The oath she had been forced to speak upon Gustavson's ascension to the throne felt brittle on her lips.

"Twattle. Tell me the truth."

She didn't dare.

Stasia slanted a look up at King Maximilian, trying to gauge his motives, but his countenance was impossible to read. "Why would I tell Your Highness anything less than the truth?"

"Because you fear him," King Maximilian correctly guessed.

Of course she feared her uncle. He was a murderous snake waiting to strike. She had only reached the age of five-and-twenty because of her use to him as a pawn in the most advantageous marriage he could secure for her. Presently, King Maximilian. But only because previous suitors had failed to pass Gustavson's tests. And none of them had been nearly as powerful or wealthy.

"Why should I fear him?" she asked with false brightness, forcing another smile. "My uncle has blessed us all with his benevolence."

Sweet Deus, what a lie. She hated the way it weighed on her heart. *Mama, forgive me*, she prayed. *I only tell these lies for the sake of the kingdom and the lives of my siblings.*

"Benevolence," King Maximilian spat.

"You disagree, Your Highness?"

"Prevarication makes me unhappy, Princess Anastasia, and when I'm unhappy, those around me must pay the price."

"I do not doubt it," she said.

"Anyone who *has* doubted me has learned the error of his ways," the man at her side drawled, his voice cold. "Often, with blood."

They were speaking quietly, voices hushed, an outward show of civility for the benefit of her uncle, who had told Stasia in no uncertain terms that she must make this match.

Or forfeit her life.

The healed lashes on her back still seemed to sting and burn as she moved, the heat of the day sending perspiration trickling down her neck, between her shoulder blades, and lower. Her uncle had wielded the whip himself. Yet another reminder of why she must accept this marriage.

"Blood," she repeated now, wondering if King Maximilian threatened her life as well.

They stopped before a fountain that had been commissioned by her uncle, a towering monstrosity bearing one of the old gods of the sea. Gustavson had spared no expense in changing the August Palace to his liking. It bore precious little resemblance to the chambers and halls she had known so well.

"It is the currency most dear to man. Even the greediest of kings will cling to his life and forfeit all his riches."

"You speak from experience, Your Highness?"

"I've conquered my kingdom and laid my every enemy to ruin, Princess. What do you suppose the answer to your question is?"

A shiver rolled down her spine despite the sweltering sun above. "Are you threatening me, Your Majesty?"

"Warning you. When we marry, your allegiance will be to me. Anything less will end poorly for you."

He said it as simply as if he were speaking of the cloudless sky overhead.

Her allegiance would always be to Boritania. To her homeland. Her family. But she had been pretending otherwise for years, and it would be no different when she was married.

She inclined her head. "My allegiance will be yours alone."

Another lie in a string of so many. She no longer counted them.

"And what of your family?" he asked, voice low. "Specifically, your brother?"

"Reinald is gone," she said numbly, for she knew that Gustavson had arranged for her brother's murder but wasn't able to prove it.

"Your *other* brother, Princess."

Shock washed over her. No one spoke of Theodoric. It was forbidden.

"I have no other brother," she lied again swiftly, using the words she had been trained to say following Theodoric's exile. Anything less was treason and punishable by death.

"He is very much alive and living in London," King Maximilian said. "He uses another name."

Hope leapt in her heart, but she tamped it down, for that delicate emotion had no place in her life. "Why do you tell me this?"

"Because I want to see Gustavson overthrown, and I believe your brother is the only man who can do so."

The blunt revelation made her sway, nearly losing her balance. She stopped, forgetting the role she was meant to play for a moment. Forgetting about the possibility of incurring her uncle's wrath.

"I've shocked you."

King Maximilian's grim observation cut through her whirling thoughts.

She inhaled a deep breath and then slowly exhaled, formulating her response. "How can that be done when my brother has been in exile for ten years?"

It was a dream, what the king was speaking of—to have her brother back in Boritania where he belonged. To overthrow the usurper Gustavson and make him pay for what he had done to their family. And yet, she wasn't certain if she could trust the diabolical man at her side. He was dangerous, to be certain. Impossible to read.

But if what he said was truth, he was also about to give her a chance to save her homeland from ruin and corruption at the hands of her uncle.

"I have a plan, Your Royal Highness," King Maximilian said. "All you have to do is pledge me your loyalty and promise to become my wife, and together, we will see Boritania restored and the rightful king upon her throne."

Stasia didn't hesitate. "You have it."

As they continued on the path leading them back to Gustavson's dais, she fervently prayed to the gods that she hadn't just made a bargain she would live to regret.

CHAPTER 1

The first time he met Her Royal Highness, Princess Anastasia St. George, she offered him a king's ransom in jewels to help find her brother, an exiled Boritanian prince.

The second, she asked him to take her virginity.

It was a gray day laden with fog, thin mist falling beyond the windowpanes on the opposite end of the chamber. The princess had arrived at Archer's town house unannounced and uninvited, two facts which displeased him greatly. And despite all logic and common sense, he wanted to feel her lips beneath his with the fiery passion of a thousand burning suns.

Despite that aberrant desire, his answer was swift and curt. He didn't dabble in deflowering spoiled royalty.

"I'm afraid I cannot, Your Royal Highness."

Beneath the brilliant purple of the cape she hadn't removed for her unexpected call, she gave a delicate shrug, as if his response was of no concern. "I shall have to find another man willing to aid me, then."

He was beginning to think the woman was a Bedlamite.

"Another man?" he repeated in a growl.

Did she mean to imply that any chap with a ready cock would suffice for the task? Had she chosen him out of *convenience*? And why did the notion rankle him so? It was hardly his concern who the stunning woman before him bedded or why.

The princess folded her hands demurely in her lap, looking effortlessly regal with her chestnut hair in a chignon and a myriad of perfect little curls at her temples. "If you don't wish to help me, then I must find someone else."

This, she said as if it were the most reasonable of utterances. As if she offered her maidenhead as a common occurrence. He shouldn't be curious. Nor should he be entertaining the twin sharp edges of jealousy and lust, but they were nonetheless a blade carving through him, preparing to lay him low.

Archer rested his elbows on the polished rosewood desk between them, leaning forward. "How do you propose to find someone else, Princess?"

"I don't desire to attend a house of ill repute for the obvious risks involved to my reputation," she said, frowning. "However, if I'm left with no suitable alternatives, I suppose I must consider it. Tell me, Mr. Tierney, are there discreet brothels for ladies in London, or do they only serve the appetites of gentlemen?"

Did madness run in the Boritanian royal line? It was the only explanation; he was sure of it. And yet, she sat opposite him calmly—her English as flawless as the rest of her—undeniably lucid. Holding his gaze without shame. Elaborating upon her utterly asinine plan to give her body to a stranger as if it were unexceptional.

"You cannot go to a brothel," he told her.

She arched a finely shaped brow. "Why can I not?"

Because the thought of her with some faceless man—of

another man touching her at all—made him long to send his fist crashing into a skull. But there were other reasons, more important reasons, he would provide. Reasons that didn't make him sound so bloody muttonheaded.

"You are a princess," he said instead.

A small smile curved her lips, as if she were amused by his pronouncement. "I would take care to hide who I am, Mr. Tierney. Naturally, any establishment where I might obscure my face with a mask for the duration would be a necessity. I'm no fool. How do you suppose I have managed to escape my uncle's guards thus far?"

"I would imagine you've been slipping laudanum into their tea or something equally cunning," he drawled.

Her smile grew, and the full effect was like a blow to the gut—for a moment, he felt light-headed. Until he firmly tamped down the sensation and reminded himself that desiring the woman before him was the height of foolishness. And he hadn't lifted himself from the bowels of London to his current height by doing stupid things.

"I do like the way you think, Mr. Tierney," she said smoothly. "However, my methods are far less diabolical, I'm afraid."

He waited for her to elaborate, but she didn't offer an explanation for the feat she had performed on two occasions thus far. He had eyes and ears everywhere, and his men had sworn to him she had arrived and departed alone. Just as he had been assured that the jewels she had offered him in payment were genuine.

Archer lost his patience. "You aren't inclined to tell me what your methods are?"

Dark lashes swept over icy-blue eyes, keeping her secrets. "Perhaps I prefer to make you wonder."

"Is it not dangerous to you, stealing away from the king's guards?" he pressed, for he did not doubt it was.

From the moment she had first come to him seeking his help in finding her exiled brother, Archer had turned his attention toward learning everything about her and the royal family of Boritania that he could. Her uncle, King Gustavson, was known for his iron rule.

Another shrug, her delicate shoulders rising and falling beneath the fabric of her cloak. "It is a danger I happily risk."

He didn't begin to understand her, and despite his best intentions, that intrigued him.

"Why do you want this?" he bit out, thinking again of her proposal, although he knew he should not. "Not the search for the exiled prince, but...the rest."

The loss of her virginity, he meant, but he couldn't speak those words aloud for fear of the effect they'd have upon him. Already, the notion of making her his, of having her beneath him in bed, was a sensual taunt he couldn't quite excise from his mind. Enough to make his blood simmer and his trousers grow far too snug.

"I prize my freedom," she said. "For ten long, merciless years, I have had to sacrifice it for the good of my people. And soon, I'll enter an arranged marriage for the same reason. I want something that is my choice alone. Something that is for me, before I must resume my duty. This time I spend in London may well be the only chance I have. If you're not amenable, I'll find someone else who is."

The devil she would. A strong, protective instinct rose, one that wouldn't be quelled. Because he understood, to his marrow, how it felt to sacrifice himself for others. He'd been doing it from the time he'd been born as the illegitimate son of a marquess and a London actress.

"You are intent upon this course, Your Royal Highness?"

She held his gaze, unwavering. "I am."

Heat unfurled through Archer, the air in the room seeming suddenly heavy with possibility. "Then prove it."

Then prove it.

Three words from the wickedly handsome man's lips before her that Stasia hadn't expected.

But then, Mr. Archer Tierney was laden with mysteries and temptation. Shrouded in darkness, countenance hewn from granite, voice as cold as the green stare holding hers captive. Dangerous, was what she had been told. Or at least, what Tansy had reported back to her after making discreet inquiries on her behalf when they had first arrived in London.

Stasia had known she was taking a risk, coming to Tierney with her request. From the moment they had first met, she had been drawn to him in a way she couldn't deny. In the old beliefs of her homeland, fate was an impossible force to resist, and she knew in her marrow that this man was meant to be hers, at least while she still had her freedom.

He wasn't just sinfully handsome, with his mahogany hair and tall, muscled form. He carried himself with power and grace and barely leashed civility. He bore the cool poise of a man who could sink his blade deep into the heart of his opponent whilst holding his gaze and never once flinching. A man who took what he wanted without asking.

A man she very much wanted to take *her*.

Still, she hadn't anticipated such a response. But there was no retreating now. She had come this far, all the way to the dragon's lair. Her chin went up. She had faced far more formidable foes without cowering. Her enemies within the unlawful king of Boritania's circle were many.

"How shall I prove it?" she asked him defiantly.

His upper lip curled, and somehow the sneer served only to heighten the potency of his allure. "You expect me to believe a coddled, spoiled princess who has been treated gently all her life can merely walk into a brothel and give herself to the first willing man?"

His voice was low, but there was a bite to his tone that might have instilled fear in her had she truly been the spoiled princess he believed.

If he knew what she had endured these last ten years of her beloved brother's exile, living in the shadow of her evil uncle's wrath, she had no doubt Tierney would eat those words.

"I expect nothing, Mr. Tierney," she said calmly. "You may believe whatever you wish."

"Stand."

His curt order took her by surprise. No one commanded a royal of the House of St. George. It was her birthright to take precedence over every other soul in the room unless the usurper king was within.

Stasia remained seated, ignoring Tierney's directive. "I haven't given you leave to speak to me so boldly, sir."

"You just asked me to take your maidenhead, and you've arrived at my town house uninvited and unannounced," he pointed out bluntly. "That damned well gives me leave to speak to you however I like."

He was challenging her. She liked it. As Gustavson's niece, no one in court ever dared to defy her, dreading his reprisal. The lack of opposition—along with the fear of her uncle that she possessed as well—had long since grown tiresome.

"Of course it doesn't," she countered smoothly, refusing to wilt beneath Tierney's steely regard.

"You do understand what losing your virginity to a man like me entails, do you not, Your Royal Highness?"

A man like *him*. Hadn't he just told her he could not? Was he questioning his refusal?

Heat crept up her throat. Not because she was ashamed of the request she had made. But because she was thinking about Archer Tierney touching her. Thinking of what he must look like stripped of his garments. Thinking of him buried inside her. Of the two of them joined, body and spirit.

She swallowed hard. "I understand fully."

He shook his head, jaw rigid and unyielding. "I don't think you do. Because if you did, you never would have come to me alone, in the depths of the night."

Stasia would own that she had taken a risk. But after many careful years of planning and plotting, whilst knowing she would be forced to marry King Maximilian of Varros, she was more than prepared to court danger. She had to, in order to find her beloved brother Theodoric alive. And she could not lie. The small taste of freedom she had enjoyed in London, beyond the reign of her fiendish uncle, had emboldened her. Had made her want something selfish before she must resign herself to a life of misery and duty.

As had the way Archer Tierney had looked at her when they had first met, as if he were disrobing her with his eyes. As if he could show her untold pleasures. As if she might turn to flame beneath his knowing hands.

"You misunderstand me, Mr. Tierney," she told him, refusing to look away or show any sign that his gruff demeanor and harsh words intimidated her. "That is precisely why I have come."

"Then you will do as I say, Princess." He leaned back in his chair, his long fingers gripping the carved wood of the armrests. "And stand."

Was this a game? Did he test her to see if she would falter in her resolve? Or was he attempting to change her mind?

They stared at each other, at an impasse for what seemed an eternity but must have only been a moment.

"Stand," he growled into the silence. "Or get out of my bloody house."

Very well. If he wanted to see her mettle, she would show him.

"As it pleases you, Mr. Tierney." Head held high, Stasia stood, holding herself with the regal bearing she had been taught from an early age that she must present at all times.

Never show anyone weakness, her uncle often said, his voice like the lash of the whip he liked to use against anyone who defied him. Stasia had the scars on her back to prove it. The beating had only made her stronger, and now she would use that strength to destroy him.

But first, she had to find her brother.

"Your cloak," Tierney said quietly, his voice like warm silk to her senses. "Take it off."

Her fingers found the clasp at her throat, unfastening it. Slowly, she shrugged it from her body, draping the royal Boritanian purple garment over the back of the chair she had vacated. As she did so, her gaze never wavered from his. The tension in the room was thick and palpable, and a new awareness settled over her, making heat pool between her thighs and her nipples tighten behind her stays.

He remained seated as she removed her cloak, an insult to her station that she had no doubt was intentionally committed.

"Come here."

He crooked a finger, beckoning like some manner of sinful king seated upon a throne of hedonism. And heaven help her, she wanted to join him there. But she wasn't so easily swayed.

"Why should I?" she asked boldly.

Tierney smiled, and dear, sweet Deus, she felt the effect of that smile to her toes. That smile was wickedness personified, and with his sensual lips curled upward, his masculine beauty was enough to make her heart pound faster.

"Because I'm going to show you how wrong you are, my sweet, innocent princess," he drawled.

A challenge.

She couldn't resist.

And she intended to be the one who proved him wrong.

Stasia moved, circling his desk, closing the distance separating them. The civility with which they had been conversing dissipated as the last barrier keeping his body from hers was removed.

Watching her with a hooded gaze, he extended a long leg and used the heel of his gleaming boot to push back his chair so that he faced her as she approached. His legs were splayed wide, his thighs encased in snug trousers that showed the lean musculature of his form. His waistcoat was spare and black, his cravat snowy white and simply tied. His shirt sleeves provided a stark contrast to his waistcoat and trousers. It was as if good and evil were met in one.

She stopped at his boots, the air of challenge crackling hot in the air around them. "Show me, then, Tierney. I grow weary of this game of yours."

His smile deepened as he gave a harsh little laugh. In the next moment, he stood and his hands were on her waist, clamped and firm. He lifted her, turning. In a blink, her bottom was on his desk, his hands sliding down to her thighs. He moved closer so that she was trapped on her perch, stranded on his desk with his big body pinning her in place.

The forbidden flesh between her legs pulsed.

"If you were mine, I'd ask you to lift your gown," he said, his voice deep and rough now, almost feral. "To pull the hems of your dress and petticoats and chemise all the way up until they were pooled in your lap."

The fight fled her, replaced by an aching, burning need.

She fisted her fingers in the muslin of her skirts, ready to do what he had just described. To do whatever he asked of her.

But Stasia had been fighting for ten years, and she wasn't going to surrender now.

"I don't belong to any man," she protested, although her voice was vexingly breathless, giving away the effect he had on her. "Even if you bedded me, I wouldn't be yours."

One day soon, she would become King Maximilian's. She thought of him: icy, disinterested, harsh, and bitter. He was as handsome as he was callous and cruel. He didn't want her; he craved the power a marriage to her would bring him. And she, in return, didn't want him. Their marriage bed would be cold and passionless. There was no spark between them. Not even a speck of what she felt whenever she was in Archer Tierney's presence.

For Tierney, she burned.

"Wrong, Your Royal Highness," he said, stroking her jaw in the faintest of caresses and making everything inside her melt.

Bringing her back from the grim thoughts of the future awaiting her.

His touch was fire. She wanted more.

"No one dares to tell me I am wrong," she managed to say coolly.

"Someone damned well should have before now." His fingers hooked lightly around her ear, tucking the curls framing her face away with a gentleness that made her stomach flip. "If they had, I daresay you wouldn't be here, offering your innocence to me."

He withdrew from her, the absence of his touch leaving Stasia bereft.

"I asked, and you refused," she reminded him. "But I am more than happy to offer myself to another. Perhaps even this very night."

His jaw tensed again, and he tipped his chin up, considering her with glacial resolve. "Lift your skirts, Princess."

Her fingers clenched in the muslin. Her body was newly awakened, and every part of her felt greedy and ravenous. She told herself she was following his command to prove him wrong.

But as she bunched up the fabric and pulled her hems past her knees, she had to acknowledge that it was far more than that. She *wanted* to lift her skirts for this man. Wanted to do everything and anything he demanded of her. Longed for him as she had never longed for another.

His heated gaze flicked to the stocking-clad limbs she revealed.

"Like this?" she asked defiantly. "Is this what you believed I wouldn't do?"

"All the way to your lap," he bit out instead of answering.

She continued, cool air kissing her legs through thin silk, past her garters, exposing the bare tops of her thighs, careful to keep them pressed together. It was shameless, half her body on display. But she wasn't embarrassed. Not in the slightest. She didn't recall ever feeling more alive.

Her lips had gone dry; she licked them, keenly aware of his stare on her legs. "Have I proven myself now?"

His gaze lifted to hers, his lips tilting upward in jaded amusement. "Hardly. Show yourself to me."

Show herself to him? What more could he wish?

"I'm afraid I don't understand."

"Before a man buys a horse, he inspects it thoroughly."

His voice was like smoke, curling around her. But sinful and soft, too. A caress in itself. But his words were another matter entirely. He had her thoroughly confused.

"What has a horse to do with the matter of another man bedding me?"

A brow rose in challenge. "Another man?"

Did that mean he had changed his mind? Her foolish heart leapt.

"Since you have declined to perform the task, it stands to reason that I must seek someone else," she explained with a patience she didn't feel.

Inside, she was heated and confused and filled with yearning and desire.

He shook his head, the smile leaving his sensual lips. "You're not going to find another man, Princess."

Her breath quickened. "Why were you speaking of horses?"

"An explanation, love. I wouldn't buy a horse without examining him, and I won't bed a woman without knowing what awaits me."

Some of her ardor cooled. How...transactional. She severed the connection of their gazes and glanced down at herself. Her fingers remained clenched on her skirts, holding them so tightly that her knuckles were white.

Her stare snapped back to his. "I'm not a horse, and you aren't buying me."

"If I'm to take the risk of bedding you, I want to see my reward. Spread your legs for me, Princess." He paused, his tone mocking, challenge glittering in the depths of those green eyes. "Or get out."

She inhaled slowly. She could do this. She *wanted* to do this.

Wanted him.

Yes, her mind was made now. It had to be Archer Tierney or no one else.

Stasia took a deep breath and slowly parted her knees.

CHAPTER 2

All the air fled Archer's lungs, and need—violent, dark, and potent—knifed through his body, making his cock stand to attention.

He hadn't believed she possessed the courage to do it.

He had sworn she would whip her skirts back down to her ankles, shocked. That she would sweep from his study with august disgust and flee into the night, her reckless invitation forever forgotten.

But no. Princess Anastasia was still perched on his desk, holding his stare in challenge, and her legs were moving. Opening. The mouthwatering expanse of her creamy thighs above her garters called for his hands, his mouth, his teeth. My God, he wanted to bite that pliant flesh. Wanted to mark her as his, even as he knew that he couldn't.

He had to put an end to this madness.

His hands shot out, eager for her smooth, silken skin. Unprepared for the heat and decadent temptation of her. He caught her hips, holding her still, keeping her from exposing herself to him any more fully, even though it was sheer agony to do so. He wanted to see her pretty pink cunny more than he wanted to live another goddamn day.

Wanted to know if she was as wet from their little battle of wills as he was hard.

"Stop," he rasped, as much to himself as to her.

Because if this show of determination progressed any further, he was going to fuck her right here on his rosewood desk. He was going to take everything she offered him and more.

But he couldn't do that. She was a virgin and she was a princess promised to wed another, and she had paid him a fortune to find her brother. And he wasn't precisely a man of honor, nor a gentleman, but even Archer possessed an inconvenient conscience that chose to rear its head on the odd occasion.

Her lashes fanned over her eyes, those full, berry-red, bed-me lips of hers parting on an irritated sigh. "I thought you wanted to inspect me like a horse, Tierney."

Christ. She was using his own callous words against him. He had been attempting to teach her a lesson, and he was failing utterly. She was so deliciously daring, a lure the likes of which had never perched on his desk and lifted her skirts all because he had asked it of her. Her skin was silken and hot, her hips deliciously curved. He wanted to glide his palms higher. To take her hems all the way up. To explore her lavish, womanly form in every manner he could.

"You deserve better than this, Princess," he ground out, trying to ignore the ache in his ballocks, the ruthless need to drive himself inside her. "A quick shag on the desk isn't any way to lose your maidenhead."

"You're toying with me." Her eyes narrowed. "I don't like it."

Oh, the toying he wanted to do with her. Not this sort. He'd start with that mouth of hers. Work his way down her throat, to her breasts. Would her nipples be hard and begging to be sucked? Somehow, he couldn't shake the feeling that Princess Anastasia would be every bit as bold and direct in bed as she was outside it.

He swallowed hard against a wild rush of lust. *Not mine*, he told himself. *I can't have her.*

But what if he *could* have her? What if he took what she offered? Surrendered to the desire thundering through his veins?

"Wrong," he growled. "I'm proving to you what a foolish idea it is to attempt to give yourself to a stranger."

"I didn't ask you to prove anything to me." Her blue eyes flashed with icy fire as she considered him with a regal regard. "I asked you to bed me."

Saint's teeth, this princess was going to be the death of him. His resolve was weakening by the second, obliterated by the need to surrender to the temptation she presented. The yearning to give her what she had asked for and more.

"You don't want this," he protested, but he was thinking again of her reasoning—that she longed for something for herself.

I want something that is my choice alone, she had said. *Something that is for me, before I must resume my duty.*

"Don't tell me what I want," she said, her voice husky.

There was desire in her tone, matching the lust burning inside him. The way she looked at him, the way she defied him, the way she carried herself. There was something deeply intoxicating about Princess Anastasia St. George, in a way that transcended her beauty.

He couldn't let her go.

Archer's body moved of its own volition, his head dipping, and he sealed his lips over hers. Lightly at first and then deeper and harder as his control gave way. Her mouth was smooth and full and responsive, so responsive. The scent of her, exotic and floral, sweet orange and jasmine, enveloped him. Everything about her was lush and decadent and rare, as if she were some ancient goddess brought to life, to lay him low. And he was lost to the potency of his reaction to her.

Still gripping her hips, he stepped between her parted thighs. She made a needy sound low in her throat, kissing him back as she twined her arms around his neck, holding him to her. He was suddenly ravenous. He wanted her tongue, wanted her teeth, wanted her panting and breathless, her mouth swollen from his kisses, every inch of her lovely body bared to his gaze.

To fuck and fill her. To make her his.

The intensity of his reaction astounded him.

Terrified him, if he were brutally honest, and he was a man who feared precious little.

She's not for me, he reminded himself. All while the cutthroat within him who had been forced to make his living in a rough and cruel world chanted victoriously. *Mine, mine, mine.*

Mine as he licked into her mouth, tasting her for the first time.

Mine as her tongue writhed against his and she tangled her fingers in his hair.

Mine as his fingers trailed higher, pushing up her gown and petticoat and chemise, seeking more of her.

He'd never been afraid to seize what he wanted before. Money, power, houses. He had ruined men without compunction. Nothing and no one had stood in his way. Why not take this beautiful princess for his own, too? She had come to him. Had chosen *him*.

Of all the men in London who would have fallen at this beautiful princess's feet and kissed her hems in awe, she had offered herself to the bastard son of a marquess who had scrabbled and clawed his way up from the depths of the city's seedy underworld. Her sheer, reckless daring ought to be rewarded.

And wouldn't he give her satisfaction? Wouldn't he touch her more tenderly than some thoughtless stranger? The things he could teach her…

He was a sinful and wicked man, and with the princess's tongue gliding along his, her breasts crushed against him in willful invitation, the last attempts at clinging to his rapidly dwindling conscience failed utterly. He was going to bloody well have her.

But first, he would show her the pleasure she deserved. He would show her the difference between a man who would take her solely with his own needs in mind and a man who would make love to her gorgeous body until she was trembling and weak and her cunny was soaked and aching for fulfillment.

With great reluctance, he left her lips, dragging his mouth along her jaw, not stopping until he reached the whorl of her ear. Her ragged breaths gratified him, imbued him with even more desire. She wanted him every bit as much as he longed for her. They were well matched in their passion, if not their stations.

"If you're going to give your innocence away, make sure the bargain is worth your while, Princess," he whispered, slowly trailing the fingers of his right hand higher, along her inner thigh. Velvet-smooth softness greeted him along with the heat of her center. "This is why you can't offer yourself to any man with a cock. Not every chap knows how to make a woman come, and even if he does, he might not give a damn."

Relentlessly, he moved his fingers to the juncture of her thighs, tracing lightly over her seam. And God's bones, she was wet. So fucking wet. He had to grit his teeth against the animalistic surge of need the discovery incited within him.

Wet from a kiss.

Wet from their banter.

Wet and ready and waiting for him to touch and tease and pleasure.

"C-come?" she murmured, the innocent befuddlement in her tone enough to make him groan.

Gone was the steel-eyed princess who had waltzed into his study and coldly offered him her virginity. In her place was someone softer and hesitant. Someone vulnerable.

The knowledge was like a vise closing on his heart.

He laughed. What a lamb she was, being led to slaughter. But she had come to him with this request, had she not? He would have relegated himself to the task of searching for her brother alone. The idea had been hers. But it had infected his mind like a curse, and now he was nothing but a man controlled by his hard prick.

"Come," he repeated, giving her another slow, light stroke with his forefinger alone. "It means to find your pleasure, Princess. To orgasm. To experience true ecstasy, whether at the hands of yourself or another."

"Oh," she said with feeling.

And damn it if his cockstand didn't grow more determined at her tacit acknowledgment that she had given herself such pleasure before, but that she hadn't recognized the name for the act. Boritanian was her native tongue, but her English was remarkably good. One could almost forget that she hailed from a foreign kingdom.

That she was a royal princess.

Except everything about her felt different and rare and beyond his filthy reach. A man could bring himself up from the dirt, but he could never become anything more than what he'd been born to be, not truly. That was the lesson Archer Tierney had been forced to learn in exacting measures.

And yet, here he was, with his hand up Her Royal Highness's skirts. Petting her very drenched, very wanton cunny.

"You've done it before, haven't you?" he murmured, taking the lobe of her ear in his teeth and nipping as his finger made another deliberate swipe, gathering her wetness on his fingertip. "Touched yourself."

When she didn't respond, he parted her folds, glancing over the swollen bud at the apex of her sex. Her hips jerked.

"Your answer, Princess," he demanded, settling his lips at the hollow behind her ear and inhaling deeply of her divine scent.

He was sure that nothing—not even heaven itself—would ever smell as bloody good.

"Yes," she hissed, giving him what he wanted.

"How wicked of you." But he was smiling as he said it. Smiling as he dragged his lips down her throat to where her pulse beat fast and frantic.

"You don't sound particularly shocked," she murmured, tilting her head back, clutching his shoulders.

"Nothing shocks me, darling." He couldn't resist giving her an openmouthed kiss, sucking a little on that very sensitive skin.

Would he leave a mark? If he did, she would have to put her powder or a fichu to use, to hide the evidence. He told himself it shouldn't matter, that she had offered herself up to him. That he should take whatever he wished.

And yet, he couldn't help but think of her returning to the town house the king of Boritania had leased. Returning to those dead-eyed guards her uncle had forced upon her. He didn't like it.

"Since you've brought yourself to orgasm, then you understand the difference," he said, swirling over her pearl again. "There are some men who would only concern themselves with slaking their own lust. They wouldn't give a damn about your satisfaction. They would fill up your pretty cunny and take you until they came and then leave."

"Don't...talk about them," she muttered, nails digging into his shoulders through his coat and shirt. "I don't want to think about anyone else. I only want to think about you."

She wasn't thinking of the faceless prospects for taking her maidenhead, he suspected, but of the husband she would soon be forced to marry. Fair enough. He didn't want to think about that either. Not when she was in his arms.

Not when her cunny was soaked and hot and restless beneath his questing fingers.

"You deserve to be taken gently," he said against her skin. "To find your pleasure. To come over and over again."

She writhed into his hand, a breathy sigh falling from her lips, and for the first time in their admittedly brief acquaintance, Her Royal Highness, Princess Anastasia St. George didn't have a single retort to offer him. Not a word.

He smiled and tongued the hollow of her throat, applying two fingers to her pearl and swirling over her with increased pressure and speed. Archer couldn't lie. He was touching her now for his own benefit as well as hers. Touching her because he couldn't stop.

"How does this feel, Princess?" He kissed the delicate protrusion of her collarbone, strummed her sex as if she were an instrument, his to play.

"Good," she admitted, her tone grudging.

The cost to her pride was no doubt stunning.

His grin deepened. She was stubborn and bold and unique. Sharper than a blade. Intelligent and cunning. What she might be capable of, he could only begin to guess. And it made his cock twitch.

"Faster?" he asked, devoting himself to his craft, to this woman's pleasure. "Slower? Harder or softer? Tell me what you want, what you need."

"Faster," she bit out. "Harder."

He ought to have known.

Archer kissed the swell of her breast through her bodice, tempted to drag the fine muslin down and reveal her but deciding against it. No need to test the bounds of his restraint too much. As it was, he wasn't certain he could let her go tonight, which he must. Because this was a demonstration. He was teaching her a lesson in the power she had over a man and the pleasure she was owed. He wasn't going to take her now, regardless of how much he longed to.

Sensing she was near to reaching her pinnacle, he took her mouth again, kissing her slowly, deeply as his fingers flew over her slick bud. She stiffened and shuddered against his hand, thrusting her cunny into his palm as her release washed over her, moaning into his kiss. He stroked her until she was limp, and she was no longer clawing his shoulders but grasping handfuls of his coat, holding him against her.

He couldn't wait to have her completely.

But not in this fashion.

She deserved better than a frantic coupling on a desk.

He tore his mouth from hers, need for her burning through his veins, and found the presence of mind to form coherent thought. To feign the pretense of control.

"Not like this," he told her.

Her arms were yet curled around his neck, her lips deliciously swollen from his kisses. "How, then?"

"In my chamber. In my bed."

Even as he said the words, he wondered what he was doing. What he was thinking.

She was a virgin, for God's sake. A princess. Promised to another. He could find someone else to slake the need she'd brought to life within him. But a part of him was convinced that no one else would do.

"When?" she demanded. "I haven't much time before my

uncle's guards will check on me and find me missing tonight."

The reminder of her precarious position was like a hot coal burning in his gut. "How soon can you steal away again?"

Her tongue flicked over her lower lip, leaving it glistening. "Tomorrow."

He couldn't resist taking her mouth again. He dipped his head, their lips fitting perfectly together. Her swift inhalation was his invitation to deepen the kiss. Just for a moment. Then another. Until he was feeding her kisses and her fingers were slipping through the hair at his nape and she was twining herself around him. She tasted sweet and decadent and like everything he couldn't possibly have enough of.

When her tongue glided sinuously against his, he couldn't suppress his moan of approval. She pressed into him more firmly, trapping his aching cock with her softness as her hips tightened around his in instinctive welcome.

If he didn't take care, he'd lose control altogether. Forget his every good intention. And for a man like him, that would prove very bad indeed.

Reluctantly, he raised his head, ending the kiss for a second time. "Come to me tomorrow, then. I'll be waiting."

Her lips were puffy and parted, but she nodded, eyes glazed with desire. "Tomorrow."

The time between now and when he'd have her in his arms once more loomed like an eternity. He couldn't recall ever being so firmly drawn to another. Wanting a woman the way he yearned to possess this one.

It required all the restraint he had to disentangle himself from her embrace and take a step in retreat. To release his hold on her and flip down her skirts, hiding those beautiful limbs from his greedy view.

She looked as dazed as he felt by the power of their

mutual desire. There was no denying the attraction burning hotter than all the fires of Hades between them.

"Until then, Princess."

Without waiting for her response, he turned and stalked from the study, leaving her perched on his desk. Because it was either walk from the chamber or take her right then and there, and the need pulsing inside him couldn't bloody well be trusted.

He found his hulking butler and oldest friend, Lucky, whose sobriquet had been chosen long ago with tongue firmly in cheek. "Have three of my men follow the lady home," he bit out curtly. "Her safety is of the utmost importance."

"Aye, sir," Lucky said with a nod. "It'll be done."

Archer paused as thoughts of the princess flitting about London alone curdled his gut. "Oh, and Lucky? Tell them I'll kill them myself if any harm befalls her."

That settled, he called for his carriage, intent upon resuming his search for the missing Boritanian prince.

"Any word, Your Royal Highness?" Tansy asked quietly the moment Stasia slipped through the casement and back inside her chamber.

She knew what word her loyal lady-in-waiting was referring to—the search for Theodoric. Neither of them would speak her brother's name aloud within the walls of her uncle's town house, however, for fear of being overheard. When Theodoric had been exiled, everyone in the kingdom had been stricken from speaking his name, upon punishment of death. And although they were a long journey from home, Gustavson's guards were an omnipresent warning, milling within the halls and chambers of the otherwise perfectly elegant and civil town house.

"Not yet," she answered, removing her cape as Tansy hastened to close the window as quietly as possible at her back. Thank heavens for the positioning of the tree in the gardens below; it ensured her ability to leave her room after darkness fell, entirely undetected. "Mr. Tierney assures me it isn't an impossible task. He has eyes and ears everywhere in London."

"There is hope remaining, then?" Tansy asked, her tone steeped in concern as she appeared before Stasia, taking her outer garment from her.

"As much as is possible," she responded with equal care and quiet, lest anyone lingering in the hall beyond overhear their conversation.

She didn't want to allow her own hopes to rise too high that they would find Theodoric alive. Or that he would be willing to return to Boritania if they did. Or that he would agree to King Maximilian's plot. Her life was laden with uncertainties.

"Promising," Tansy murmured, her shrewd eyes traveling over Stasia's form. "You're injured, Your Royal Highness."

She realized that her lady-in-waiting was referring to her neck.

And then her cheeks went hot as the reason for the mark rose in her memory.

She covered the mark Tierney's mouth must have left on her sensitive skin. "It is nothing."

"I warned you of the danger," Tansy added, frowning severely. "London is rife with footpads. How have you been harmed? Was anything stolen?"

"It wasn't a footpad," Stasia said.

Tansy was fretting with the cumbersome cloak, as if it held all the answers to her questions. "Then what was it? The guards may take note if it doesn't heal sufficiently soon. We'll need an explanation. If they suspect anything is amiss…"

"They'll suspect nothing," Stasia reassured her, hoping she was right.

Tansy was adept at creams and powders that were capable of covering bruises. Life in Gustavson's court had necessitated the art of subterfuge in more ways than one.

"It was him, then?"

Her lady-in-waiting was far too intelligent. Their relationship was close. In many ways, Tansy was the only confidante she possessed. Stasia loved her sisters Emmaline and Annalise, but they were younger than she, and they had lost both of their brothers at two different times and in two different ways. Their parents were dead, their father from an illness and their mother at their uncle's hand. No one else could be trusted, particularly not with all the snakes Gustavson had brought into his court. And now, she was entrusting Tansy with her life.

But that didn't mean she wished to speak with Tansy about what had happened in Archer Tierney's study, on his desk. Nor with anyone.

She ignored the question and skirted her lady-in-waiting, crossing the chamber before kneeling to remove her boots.

But Tansy had followed her, and she knelt with her. "Allow me, Your Royal Highness."

"I can manage on my own," she denied, making short work of the knot she had tied in the laces of her left boot.

"King Maximilian will be furious," Tansy said, whisking Stasia's fingers aside so she could remove the boot herself. "You cannot risk issue coming from such recklessness. The line will be called into question when you marry."

Her snug leather boot was plucked free, and Stasia flexed her toes, not liking that Tansy was correct.

"King Maximilian needn't know," she countered calmly,

before switching knees and offering her right boot to her lady-in-waiting, allowing her to untie the knot this time.

"You are being careless," Tansy muttered to her laces.

And yes, she was. But Stasia didn't appreciate the reminder. Her lady-in-waiting was overstepping her bounds, but that had been the nature of their relationship for some time.

"I am being free," she countered as Tansy pulled off her second boot. "For the precious little time I have remaining before I must wed King Maximilian, I am being a woman who can make her own decisions. One who is able to decide what and whom she wants."

And she wanted Tierney.

Wanted him with a fire that threatened to sear her very soul.

Wanted him enough to risk everything she held dear.

Wanted him in a way she would never want the cold and terrifying King Maximilian.

"There is great danger in a free woman," Tansy said, rising with the boots in hand. "Why do you think your uncle wishes for you to wed?"

"To increase his power and coffers," she answered with distaste. "Gustavson doesn't fear me or see me as a threat to his reign. He never has."

"It isn't in my place to say you are wrong, Your Royal Highness." Tansy brushed her boots, her gaze averted.

"But you think I am wrong," Stasia finished for her, following the lady-in-waiting across the chamber, frowning.

"I would never presume to do so."

"Tansy," she bit out. "Be honest with me."

Her lady-in-waiting sighed. "You must take care. I worry for you. You are every bit as much a threat to King Gustavson as Reinald was."

"I am his biddable and loyal niece," she said bitterly.

"About to make a most advantageous match with the suitor he has chosen for me."

"If word reaches your uncle…"

"Word won't reach my uncle," she said with more assurance than she felt.

In truth, every moment she spent beyond the walls of the town house was a grave risk, and she knew it. But it was one she was willing to take for the good of her kingdom and people.

"If you go to your marriage bed without your innocence, King Maximilian will know," Tansy murmured, carefully keeping her voice hushed.

She didn't want to think about the king or the thinly veiled threats he had made regarding her loyalty to him. As far as she was concerned, her loyalty would begin when they were married. These last, fleeting moments of liberty in London were hers alone.

"You know how I feel about the king," she reminded Tansy. "He is a terrifying brute."

"One who is in London for the announcement of your betrothal and may have his own men watching you, given that he has arranged for your use of his carriage." Tansy was somber as she organized the brushes and other items of Stasia's toilette on a silver tray. "You must take greater care, Your Royal Highness. If you should fail…"

"I will not fail," she vowed fervently. "I haven't lost sight of what must be done."

Tansy gave a reluctant nod. "I will fashion a cream for you to cover the mark."

Relief made her exhale the breath she hadn't realized she'd been holding. "Thank you, Tansy."

"I pray you protect yourself," Tansy added quietly, her voice weighed with worry.

"I will."

But even as she made the promise, Stasia knew that despite her lady-in-waiting's warnings and regardless of the inherent danger, she was going to give herself to Archer Tierney when next she saw him. Nothing and no one would stop her.

CHAPTER 3

One of Archer's favored mercenaries, a man known only as Beast, was currently seated in the same chair Princess Anastasia had occupied the night before. Upon first examination, the two could not have been more disparate in appearance. Beast was unsmiling and cold, his hazel stare harder than flint, his nose a long blade in a brutally masculine visage. The princess had bright-blue eyes, was beautiful and feminine, her lips full and kissable, her nose smaller and slightly upturned, her chin softer, though no less determined.

But on closer inspection, that was when the similarities became apparent.

Archer would give his eyeteeth if the man who had just finished delivering a report on his latest post guarding the Duke of Ridgeley's town house wasn't exactly the Beast— Prince Theodoric Augustus St. George—whom the princess was seeking.

"If that is all," Beast said, "I should return."

There was a reason Archer had chosen Beast to play bodyguard for a duke who was in peril. The man was dangerous and fearless, a deadly combination. He would entrust him with any task without hesitation. But he had never for a moment supposed that beneath the man's cold, harsh façade lay a royal prince.

"Just a moment, if you please," he said, staying Beast when he would have departed before they could discuss the true reason he had summoned him. The matter of the man's true identity. "There's someone who's been making inquiries about you."

"I'm afraid my services aren't available at the moment," Beast replied wryly, clearly misunderstanding him.

"It's not your services that have been asked after," Archer said, pausing to study the mercenary he had known for so long, wondering at the truth hidden in secrets, wrapped in lies. "A lady," he added, weighing his words to watch the other man's reaction.

"What is her name?" Beast asked, looking very much like a man struggling to keep his face an expressionless mask.

Time to truly test his reaction.

"She claims to be Her Royal Highness," Archer said slowly, watching Beast's countenance for the slightest hint of a reaction, of recognition, "Princess Anastasia Augustina St. George."

He wasn't disappointed.

The other man went pale, his jaw going slack, shock passing over his features.

"Stasia?" he asked.

It was more than likely true, then. Beast was almost certainly the exiled prince.

Stasia. The pet name suited her. Perhaps he might use it upon their next encounter.

Archer drew on his cheroot and calmly exhaled a cloud of smoke. "A mercenary who knows a Boritanian princess. Rather an intriguing development, if you ask me."

"When did she come to you?" Beast demanded.

"Yesterday," he told him mildly, inhaling again from his cheroot, which was nearly down to a nub now.

He almost knew a moment of pity for Beast, except that the man had been lying to him for years. Archer didn't like liars, even though he had misled his fair share of culls. Hell, he didn't like a lot of things, but that was neither here nor there.

"Why should you think she was looking for me?" Beast asked, tipping his chin back, having regained enough of his composure to turn a questioning stare upon Archer in return.

Had he expected a calm admission? If so, he'd been destined for disappointment. Beast, never a man of many words, didn't appear to be inclined to surrender even a modicum of details.

"Because she said she was searching for her brother." Archer stopped to toss his cheroot into the grate of the fireplace, having had quite enough of it. "The exiled Prince Theodoric Augustus St. George, a man she had reason to believe has been living in London and calling himself Beast."

Beast's jaw tightened. "I've never heard of him."

More lies, then.

"Indeed," he drawled. "And what am I to tell the princess, should she lower herself to pay me another call?"

No need to reveal to Beast that the princess would be paying him another call this very night, nor the reasons for that visit.

Beast had already risen from his chair.

He held Archer's gaze, looking haunted. "Tell her that her brother is dead. I killed him myself."

With that grim pronouncement, he quit the chamber, leaving Archer to stare after him as the door slammed soundly closed.

"Goddamn it," he muttered, standing as he raked a hand through his hair.

What had he expected, that a man who had been hiding who he was for years would simply be overjoyed that his sister was searching for him? And what would he tell the princess when she returned? The thought of disappointing her was like a leaden weight in his gut.

Why did he care? He scarcely even knew her. Likely, it was the fortune she had paid him for his services. Yes, that was all it was.

He stalked out of his study, determined to distract himself. "Lucky?"

His butler appeared, scowling. "Wot you want, sir?"

He and Lucky had come a long way from the pugnacious lads who had been abandoned, but some things never changed. Lucky had as much polish as a candlestick at the bottom of the Thames, and he always would. Archer didn't give a damn. Lucky had saved his life, and that was a bloody favor he intended to repay into eternity. Even in Hades, when they likely both ended up there one day.

"Tell me about the conveyance the lady has been traveling in for her past visits," he requested.

Previously, he had settled on the word of his men, passed to him by Lucky. But there was something about the heaviness of his meeting with Beast, the man's denial, and his own connection with the princess combined, that wouldn't allow Archer to cease thinking about the notion of her gadding about London in the night. Whose carriage was she traveling in, and why? He'd been assured it was a private chaise, not a hired hack.

"Expensive," Lucky reported without hesitation. "Belongs to someone 'igh in the instep. Waits for the lady beyond the mews. The men make certain she arrives safely each way."

"Don't send the men tonight to watch for the lady," he said, his mind made up.

"Aye, sir." Lucky nodded, his countenance unchanged. "She'll not be coming this evening, then?"

"She'll still be joining me," he said, trying to keep the word *coming* and thoughts of the princess separate in his mind and failing. He cleared his throat, which had suddenly grown thick. "I'm going to escort her tonight, however."

As trusted as each of his men was, Archer didn't want any of them trailing her discreetly. Not after the unsettling interview he'd just had with Beast. Nor did he want her traveling in some other gent's fancy chaise. Those weren't the only reasons, but he wouldn't allow himself to think about the others. No, tonight, he was going to steal his princess off the street and bring her to his lair himself.

˷

STASIA WAS APPROACHING the carriage King Maximilian had sent for her use, cloak drawn firmly around her, when an arm went around her waist, hauling her against a hard body. Her heart leapt, fear making her gasp.

"Hush." Warm, familiar lips grazed her ear, the velvet-rich voice promising untold sins familiar, too. "Don't scream."

It was Tierney. But why was he here, scarcely any distance from the king's chaise, holding her as if he had a right to do so?

You gave him the right yesterday, her conscience reminded her.

She swallowed hard against a rush of longing mixed with worry. "What are you doing?"

"I'll be escorting you this evening, Princess," he said quietly in a tone that brooked no opposition. "Send your carriage away and tell the coachman you've changed your mind, that you'll require him a different night."

As quickly as he had caught Stasia, he released her, stepping away to melt into the shadows from whence he had come. Leaving her to do his bidding. She moved swiftly to the carriage, not wanting to arouse the coachman's suspicion, lest he report anything untoward back to King Maximilian.

To her relief, the coachman didn't question her request. The jangling of tack and clatter of wheels reached her as she watched the chaise driving away. Tierney returned from the shadows, sweeping an arm around her and guiding her quickly around the corner of the street to where another carriage awaited. Like King Maximilian's chaise, it was unmarked.

Wordlessly, he handed her up before joining her inside. The door closed, enveloping them in privacy. Within, the Venetian blinds were closed, and a carriage lamp flickered cheerfully, illuminating the sumptuous Morocco leather squabs. Instead of seating himself on the opposite bench, Tierney folded his tall frame into the squab at her side before hauling her effortlessly into his lap.

He tugged the hood of her cloak, making it fall down her back. She turned toward him and was about to protest his high-handedness when his mouth covered hers. All thought of objections was dashed by the possessive heat of his lips. She grasped the lapels of his greatcoat, holding him to her as she opened for his questing tongue. All the worries and fears that were never far from her mind dissipated, replaced by the searing need for more of this man.

His tongue teased hers, dipping into her mouth like a thief, stealing her ability to resist him. Beneath her bottom, the evidence of his own desire stirred, thick and long and hard. The urge to climb astride him rose. She couldn't seem to get enough. His lips were firm and demanding, slanting over hers possessively.

She made a helpless sound of need, tugging him closer, her body suddenly immersed in flame. Every part of her was alive, from the ache between her legs to the tightness of her nipples. She felt restless and dangerous, and she wanted more of the pleasure he had shown her the night before. Wanted his fingers on her intimate flesh, stroking and bringing her to shuddering release. Wanted more than that, even.

But Tierney ended the kiss then, tearing his lips from hers.

"Whose is it?" he demanded.

She blinked, her mind muddled by desire. "I don't understand."

"The chaise," he elaborated curtly. "To whom does it belong?"

King Maximilian's carriage, he meant.

"It belongs to the man I'm going to marry," she admitted, not wanting to reveal precisely who that man was.

Their betrothal had yet to be officially announced. The ceremony surrounding it was King Maximilian's idea. He wished to align himself with the monarchy, and Gustavson wished for anything that would bring him more power and legitimacy. What her uncle didn't know, however, was that King Maximilian was also using their London betrothal as an opportunity to find her brother, and that Stasia herself was making it possible.

"When you're coming to me, you'll use my carriage," Tierney said, his voice crisp and unyielding. "Not his."

A demand, as if she hadn't the right to refuse him. His green gaze glittered in the low lamplight.

"If my uncle's guards see me entering his carriage, there will be far fewer questions asked," she pointed out.

His lip curled. "What kind of a man allows his woman to flit about London in the night alone?"

One who couldn't afford a connection to inquiries being made into an exiled prince. King Maximilian had given her the use of his carriage and his guards, but she had to uphold her end of their bargain. Finding Theodoric.

Not kissing Archer Tierney senseless.

That was a betrayal King Maximilian wouldn't forgive, and the reminder sent ice to chase some of the warmth burning inside her.

"It doesn't matter," she said. "You needn't concern yourself with my means of travel."

Tierney considered her, his stare hooded, his expression indecipherable. "Does he know what you do when you take his chaise?"

"He knows I am searching for my brother," she said primly, attempting to remove herself from his lap.

But Tierney's hands were on her waist, his grip possessive, keeping her from fleeing. "Does he know you begged me to fuck you?"

His words were as harsh as his tone. She knew he was saying something unkind, that he was likely referring to her improper proposal, and yet, she didn't understand. Boritanian was her native language, although English felt comfortable on her tongue.

"What does that mean, *fuck?*" she asked, repeating the word he had used, an unfamiliar one to her.

Her English was strong, but apparently not strong enough.

"Bed you," Tierney said. "Fill you with my cock. Make you mine instead of his."

It was as she had suspected, then.

Her chin went up. "I didn't beg."

His lips twitched. "You know what I mean, Princess. You

were shameless on my desk last night, lifting your skirts for me, spreading your legs. Do you think this paragon of yours would be pleased to know it?"

She thought King Maximilian would likely kill her with his bare hands if he discovered what she had been doing. His warning words in Boritania echoed in her mind. *Anyone who has doubted me has learned the error of his ways. Often, with blood.*

"He doesn't know about my…request," she managed. "Now let me go, if you please."

If he was intent upon being rude, then she very much wished to sit on the opposite squab, without his maddening scent and heat surrounding her.

"Why not allow your betrothed the privilege of taking your maidenhead?" he asked, ignoring her request.

"Because I have no choice but to marry him, but I do have a choice in whom I give myself to for the first time," she explained tartly. "I'm currently rethinking the wisdom of my choice, however."

"Mmm," he hummed, one of his hands sliding from her waist to cup her breast over her cloak and gown. "Liar."

Her back arched, her traitorous body confirming his softly spoken accusation.

"Why do you care how I arrive to your town house?" she asked.

"Because while you're mine, I don't want you in his carriage," he said, rolling his thumb over her nipple.

And heavens, even through her stays, the touch was as incendiary as his words. While she was *his*. Why did she like the sound of that, the wicked promise it held, so much?

"You cannot dictate to me, Tierney," she argued, frowning at him. "I do as I please."

"Wrong, Princess," he drawled with the air of a man who

knew how to get what he wanted and did. Often. "You'll do as *I* please."

She didn't know how a man who hadn't been born to privilege and power could hold himself with such regal authority. He commanded as if he were a king. His hand moved from her breast, sliding with slow deliberation along her chest and then higher, curving around her throat to cup her nape. Perhaps she could allow him this one victory. After all, she wouldn't be seeing him often. Never again after she was a married woman.

The thought left her cold. Filled her with dread. What would it be like to be married to King Maximilian, far beyond this man's reach? The future loomed, bitter and unwanted.

"Say it," he said, stealing her attention again, his gaze dipping to her mouth.

She wanted him to kiss her. Wanted his lips on hers.

"Say what?" she asked, breathless and confused again.

He drew her nearer with the hand on her nape. Slowly. Carefully. It wasn't a show of force but a show of his dominance. Of how much she wanted him.

A slow, satisfied smile curved his sensual lips. "That you'll do as I please and use my carriage only."

She should deny him. Tell him no. She was a royal princess of the House of St. George.

But then he kissed her, and all her resolve turned to ash, burned by the fires of desire. She kissed him harder, ravenous for him, and he gave her everything she wanted, kissing her with equal ardor. Kissing her so deeply and passionately that she knew no other man's mouth could ever compare. She was ruined for anyone who would come after him. When he caught her lower lip in his teeth and nipped, she moaned.

He licked away the sting, then kissed her jaw, her throat. "Tell me, Princess."

She was helpless, unable to deny him.

"I'll use your carriage," she said, knowing she would promise Archer Tierney anything he wanted.

"You're damned right you will."

Even in triumph, the man didn't possess a speck of humility.

Someone ought to teach him a lesson in it. But the smile he gave her was beautiful, sinful, laden with victory, and to her dismay, she couldn't seem to summon a hint of regret at her capitulation as his carriage carried them through the darkness to his town house. Nor did she regret it as he rewarded her with more wickedly delicious kisses along the way.

CHAPTER 4

"*He* said that my brother is dead?"

Worry etched the princess's lovely face in a rare show of emotion, and Archer wished he had simply carried her to his chamber when they had arrived at his town house, rather than settling into his study to talk instead. After spending the carriage ride with her in his lap and her mouth on his, he'd wanted nothing more than to pursue the second bargain she had made with him rather than the first.

But she was paying him a bloody fortune, and he had a reputation to uphold. Business had to come first.

"Specifically, he said that he had killed your brother," he told her, reminded that he had a task at hand.

"This man murdered my brother? How can you report this to me so callously?" she demanded, throwing up her hands in a fiery gesture as she stormed toward him. "You spent the entire carriage ride kissing me, when you knew Theodoric was..."

Her words trailed off on a sob, and she stopped midstride, pressing a hand to her mouth to stifle the sound of her anguish. Something inside him turned soft where previously only hardness had been. Stern angles and a complete lack of caring for anyone who wasn't himself, Lucky, or one of the few people he allowed into his circle.

He found himself going to her, taking her into his arms.

"I don't believe your brother is dead," he reassured her, stroking a calming hand down her spine. "Beast called you Stasia."

The shortened name felt right on his lips, his tongue. Felt as right as she did in his arms, her cheek pressed to his chest.

"Stasia is Theodoric's name for me." She pinned him with a searching glance, her brow furrowed. "But I prefer it to Anastasia, particularly since Theodoric has been gone. It reminds me of him."

Her admission further cemented his suspicion that Beast and Prince Theodoric were the same man.

"Just what I thought." As he watched, a tear that had been glittering in her eye slipped free and spilled down her cheek. The urge to dry that one drop, to catch it on his tongue, was ridiculously strong. He resisted by the thinnest of restraint.

"Others in court know that I prefer to be called Stasia," she said, taking her lower lip in her teeth. "It is common knowledge. This man calling me by that name isn't sufficient proof that he is my brother."

Good God, how was he to concentrate when she presented such undeniable temptation? He had to force himself to recall the true reason she had come into his life, which was not to torment him with desire but to solve the mystery of where her brother was now.

"I am reasonably certain that Beast *is* the brother you are seeking," he said, struggling to keep himself under control, no easy feat with her lush form pressed against him. "He was surprised to learn you are here in London and searching for him. He couldn't hide his reaction. I strongly suspect he doesn't want to be found. I'll need to do a bit more digging to be certain."

Beast had always been aloof. A man who was hard to know. Daring and cutthroat when he needed to be, not shying away from making a man pay his debts in whatever means proved necessary. An excellent ally to have on Archer's side. He'd never once, in all the years of their association, suspected the man of secretly being an exiled Boritanian prince. Not much shocked him these days, but the arrival of a royal princess at his town house, requesting his services, certainly had. And when she had given him the few details she possessed to aid in the case, he'd been astounded to learn her brother was believed to be calling himself Beast when there was a Beast within his own band of rogues, thieves, and mercenaries.

"But why wouldn't he want to be found?" the princess was wondering. "When you told him that I was looking for him, why would he tell you that he is dead? I don't understand."

"Why was he exiled?"

She stiffened in his arms before withdrawing. "I don't wish to speak of it."

With that grim pronouncement, she turned away to resume pacing the length of the chamber. But if she thought to elude his question so neatly, she was wrong. He held the upper hand in all their dealings, whether it related to her lost brother or to her body.

"If you don't tell me, I'll do some digging," he drawled, extracting a cheroot from its silver case. "It will take me longer, no doubt, to find your brother. But if that's what you prefer…"

He allowed his words to trail away with an indolent shrug before lighting his cheroot on a nearby candle.

She stalked back toward him, her face a study in determination. "I don't have much time. I need him found."

Interesting.

He inhaled and then exhaled slowly, stroking his chin as he watched her, trying to remain impervious to her clear agitation. "Then tell me why he was exiled." Compassion for her had him adding in a gentler tone, "I need to understand as much as I can about the circumstances, Princess. It's a part of my job."

Her chin went up, her nostrils flaring, and she looked like a warrior queen preparing to do battle. She was utterly magnificent.

"He was exiled for refusing to renounce our mother the queen," she said quietly. "First, they tortured and starved him in the dungeons. And when he was near death and still refused to call for our mother's head, my uncle agreed that he could be sent away. His return to Boritania is punishable by death."

Sweet Christ.

And Archer had thought himself ruthless. What the hell had happened within the small kingdom of Boritania to cause such a rift? He searched the princess's gaze and saw pain and sadness glittering back at him.

"Your mother," he said quietly, fearing he knew the answer, for her uncle currently sat upon the throne. "What happened to her?"

"She was sent to the gallows for treason."

She looked so alone, stoically standing at the center of his study, a princess without anyone to support her. No courtiers or hangers-on, her family shattered. Little wonder she faced him with such reckless boldness. He suspected she had been through hell on earth, and he understood what that was like all too well.

"Your brother's struggles were for naught, then?"

"He did what he could. He was the eldest, and as such, many burdens fell upon him." She shook her head, dashing at more tears with the back of her hand. "He suffered dreadfully, from what I understand. I was forbidden from seeing him before his exile."

Archer tossed his cheroot into the fire and went to her, reaching into his coat for a handkerchief, the urge to comfort her rising above all else. He reached her side, offering her the linen square.

"To dry your eyes," he said softly.

She hesitated, looking for a moment as if she were too proud to make such a concession. But then she relented, accepting the offering, their fingers brushing. Despite the heaviness of the moment, the touch of her skin on his sent awareness roaring through him.

"Given the circumstances, you cannot be surprised he wouldn't welcome your arrival in London with open arms," he said as gently as he could muster. "Likely, he doesn't trust you. And I can't say I'd blame him, were I in his boots."

"I have no intention of hurting my brother," she protested, dabbing furiously at her eyes with his handkerchief, as if the notion were so offensive she might begin spewing fire. "All I have wanted, for these many years that he has been gone, was for him to return home to Boritania. It is all I still want. He belongs in our kingdom, not here in a foreign land. He is a prince of the blood."

"His return is punishable by death, however," he pointed out. "One can easily see why he would remain in London. Your uncle the king would have him executed, would he not?"

She shook her head. "I don't want to speak of that."

He raised a brow. "Ignoring the truth won't make it any less true, Princess. Your brother has been exiled. He won't be able to return to your homeland without forfeiting his life."

"There are other circumstances at play," she said coolly. "Circumstances of which you know nothing."

Archer was about to demand to know just what those circumstances were when the loud, undeniable growl of hunger severed the silence. The rumble was unmistakable, and it had come directly from the august Princess Anastasia herself.

"You're hungry," he noted, not giving a damn if he was being far too familiar. They'd already crossed the bridge of propriety and set it bloody well on fire.

Her cheeks went pink. "I'm not."

He wasn't surprised she would deny it, nor lower herself to the pedestrian need for sustenance. But he wasn't going to allow her to starve. Not when she was at his town house. Not when she was in his care.

"Then you have a snarling, feral wolf trapped somewhere within your gown."

Her color deepened. "The only snarling wolf in this chamber is you, Tierney."

"When was the last time you supped?" he asked, unperturbed by her charge.

"I took some tea and toast at breakfast."

"Good God, are your uncle's guards starving you?" he demanded, aghast.

He was prepared to go to battle for her.

"Of course not," she snapped. "It is the only way I can slip away from them, by feigning an illness. My lady-in-waiting has told them I'm terribly ill and that I am scarcely able to take any food. They fear contracting my contagion themselves and won't come near my chamber."

The selfish bastards. If anyone needed to be sent to the gallows, it was the king's guards. She could have been dying in truth, and they were too craven to offer her any aid. He thought then of the manner in which she had avoided his question the day before when he had asked if she slipped laudanum into their tea. *My methods are far less diabolical, I'm afraid.*

The clever minx.

"Have they not sent for a doctor?" he asked. "Surely the illness of a Boritanian princess would merit such a call."

"They did." A small, sad smile turned up the corner of her lips. "They sent for the physician of the man I am to marry. The doctor has been paid well to give credence to my lie."

There it was again, the specter of the man she was meant to marry. Archer didn't like the reminder, nor did he understand the full implications. Why was her soon-to-be-betrothed aiding her in the business of finding her brother? He sensed that there was far more to the story than what his wily princess had thus far revealed.

And he intended to find out everything.

He offered Princess Anastasia his hand. "Come with me."

She eyed his hand dubiously. "To where? I cannot be seen alone with you."

"To my kitchen," he said. "My chef has long since gone to bed for the evening, but I'll not have you going hungry. I'll cook for you, and you'll tell me more about your brother, your uncle, and your homeland."

She hesitated, looking tempted and yet uncertain.

He wiggled his fingers. "Come along, Princess. I won't bite."

She placed her hand in his.

"Unless you ask very nicely," he added with a teasing grin, lacing his fingers through hers.

Her lips twitched with suppressed amusement. "We shan't have to worry about that, then."

He guided her to the door of the study, chuckling. "I have a suspicion I'll prove you wrong. And we'll both enjoy every moment of it."

∼

ARCHER TIERNEY HAD *COOKED*.

And for her alone.

A hearty mutton stew with apricots and haricot verts. It had been rich and delicious, and she had eaten with abandon, not having realized just how truly hungry she had been. In addition to the stew, he had offered something called Pica Lilla, which she discovered to be a delightful, sweet pickle she'd never heard of before. Some bread and cheese completed the surprisingly delicious meal. They had eaten in his elegant dining room without a single servant to wait upon them, and Stasia couldn't recall when she had ever enjoyed a meal more. No pomp or pageantry of the court. No eyes watching her and waiting for her to make a mistake. No aching sense of loneliness.

The lack of formality was refreshing, but the company was even more alluring. So much so that he had cozened much of the story of her past from her by the time she had eaten all she possibly could. He was deceptively charming when he wished to be.

And that, she was beginning to discover, was decidedly dangerous.

"And for the last ten years, you've been living at court, doing the bidding of your brother and uncle?" he asked, his brilliant green gaze holding her in thrall.

"Since my father's death, my uncle has always held all the power," she answered, unable to keep the bitterness from her voice. "My brother Reinald was a pawn who served his purpose and was removed when he was no longer an asset to Gustavson."

A shiver crept down her spine at the mystery of Reinald's disappearance. She knew in her heart that her brother was dead, likely killed by one of her uncle's men. His disappearance without explanation had caused many questions to swirl at court, but Gustavson had declared himself king in the absence of other male St. George heirs. Fear of her uncle and the torturers in his dungeons had led to the silent acceptance of Gustavson as the new king.

"Removed," Tierney repeated, stroking the sharp angle of his jaw with his long fingers. "Forced to abdicate, do you mean?"

Tears stung her eyes. "Murdered."

The lone word and all its implications hung between them, heavy as the silence that followed.

He muttered an oath. "I'm sorry, Princess."

There was true compassion in his voice, in his eyes. A tenderness that was unexpected from such a hard, harsh man. She had spent the past decade fearing for her life, fearing for her sisters, mourning her parents, terrified of her uncle's cruelty and tyranny. She had endured lashes and every manner of degradation and deprivation fathomable. Through it all, Stasia had prided herself on her strength, her indomitable determination. And yet, there was something about the softness in Archer Tierney's voice—the caring— that made her feel so very vulnerable.

She swallowed against a knot of emotion rising in her throat, stifling a helpless sob that her pride refused to release. "You needn't pity me. Others have endured far worse than I have. I am a coddled, spoiled princess who has been treated gently all her life, after all."

She couldn't resist the jibe. Perhaps it was small of her to throw his words back at him. But his opinion of her had stung.

He winced. "Not so coddled, I begin to see. Nor spoiled and gently treated. I'm sorry for judging you without knowing you, Your Royal Highness."

The formality of her title felt wrong coming from the man seated opposite her at his elegant table.

"Call me Stasia, if you please," she said softly.

He considered her for a long moment, and she was convinced he would refuse.

"Stasia," he repeated in his velvet-and-sin voice.

It wrapped around her like an embrace. And despite the sadness that overwhelmed her at the discussion of her painful past, warmth blossomed, chasing some of the chill.

She took a sip from her wine to quell her sudden discomfiture.

"Your uncle," Tierney said into the new silence. "Tell me more about how he came to be king and what happened to the brother you are seeking here in London."

Grateful for the return to the matter of Theodoric and finding him, she placed her wineglass back upon the snowy table linen. "My father was ill for some time. On his deathbed, his mind was frail, and he was easily manipulated. My uncle was able to persuade him that my mother had poisoned him and that she was the reason for his illness. My father made a royal decree that every child in his line must renounce my mother and demand that she be sent to the gallows. I was a girl of fifteen at the time, terrified of my uncle's growing power over the court and my father, afraid that I would be sent to the dungeons. My sisters Annalise and Emmaline were only ten. I did what I felt I should to protect them and acted as my uncle and father commanded. My brother Reinald became king when my father died, but he was always under Gustavson's control. I saw very little of him after he assumed the throne. We were never free to speak openly with Reinald. Often, he would remain in the king's chambers for weeks at a time. And then, there came a day when Reinald was gone, and our uncle declared himself king."

Her voice broke on the last, for grief over what had become of her brother and mother, and pain over what had ensued after Gustavson took the throne. He had systematically destroyed all the prosperity in Boritania, his greed and corruption eating the court and the kingdom alive. Exacting his vengeance on anyone who dared to defy him.

She took a deep, shaky breath before continuing. "So, you see, that is why I search for my lost brother Theodoric. The last hope for Boritania and my sisters rests in his hands."

Tierney's countenance was grim, a muscle ticking in his jaw. "What of you?"

She held his stare. "I will happily sacrifice myself for the good of my people and my family. I should have done so before. I should have been as courageous as Theodoric and refused to renounce our mother. There is not a day that passes when I don't think about the choice I made with deepest regret. I'll do anything to find my brother and repent for my sins."

"Even if it means entering a marriage you don't want."

She nodded, thinking of King Maximilian and his cold ruthlessness, the bleak future awaiting her in a loveless marriage with a man she feared. "As I said, I'll do anything."

"And endangering yourself by searching for your exiled brother."

"Yes." She couldn't bear to hold his gaze any longer, for the emotions swirling within her were too strong, and she didn't want to show him her vulnerability. She glanced down at her hands in her lap, realizing that she was worrying the fabric of her gown, wrinkling it hopelessly.

"Stasia, look at me."

His voice was gentle. Achingly so. She obeyed reluctantly.

"You are every bit as courageous as your brother, if not more so," he said. "I was an arse for calling you spoiled and cosseted. You are so damned strong."

Once again, she had to break the connection of their gazes, but for a different reason entirely.

"Thank you," she murmured.

There was the soft sound of his chair scraping the carpet, and then he was at her side, offering her his hand. "Come with me."

She didn't hesitate. Stasia placed her palm in his and allowed him to help her from her chair. In silence, he led her from the dining room and to the elegant staircase. As they ascended the stairs side by side, it occurred to her that she would follow this man to the gates of Hades and beyond. That was how right it felt to be at his side, in his care, their fingers entwined.

And in their own way, those discoveries were every bit as frightening as the future awaiting her.

CHAPTER 5

Archer Tierney didn't lead her to the gates of Hades. Instead, he took her to his bedchamber.

Candles were lit within, bathing the sumptuous interior in a warm, flickering glow. The large room had an opulent Aubusson with an intricate pattern of roses and ivy in shades of rich red, green, and gold. The walls were red and hung with gilt-framed paintings. A hasty perusal revealed a stormy landscape, a nautical scene with a large sailing ship, and a haunting painting of a ruined temple.

The furniture was sleek and carved from mahogany, ornamented by brass. At one end of the chamber stood an imposing four-poster hung with velvet that matched the walls.

There was no question of where he had brought her.

The chamber even bore his scent.

The door closed at their backs, leaving them as alone as they had been in the dining room below. And yet, given the nature of the room in which they stood, a staggering intimacy accompanied their seclusion.

Had he decided to take her innocence now? There hadn't

been even a hint of seduction in him as they had dined earlier. He had been nothing but the solicitous host, making certain she ate her dinner. His questions had been professional in nature; she did not doubt he asked them to aid him in his quest to find Theodoric on her behalf.

"You've brought me to your bedchamber," she said, turning toward him, their fingers still laced together, their palms kissing.

He was solemn as he regarded her, his expression otherwise unreadable. "Do you not wish to be here?"

The question caught her by surprise. But her answer remained the same as it had always been from the moment she had decided to give herself to him.

"Yes," she said simply.

He tugged her into his chest, his strong arms surrounding her, holding her in an embrace she hadn't realized she had needed so much. Not until he nuzzled the hair at her temple, inhaling slowly as if he lived to breathe in her scent. And it occurred to her with sudden, startling clarity that no man had embraced her since her brother Theodoric had come to her, fearing he would be taken away to the dungeons. That had been just before palace guards had arrested him.

Before her entire world had been torn so brutally asunder.

A shiver passed over her, emotions rising within that had long been held inside. Emotions she'd never had the luxury of acknowledging.

"Stasia."

Nothing more than her name. As if it were a prayer.

She held him tightly, closing her eyes and taking comfort in his warmth and his muscled, masculine body.

"You should call me Archer," he added.

"Archer," she repeated softly.

They were quiet, the only sound the faint crackling of the fire in the grate at the other end of the chamber.

"I like the way my name sounds on your lips, Princess."

"So do I," she admitted.

She liked *everything* about him. Liked the way it felt, being held in his arms. Liked being alone with him. Liked the deep timbre of his voice when he said her name. Liked his callused hand in hers, his vibrant, emerald gaze drinking her in, his raffish charm, his innate sensuality. Liked his sharp jaw and steely determination.

"You're trembling. Why? Do you fear me?"

"I fear nothing," she lied.

For that wasn't true. She did fear the future. Feared what she would do should her uncle's guards uncover her deception. Feared what would become of her sisters and her homeland if she couldn't find Theodoric or if he refused to return to Boritania. Feared marrying the cruel king.

"I think you are astonishingly adept at presenting yourself to the world as if you don't," he said, his hands sweeping up her spine in a slow, comforting caress, his lips grazing her ear as he spoke.

How perceptive he was. Alarmingly so. She had never met another with his ability to cut her to her heart. She felt as if he saw her, as if she were more exposed to him than she had been the day before in his study, with her gown and petticoats raised to her waist.

"I've had to be," she said simply instead of arguing, for doing so was a moot point.

The man holding her so close was not one whom she could easily fool.

She didn't even dare try.

"You've been alone, at the mercy of a ruthless man."

She shouldn't agree with him; to voice such an opinion of the king of Boritania was treasonous. Punishable by death.

"Yes," she whispered, clinging to Archer more tightly, clutching the fine wool of his coat.

"And this man to whom you have promised yourself. Is he ruthless as well?"

She didn't want to talk about her future husband now. She stiffened, ice creeping into her heart at the thought, the heavy weight of dread filling her.

"You needn't answer," he said softly. "I already know."

Her eyes fluttered closed. If only she could preserve this moment. Remain forever in it, safely ensconced in Archer Tierney's arms. He felt like home to her. The way Boritania once had, before time and her uncle's wrath had destroyed it. How was it that a man she scarcely knew could make her feel so at ease?

"He is the man I *must* marry," she forced herself to say, taking a deep breath and tucking his scent into her lungs, holding it there as if she could forever keep it. "Let us not speak of it further, if you please."

"Whatever you want, Princess. Let me take care of you tonight."

She didn't know if he was asking permission or commanding her. Either way, she was helpless to resist.

"Please."

He kissed her temple, her cheek, then drew back to stare down at her. His fierce male beauty stole her breath.

"If you want me to stop," he told her softly, "say the words, and I will."

Her heart thundered. "You will do it, then? You'll bed me?"

She hadn't been certain. But then, with him, she never was. The night had taken them on many meandering paths, only to return them to this one. The path that made her body ache with longing. The path that made her greedy for the only part of herself she might give on her own terms—once and then never again.

"I'll take care of you," he repeated, not truly answering her question. "You've dedicated your life to living beneath the whims of others. Even in your marriage, you'll be giving yourself away for the sake of your kingdom. Your time in London, the first freedom you've tasted in ten long years, has been devoted to finding your brother. You deserve to be the spoiled princess I originally believed you to be. Even if only for a night."

How tempting it was, the offer he presented. And yet, she noted he hadn't confirmed he would do as she wished. He hadn't conceded their battle of wills just yet, she realized. And the notion left her feeling strangely thrilled.

"Will you let me?" he asked.

How could she deny him? The answer was as plain as the candles burning on a candelabra behind him, illuminating him in a golden glow.

"Yes."

He gave her a slow, sensual smile that made heat creep over her. He took her lips in a lingering, sweet kiss that left her wanting more when he ended it abruptly to withdraw from her entirely.

"Good. Turn for me."

She balked at his orders. He was always so swift to command her, and although she was no stranger to obeying the edicts of those in power, she was still a princess. She was not accustomed to being told what to do without question, as if it were a matter of course that the demand would be obeyed.

"Turn, Stasia," he repeated gently when she remained as she was.

Slowly, she pivoted, presenting him with her back, her

petticoats and gowns swishing about as she moved. "As you wish."

His hands landed on her waist in a possessive hold that took her by surprise as he pulled her snugly against him. So snugly that she could feel the thick length of him prodding her lower back.

And then there was his voice, low and deep and delicious in her ear, his breath hot over her skin as he said, "You are mine until dawn, Princess."

Dawn? Even as a new languor swept over her, along with it came the swift lash of concern.

She jerked her head to the side, their gazes clashing. "I cannot afford to be gone for so long. My lady-in-waiting is expecting me to return far sooner than that."

Tansy was already fiercely disapproving of Stasia's decision to lose her virginity on her own terms, before entering her marriage to King Maximilian. But if she feared something ill had befallen Stasia, it was entirely possible that Tansy would raise alarm amongst her uncle's guards. Stasia couldn't take such a tremendous risk. Not even for the sinfully handsome man holding her in his arms.

"I'll make certain you're returned safely and without anyone knowing," he assured her smoothly, all easy confidence and silken charm.

And somehow, she believed him. Her days in London before her betrothal was formally announced were dwindling. So too her hours of freedom. Here was her opportunity to seize what she wanted whilst she still could.

"I'm already risking a great deal by taking your carriage," she reminded him.

If word were to somehow reach King Maximilian that she had lied this evening...

No, she wouldn't think about that now.

Archer kissed her brow. "You're thinking too much, love.

Grant me your trust. I'm not a man who offers his protection lightly, but when I do, by God, I honor my word."

Her eyes fluttered closed, unable to withstand the intensity of those eyes. "I trust you."

His lips brushed over each of her eyelids, the bridge of her nose. "Your freckles are bloody bewitching."

Her eyes flew open. His mouth was on hers before she could respond. This kiss was deeper than the one that had preceded it. His lips angled expertly over hers, firm and demanding, the mastery somehow all the more erotic for their odd positioning. With his hands clamped on her, his hard body at her back, and his lips feasting on hers, she was completely at his sensual mercy.

That same forbidden, wild thrill that had burst to life inside her yesterday in his study returned. She reached for him, fingers blindly finding the back of his head, sifting through soft strands, holding him to her. They battled each other for command of the kiss, tongues and teeth colliding. She wanted, with a sudden urge that was as desperate as it was voracious, to consume him. To devour his lips and rub herself against him as sinuously as a cat. She wanted more of the pleasure he had shown her before, wanted his hand between her legs, wanted him inside her. Wanted to lose herself in mindless bliss and forget about the ugliness of the world, the pain of her past, the hopelessness of her future.

It seemed as if all things were possible. As if she had been created for this moment alone with him, as if her body had been made to melt beneath his skilled hands. She felt reckless and bold in a way she hadn't the right to be. She felt like a woman instead of a princess. Powerful and seductive rather than the royal prisoner she had become.

Archer kissed her until she was breathless, and then he tore his mouth from hers. He caught her hand in one of his, lifting her inner wrist to his lips for a kiss she felt to her toes.

"My rules tonight, Princess," he warned softly. "You do as I say."

And Princess Anastasia Augustina St. George, who had only agreed to obey the will of any man when her life and those of her sisters had depended upon it, found herself agreeing. Not because she was weak and meek, and not because she feared him. But because she wanted to surrender herself to Archer.

She wanted to be his in every way.

"Yes."

"Good." He gave her a slow, sinful smile that made her nipples go hard.

He released her and took a step in retreat, her body suddenly bereft without his heat searing her. But before she could protest, his nimble fingers were working the tapes of her gown. It loosened with expert ease that made her aware that he must have performed this task before and enough times to provide him the skilled haste of any lady's maid.

The notion sent a sharp twinge of jealousy through her.

"You've done this before."

He gave a low chuckle, not hesitating in his task. "Is that a question or an observation?"

"The latter." Her cheeks went hot.

How dreadfully foolish. Of course he must have bedded other women. He was wickedly handsome, and she hadn't a doubt that no woman could resist him when he turned his charm upon them. And why should she care? She hadn't known him then. When she left for Varros, she would never see him again. He was hers for these stolen moments only. Not for forever.

Her heart squeezed as if it were caught in the relentless grip of a vise.

"I have," he agreed as her bodice went loose. "But never for a princess."

He made her feel like a woman instead of a princess, and that was entirely new to her, something she'd never felt before. But she didn't tell him that. He was already smug enough in the effect he had upon her.

"I expect not," she said tartly instead.

"Raise your arms."

She did as he asked, and he pulled her gown over her head with one swift motion, leaving her in her petticoat, stays, and chemise. He laid her gown over the back of a nearby chair with surprising care. He was a man of such contradiction, and she was so very drawn to him, to his complexity.

Archer returned to her, this time standing before her instead of behind her. "Petticoat next."

Her heart leapt at the pronouncement. For some reason, she had believed he would leave her in her undergarments. Yesterday, he hadn't removed a single layer. But then, what did she know of lovemaking? Her knowledge was woefully sparse.

"What do you intend?" she couldn't help but ask.

He gave her a wolfish grin that turned her insides molten. "Have you changed your mind, Princess?"

Her answer was instant and visceral. "Of course I haven't."

His lips twitched, and she couldn't tell if he was repressing laughter or a smile of victory. "Arms up again."

She did as he asked. He grasped the linen of her petticoat and whisked it away as well. The garment was laid carefully atop its predecessor, and then Archer returned.

"Stays."

Swallowing hard, she turned, presenting him with her back, where Tansy had aided her with the lacing earlier that day.

He made short work of the knot, untying it with ease and

HER WICKED ROGUE

tugging so that it loosened. Her breasts sprang free, aching at their release but also from her own heightened state of awareness.

"Arms."

She obeyed his curt directive, lifting her arms so that he could remove the short stays as well. Wordlessly, he draped her stays over the chair. She licked her lips, tasting him on them—wine and freedom and sin and Archer. Everything she wanted more of. Everything that could never be hers.

He turned back to her, his gaze blazing with hunger as it swept over her. "The chemise. Will you take it off for me?"

"You...you want me naked?" Although she prided herself on her boldness, she stumbled over the question, newly self-conscious.

She had never been unclothed before a man.

"You wanted me to take your maidenhead," he drawled. "What did you suppose doing so would entail?"

"I didn't know," she admitted, cheeks going hot again at the admission of her ignorance.

If she expected him to take pity on her, she was wrong.

Archer kept her pinned in his fathomless stare. "It isn't too late, Stasia. If this isn't what you want, I'll dress you again, and you are free to go. I'll see you home in my carriage right now."

The thought of losing the opportunity to know pleasure in his arms spurred her, made her regain her courage.

"It is what I want," she said, taking the chemise in hand and hauling it up over her head before her bravado failed her.

The garment was gone. Not gone. Still clutched in one clenched fist at her side. But she was naked of everything aside from her stockings, which were tied with neat purple satin bows above her knees. Naked to his roving gaze.

She forced her shoulders back and stood for his perusal,

telling herself she would not falter. "Here is your horse then, Tierney," she told him. "Perhaps you require further inspection beyond the one you conducted yesterday."

And then she did something silly and childish. Something to distract herself from the astounding fact that she stood nude before a man she scarcely knew. Stasia took her wadded chemise and threw it directly at Archer Tierney. It hit him in the chest and dropped to the Aubusson at his feet.

He chuckled again, the sound rusty, quite as if he hadn't had much use for levity in his life. "No one would ever mistake you for a horse, Princess. Now get in my bed."

∽

NOTHING COULD HAVE PREPARED Archer for the sight of his princess naked before him, wearing nothing but her stockings, like a goddess demanding worship.

And worship he would.

Legs curved in all the right places, encased in ivory stockings embroidered with purple roses and tied above her knees with matching satin bows. Her thighs were as lush as he recalled, the prize between them begging for his mouth. Her waist was narrow above the flare of her hips, and her breasts were full and round, tipped with pink nipples he longed to suck.

And the way she held herself, her regal bearing evident in every line of her posture, her icy-blue gaze snapping with defiance as she stood before him.

Sweet God.

This woman was going to be the ruination of him. He knew it to his black, tattered soul.

It required every bit of self-possession he had to rein in his brutal, all-encompassing desire for her as she moved past him, going to his bed.

But as quickly as the fires of his need for her had begun to rage, they were as suddenly doused by the sight of her back.

Shock made his mouth go dry. He was striding for her, taking her arm to stay her progress to the bed, fury so fierce and so potent that it nearly felled him, taking Archer in its relentless grip.

"Who did this to you?" he demanded.

She turned to him, surprise flaring in her brilliant eyes, lips parting. "I don't know what you're speaking of."

He ground his molars so hard he feared they would crumble, trying to control his anger for whatever bastard had dared to lash his princess with a whip. For there was no mistaking the pattern of the scars rising in thin ridges on her otherwise smooth skin.

"Your back," he bit out. "It bears the mark of a lash."

More than half a dozen lashes, in fact. Holy Christ. The thought of anyone raising his hand against her made him ill, let alone striking her with such force that it would leave behind a lasting tracery of pink ridges crossing her spine and upper back.

Her chin went up. "My younger sisters spoke against my uncle. I took the whipping on their behalf."

Her stoic acceptance of the violence which had been visited upon her made his gut clench. As did the calm nature in which she spoke of taking on the punishment, all to protect her sisters. Belatedly, he realized he was holding her in a far-too-stern grip, governed by his body's visceral reaction to the sight of her suffering.

He released her. "I'll kill him for you."

He had it in him. His own half sister had been beaten by their half brother, the Marquess of Granville. He'd made Granville pay, with the help of his powerful friends in the Sutton family, and together they had made certain that Portia would never again be harmed by that swine. Archer would do the same for Stasia. A protective surge for her rose inside him. In that moment, he felt capable of scaling any enemy palace wall, slipping inside, and slitting the king's throat in his sleep.

Or better yet, sinking a dagger deep between his ribs while he was awake. No merciful end for such a ruthless tyrant.

"You cannot kill him," Stasia said. "He is the king, and such words are treason."

She spoke woodenly, nary a hint of emotion in her voice. And he hated that. Loathed the circumstances in which she found herself—a bird trapped in a gilded cage, a pawn for her murderous uncle without any true means of escape.

"I don't give a damn who he is," he growled. "Anyone who takes a whip to a woman as he did to you deserves to choke on his own blood as he dies."

The virulence of his reaction might have frightened another in her position, but the princess didn't even flinch at his words.

"Forgive me," Stasia said softly instead. "I had forgotten. My lady-in-waiting tended to my wounds as best as she could, but she warned me the skin would never be the same. If you prefer it, I can unpin my hair. It is long enough to hide the scars quite well."

As much as he longed to see her hair falling loose around her shoulders in all its rich glory, he would be damned if he would allow her to cover those scars just now.

She was already reaching for her hairpins.

He caught her wrist, stopping her from dismantling her coiffure. "Your hair stays as it is, Princess."

Gently, tenderly, he spun her so that she was presenting him with her bare, marked back. Once more, her strength and courage astounded him. He kissed the raised scars marring her flesh.

"These scars are a reminder of how bloody fearless and selfless you are." His lips traveled over the puckers and ridges, the pink, healed skin that was evidence of how fiercely determined she was.

"I'm hardly either of those things," she said.

"You're brave." *Kiss.* "Strong." *Kiss.* "Beautiful."

"You don't have to do this," she protested, attempting to turn around.

But Archer wasn't about to be swayed from his course. His hands clamped on her waist, holding her still.

"Yes," he countered, continuing to kiss the rest of her scars undeterred, a new and deeper appreciation for her running through him. "I do."

She held herself stiffly as he finished, the warmth of her skin and the scent of her chasing the icy chill of his discovery that she had been so viciously whipped in the past. A new resolve supplanted the old.

He turned her to face him, hands still on her waist.

The sheen in her eyes made something inside him crack and break open. Tears that she refused to shed. It was strength as much as pride that spurred her. What a fascinating woman she was. He knew he would never meet another like her.

"Tell me what you want," he said, voice raw with pent-up emotion he'd long believed he no longer possessed the capacity for.

"I want you to kiss me," she murmured.

He took her mouth without hesitation, showing her without words just how much he wanted her. Showing her how beautiful she was to him. How much her daring and fortitude made him long for her. She opened with a sigh, and he gave her his tongue, tasting the sweetness of wine and the sweeter mysteries of Stasia herself. A royal princess who fought and sacrificed herself for the sake of others.

Who dared to risk her life for a few stolen moments of freedom and passion.

He would give her that. He would give her anything she wanted.

Everything she wanted *except* taking her innocence. Because now that he understood the brutality she faced, the ruthlessness of her uncle, how could he allow her to take such a tremendous risk? He would not be the reason for any more pain or viciousness to be inflicted upon her. Regardless of how tempting the prospect of taking her innocence for himself was.

He simply couldn't do it. He cared for her far too much.

He gentled the kiss, knowing he had to proceed slowly so that he didn't lose control. The urge to carry her to his bed and bury his head between her thighs, licking her until she screamed, rose strong enough to combat the protective fury he felt on her behalf. Summoning all the restraint he had, he tore his mouth from hers, gratified at the sight of her: lashes low over her brilliant eyes, lips parted and swollen from his kisses, the color of crushed summer berries.

How lovely she was, his warrior princess who sought to protect everyone she could from her uncle's wrath. But who had been there to protect her? When her brother had been exiled and her mother sent to the gallows, she'd been left at the mercy of a vicious man. He vowed to himself that he would protect her now in any way he could, for as long as he was able.

Not long enough, he thought as he bent and scooped her effortlessly into his arms.

She made a sound of startlement, her arms flying around his neck. "Tierney!"

"Archer," he reminded her, wanting to hear it in her luscious voice.

"Archer," she repeated with less alarm. "You needn't carry

me. My wounds have long since healed, and I am fully capable of walking on my own."

"I do need," he said, aware they were echoing their conversation of only minutes earlier, when she had told him he didn't need to kiss her scars.

She was a soft, delightful weight in his arms, against his chest. Now that he had her here, the driving desire to keep her rose, maddening and futile. He could never have her, not the way he wished.

But he *could* pleasure her. He could give her a modicum of what she deserved before she went on to her loveless marriage and left him behind. And that was precisely what he intended to do.

"You are a stubborn man," she grumbled, but she failed to hide the note of appreciation in her voice.

"You like my stubborn nature," he teased, striving to lighten the moment.

He didn't want what was about to happen between them to be marred by the violence of the past.

"I don't," she said tartly. "You're too arrogant by half."

"You prefer it." He reached the bed and laid her reverently upon it, not bothering to hide his blatant admiration from her as his gaze traveled over her nakedness. "My God, Princess, you're delicious enough to eat."

And he was going to do just that.

He was still fully clothed. It didn't matter. In fact, it was likely better that he was, for the barriers between them made it harder for him to lose control and give in to temptation.

"I'm still wearing my stockings," she said, sounding breathless now. "Should I not remove them?"

There was something unbearably erotic about the way she looked in nothing but her stockings and garters. It was the single most wicked sight he had ever beheld.

"Leave them," he told her, voice thick with suppressed desire as he knelt on the bed to join her.

She was going to protest; he could see it in the shift in her countenance. But the time for talking was done. He braced himself on a forearm, stretching beside her, and bent his head to take the tip of one breast greedily into his mouth.

"Oh!"

Her soft gasp of surprise sent heat to his aching cock. *Not for you, old chap. You'll have to wait your turn*, he thought wryly. Later, he would take himself in hand to the memory of his princess, pliant and naked and utterly gorgeous on his bed, ready to give herself to him. He would think about the hardness of her nipple as he sucked. He would remember the sweet orange and jasmine scent surrounding him. The softness of her skin.

He released the turgid bud and ran his tongue in a slow circle around it before blowing a stream of hot air over the puckered flesh.

"Oh," she said again, with great feeling.

Unable to keep the grin from his lips, he flicked his gaze to her hauntingly lovely face. "I aim to earn more *ohs* from you before the night is done, Princess."

She was so regal, even lying naked in his bed, her hair still trapped in an elaborate series of braids, her jaw proud, her nose upturned in a mimicry of the defiance she inherently possessed. Sun-kissed skin so different from the pale English roses he knew here in London. And he was suddenly, viciously jealous of the sun for all the days it had been allowed to worship her face, her throat. She was tanned. Indecently so, her arms and shoulders golden, whilst her belly and breasts and thighs were pale.

"Tell me how it is that you have been able to bare so much of yourself to the sun," he said, kissing the cool, soft curve of her breast.

He could scarcely believe her tyrant uncle would have permitted it.

"I have a balcony in my chambers," she said. "It faces the ocean, and no one can see me there. I'm often relegated to my apartments. When the summer sun is warm, I sit on the balcony to read in my dressing gown. Boritania has a much warmer clime than England."

He could envision her there, his glorious princess alone on her balcony, lowering her dressing gown to bare her shoulders. His cock pulsed.

"Your skin is like honey," he murmured as he palmed her breast, swirling his thumb over the peak. "Every bit as sweet and golden."

He took her other nipple into his mouth, sucking hard, gratified by the hitch in her breath and the way she arched her back, offering more of herself to him. Her fingers tangled in his hair. He suckled and licked and nipped until she was writhing beneath him. And then he smoothed a hand down her hip, dragging his mouth along the supple skin of her stomach.

"You're still wearing all your clothing," she protested.

And he intended to continue wearing it.

"Never mind that," he said, shifting so that he was between her legs, his hands gliding over her thighs to urge them wider. "Show me your pretty cunny."

She did as he asked, legs gliding open on his counterpane, showing herself to him without hesitation. Her frank acceptance of her own sensuality and her boldness roused him in a way he'd never experienced before. His body seethed with extraordinary lust. Her sex was fully exposed like a blossom, pink and glistening with the evidence of her desire and so perfect.

Mine, roared the possessive beast within him.

For tonight, his conscience reminded him.

But he wouldn't think about the agonizingly short amount of time they had together now. Wouldn't think about anything other than making her mindless with pleasure.

His inquisitive princess was impatient and curious. "But how can we..."

Her question trailed away as he bent his head and licked her. The taste of her flooded his senses. Musky and sweet and utterly delicious. He lost control, cupping her arse in his hands and holding her to him so that he could feast. He ate her with ruthless abandon, licking and sucking and nipping until she was moaning breathlessly from the pillows, her fingers grasping the bedclothes at her sides. He suckled her pearl, lapped at her entrance with his tongue. Her thighs quivered, and he knew that she was already close.

Bloody hell, so was he.

He ground his rigid cock into the bed to stave off his own release, because he was not going to spend in his trousers like some green lad who'd never seen beneath a petticoat before. He sank his tongue inside her, her wetness coating his tongue, so hot and sleek.

Damnation.

He told himself that he couldn't sink his cock inside her the way he wanted. That this was for her. But he couldn't resist claiming a bit of her pleasure for himself. He licked her seam, returning to her swollen bud, and brought a finger to her entrance, sinking it into her tight, wet heat to the knuckle.

"Oh," she gasped out.

He paused to glance up at her. "More?"

"More," she said without hesitation.

A sensual plea and demand in one.

Fuck.

He slid his finger deeper inside, her cunny gripping him. He had to swallow against a blinding rush of need. It required every bit of control he had to keep from tearing at the fall of his trousers and releasing his cock. He wanted to be inside her so damned badly. But he would have to settle for his fingers, his tongue. He wouldn't claim her fully.

He groaned, working her sensitive flesh in every way he could. Lips and tongue and teeth, his finger gliding effortlessly in and out. She was so wet, her dew dripping down his wrist, the slick sounds of him penetrating her filling him with the fiery need to pleasure her until she was moaning and shuddering beneath him.

His restraint splintered.

He was a beast now, ravenous for her. Two fingers inside her tight sheath, fucking her fast and deep as he sucked on her swollen nub and then teased her with his tongue. She stiffened, body bowing from the bed as she cried out with her release, clamping on his fingers. He couldn't help but think of what it would be like to be inside her when she came, for her cunny to milk his cock until he filled her with his seed.

But he couldn't give in to the relentless urge to take her completely.

So he stayed with her instead, tonguing her gently as the last of her orgasm quaked through her, prolonging it and wringing every last drop of pleasure from her. He planted a kiss on her cunny and then stretched out beside her on the bed, curling her sated form against him.

It was only then that he realized he'd been so mindless in his driving need to make her come that he'd forgotten to remove his damned boots.

CHAPTER 6

The carriage rocked over the Mayfair roads, and although the spacious interior was as familiar as the back of his hand, Archer felt like a stranger inhabiting its well-appointed confines.

Like it or not—and he decidedly did not—everything had changed tonight.

He had become a stranger to himself, a man he scarcely recognized.

Because he felt something deep and indefinable for the woman tucked trustingly against his side. Something that bloody well terrified him. Left him vulnerable when he was a man who couldn't afford to be weak.

"Archer?"

Her dulcet voice interrupted his grim musings.

He glanced down to find her gazing up at him, blue eyes glittering in the glow of the carriage lamp, the hood of her cloak having fallen down her back. She was so damned lovely, and he couldn't quell the furious need rising inside him. He longed to order the carriage to be turned around, take her back to his town house, and keep her in his bedchamber for the next eternity.

He cleared his throat. "Princess?"

"Why did you not fuck me?"

Fuck her? Christ.

He frowned. "Where did you learn that word?"

She raised a brow, imperturbable. "From you."

Ballocks. Of course she had.

"I'm a bloody terrible influence, Princess," he told her, scrubbing a hand over his jaw. "Don't repeat a word I say to anyone else."

"Is it vulgar then, the word *fuck*?" she asked innocently. "You said it meant bedding. I do not know if we have an equivalent in Boritanian."

"I'm not teaching you to curse in your native tongue, Princess," he said wryly. "Even if I knew the words, you should keep them off your pretty lips."

Because if those crushed-berry lips of hers kept forming around that word, it was entirely possible that he would go mad. He'd sink to his knees and flip up the gown and petticoats he had painstakingly restored earlier and lick her until she was begging for mercy.

"Why should I?" she asked, her defiance making a return now that they were in the carriage and she was no longer lying limp and satisfied in his bed. "Because you say so?"

"Because you're a princess and a lady," he muttered, realizing how hypocritical it was, for the world's greatest sinner who had just thoroughly debauched her in his bed, to offer instruction in the vagaries of etiquette.

"But a gentleman may use the word *fuck* with impunity?"

Saint's bones.

His cock was rigid again, and he hadn't needed to come this badly in as long as he could recall. Her spirited banter and filthy mouth weren't helping matters. He would have taken himself in hand back in his chamber, but he'd been too afraid he would surrender to temptation and take her instead.

"Stop saying that, Princess."

"Or?"

"Or I'll drag you over my lap and give that pretty arse of yours the spanking it so richly deserves," he ground out, shifting on the squabs in an effort to lessen the snugness of his trousers.

"Perhaps I'd like that," she told him, the utter sorceress.

Good God, the woman was dangerous. He adored her spirit. Adored everything about her, if he were honest. From the smattering of freckles on her aristocratic nose to the soles of her dainty feet.

"I'm returning you to your town house," he reminded her grimly. "There isn't time for further sport."

Regardless of how much he wished there were.

Her shoulders tensed, the fire fading from her eyes. "You never answered my question."

Ah, yes. She wanted to know why he hadn't taken her virginity. Why he hadn't sunk inside her and fucked her to oblivion the way he so desperately wanted.

"Because I'll not be the reason that further harm comes to you, Princess," he told her, the truth torn from him.

"No one would know," she countered.

"What if the discovery is made?" He shook his head. "No, Stasia. I'll not do it."

She huffed a little sigh of indignation, the stubborn determination returning to her. "How should such a discovery be made?"

"Your husband could take note of your lack of innocence on your wedding night," he said grimly, those words like poison on his tongue, the thought of another man seeing her as he had tonight, touching her and kissing her and making her his own, like a dagger between his ribs.

He couldn't bear to think of it.

"Your lady-in-waiting, your uncle's guards," he added. "There are far too many risks. You've suffered enough, and I'll not be the reason for more pain inflicted upon you."

"Do you not think I should be allowed to decide which risks I choose to take?" she asked, all prickly defiance.

She was mesmerizing.

But she also needed someone to save her from her own courage and resolve. She needed someone to protect her, damn it.

"You can choose them as you like," he explained cooly, "but that doesn't mean I'll be complicit in them."

"That is rather upper-handed of you," she snapped.

Even in her pique, she was glorious. Of all the women in this godforsaken world, why did he have to be drawn to the only one he couldn't have?

"High-handed, you mean," he corrected her, amused by the rare lapse in her English, grateful for the distraction from the weightiness of their conversation.

She waved a dismissive hand. "Overbearing and arrogant, Tierney. That is what you are."

Ah, so she had once more reverted to using his surname. Good. They needed some distance between them.

His lips twitched. "You didn't think so an hour ago in my bed."

The princess sniffed, somehow managing to make the act regal. "That is because I thought you were a man who finished his job."

That rather stung his manly pride, but he ignored it. He was denying them both for her own good.

"There's only one job you're paying me to do, Princess, and it isn't bedding you. It's finding your brother."

"Of course." She turned away from him, directing her gaze to the window of the carriage and its closed Venetian blinds as if she might see beyond. "When will you have more word on Theodoric?"

A far safer subject. Perhaps he had successfully swayed her from her course. A pang of disappointment he had no right to feel sliced through him.

"Tomorrow," he decided, for the sooner he had Princess Anastasia St. George out of his life forever, the better off he would be.

"Thank you." Her voice was soft, her gaze still averted. "I'm running out of time before the betrothal is announced."

The reminder of the man she would be marrying was unwanted. He knew he should leave the subject alone, but somehow, he couldn't.

He clenched his jaw. "You don't wish to marry this man your uncle has chosen for you?"

"I do not," she said quietly, hands clasped in her lap.

"Then why do you not simply flee, now that you are in London?" he asked, curious. "You've demonstrated the ability to escape your uncle's guards without their knowledge. Surely he cannot force you to make a marriage whilst he is in Boritania and you are here."

She turned back to him, her smile redolent with sadness. "Of course he can. He knows I will do whatever he demands of me because if I disobey him, he will kill my sisters."

Archer hadn't been prepared for her response. It hit him with the force of a blow, knocking the air from his lungs. Good God. Her uncle was a brutal monster. He didn't know how to respond. What could he possibly say to her? Words were woefully insufficient. The urge to take her in his arms was stronger than ever, but he forced it down, knowing that if he touched her again, it would make their momentary parting that much more difficult for the both of them.

Instead, he reached for her hands, covering them with his. "I'm sorry, Stasia."

The carriage rocked to a halt.

"As am I," she said.

With his free hand, he parted the blinds, determining that they had reached their destination, near to the town house where she was staying but far enough away not to attract notice.

"We have arrived," he told her.

She nodded, her shoulders straightening. "Thank you. I should go."

The notion of her flitting away into the evening alone greatly disturbed him. "I'll escort you to the mews."

She slipped her hands free. "That won't be necessary. I bid you good evening."

She was not wrong in her refusal; she knew where her uncle's guards were stationed, and he didn't. He had no wish to inadvertently cause more problems for her or risk her being seen. But damnation, he wasn't accustomed to feeling so bloody helpless, and he didn't like it. Not one bloody bit.

"As you wish, Princess," he forced out.

With a sad smile, she drew her cloak more firmly around herself and exited the carriage. He waited for a few moments before following her into the night at a discreet distance. She moved through the shadowy streets with an eerie grace that proved she was more than familiar with wandering through London at night.

He ventured to the outskirts of the tiny garden in the rear of the town house, his eyes accustomed to the darkness. A fluttering of movement near the low-hanging branches of a lone tree attracted his attention. As Archer watched in baffled amazement, the princess climbed her way to an illuminated window and slid over the casement in a flap of ivory petticoats and royal purple silk.

∼

"You were gone for hours."

Tansy's voice was laden with a fraught mixture of worry and disapproval.

Sighing, Stasia searched the shadows of her chamber, finding her lady-in-waiting draped on a chaise longue, looking wearied and concerned, a frown marring her countenance.

"I thought you would be abed by now."

"As well I should have been," Tansy replied pointedly. "As should you."

True. Instead, she had been in Archer Tierney's bed, naked and wanton, his handsome face buried between her thighs. The thought had warmth and restless yearning colliding inside her. How she wished she were still there now. Wished she'd never had to leave.

She cleared her throat, praying Tansy couldn't read her thoughts. "You know why I was gone."

Tansy rose from the chaise longue, crossing the chamber in hushed, determined strides. "Your original purpose should not have required all evening and half the hours of the morning."

Her voice was quiet to avoid carrying; even in her ire, Tansy was nothing if not circumspect. And Stasia knew that her friend's anger had been caused by fear for her own safety. Furthermore, her disquiet wasn't misplaced. Stasia had taken another risk tonight in remaining with Archer for so long.

She opened the fastening of her cloak, allowing Tansy to sweep it away. "He served me dinner. I hadn't realized how very hungry I was after largely refusing the trays sent to me."

"For seven hours?" Tansy asked. "Pray, Your Royal Highness, do not mistake me for a fool."

There was something different about her lady-in-waiting

tonight. Her voice bore a harsh edge which had been previously absent.

"I would never think you a fool," she told her softly, reaching for Tansy's arm. "Something is amiss. What is it?"

"Of course something is amiss," Tansy hissed, withdrawing from her touch. "You are placing yourself in grave danger, acting as recklessly as you are."

A new unease closed on her heart like a fist. "Have my uncle's guards come to check upon me whilst I was gone?"

"No." Tansy's frown became more severe. "*He* came."

"My brother?" The moment the question fled her, she realized how silly it was.

Theodoric had made it plain that he had no wish to be found. The last thing he would do was venture to a town house watched by their uncle's guards and pay a social call.

"King Maximilian," Tansy announced grimly.

Icy dread chased all the burning desire that had been searing her ever since she had been alone with Archer. "He called? Why would he do such a thing?"

"You returned his carriage. He wished to know why." Tansy's capable hands were moving with uncharacteristic haste, working at tapes and removing Stasia's gown. "I was forced to meet with him on your behalf."

"Deus," she whispered. "He didn't harm you, did he, Tansy?"

"What would you do if he had?"

The bitter question sent guilt washing over her. "Did he hurt you?"

Tansy was silent, working at her petticoat, sending it to the floor in a whisper of sound.

"Tansy," she pressed, frustrated and sick with fear.

King Maximilian was capable of anything. She knew it. He had warned her. And yet, she had believed that she alone would be made to pay the price if he discovered what she was about. Selfishly, she hadn't considered if there would be ramifications for Tansy.

"This knot isn't mine," her lady-in-waiting murmured at her back, pulling at the lacing on her stays.

That was because Archer had untied Tansy's knot, given Stasia more pleasure than she had ever known, and then tenderly restored her clothing as if she were someone precious to him. Someone deserving of his care, when her actions tonight had proven that she was not deserving of anyone's care, let alone his. Good God, what if King Maximilian discovered she had been in Archer's bed? Would he have him killed as he had so many of his enemies in Varros?

She whirled to face her lady-in-waiting, unable to bear the suspense. "Tell me what happened. Please."

Her gaze roamed over Tansy's pale face, finding no hint of a bruise. But no one knew better than Stasia that scars and bruises were easily hidden.

"I told the king that his carriage had been spied by the guards near the mews and questions had been raised," Tansy said. "His Royal Highness was grateful for your caution. He was careful to play the part of concerned suitor. The guards were easily fooled. He wished for me to pass on the warning that his spies in Gustavson's court have sent word that your uncle grows suspicious by the delay in announcing your betrothal. There is word he may travel to London himself."

Stasia exhaled the breath she hadn't realized she'd been holding. "That is all?"

She didn't think it likely that her uncle would leave the haven of his court or the protection of the August Palace. Not when he was so reviled throughout Boritania for his disastrous taxes and vile corruption. To travel so far would expose him to danger, and having only recently grasped the power he had been hungering for all these years, she did not doubt that he would not do anything to jeopardize his rule. A delay in the betrothal announcement, caused by her illness, would not be sufficient reason. It was a risk that she and King Maximilian had willingly taken while they worked to find Theodoric.

"No," Tansy said quietly then, interrupting her whirling thoughts. "That is not all."

"Did he strike you?" she demanded, fresh fear that the king had somehow inflicted pain upon Tansy rising once more. "Did he threaten you or hurt you in any way? You must tell me, Tansy. I will not allow you to suffer because of me."

"No, King Maximilian did not," her lady-in-waiting said, her gaze sliding away from Stasia's, an undeniable cast of guilt setting on her features. "He did something far worse."

"What can it have been?" Alarm flared to new life, making her heart beat fast. "You must tell me, Tansy. Please."

With a shaking breath, Tansy's stare flicked back to hers. "He kissed me."

"He kissed you," she repeated, shocked. For in her interactions with King Maximilian, she had never found him to be a man given to romantic inclinations. He had never once pressed his suit. The revelation brought with it new, ugly implications. "He forced himself upon you?" she demanded to know.

"No." Tansy shook her head, her ordinarily stoic expression crumpling. "There was no force. Your Royal Highness, I am so sorry for what happened. I pray that you will forgive me and that I may regain your trust."

Stasia stared at Tansy, emotions warring within her. In all the years that Tansy had been faithfully at her side, she had only ever proven her loyalty and faithfulness. She had been the only trusted friend and confidante Stasia possessed, beyond her younger sisters. After her world had been upended, losing her mother and Theodoric, Tansy had been the rock to which Stasia had clung.

She trusted Tansy with her very life.

She didn't know how this revelation should make her feel. King Maximilian was meant to be her husband. A husband she neither wanted nor held any tender feelings toward, it was true. But for her lady-in-waiting to kiss the man she would soon wed...

"I never meant for it to happen, Your Royal Highness," Tansy added, bowing her head. "I must beg you for mercy, which I do not deserve. I promise you that it will never occur again."

"He did nothing to hurt you?" she asked, needing to be certain.

"Nothing," Tansy confirmed softly.

For now, that would have to be sufficient. She cared for Tansy far too much; she needed her friend at her side. And for the present, she was more concerned with finding her brother and—she could not lie—consumed by Archer Tierney.

"You are forgiven," she said.

Tears shone in Tansy's eyes. "Thank you, Your Royal Highness."

"Stasia, if you please. You have always been like a sister to me, Tansy. That shall never change."

Even if her future loomed bleaker than ever.

"You are the only sister I've ever known," Tansy returned, unsmiling. Perhaps she was thinking of her own troubled past.

She had been orphaned as a small child and left at the mercy of the court.

Stasia took her friend's hand, giving it a reassuring squeeze. "We shall weather this storm as we always have. Together."

Tansy nodded, still frowning. "But you need to take greater care. The danger grows stronger, and I am not certain how much longer we can continue to fool the guards or King Maximilian."

The thought of never seeing Archer again, never touching or kissing him, never being held in his arms, was like a wound torn open inside her.

"Just a bit more time," she said, hoping that it would be enough to both find her brother and cure herself of the need for Archer Tierney.

Because all too soon, she would lose him forever. And if she didn't locate Theodoric and convince him to join their cause, her homeland and her sisters would be lost, too.

CHAPTER 7

"What do ye want to know, sir?"

Archer drew on a cheroot, fixing the squirming man before him with his deadliest stare. The one that promised brutal retribution for a falsehood. And then he exhaled as if he hadn't a care in the world.

"Everything there is to know about Beast," he said.

Betram Hyde shifted again in his chair, looking distinctly uncomfortable. He was one of the men who was working with Beast to protect the town house of the Duke of Ridgely. After recent attempts on the duke's life, the duke had hired Archer and his men for protection. Their task was twofold: protect the duke and his household, and discover who was trying to kill him. Now, Archer had yet another task, one that had nothing to do with the duke and everything to do with the gorgeous princess he couldn't seem to stop thinking about.

Archer had played a great many roles in his life. Bastard son, ruthless moneylender, secret spy for the Crown. After years of entangling himself with the most dangerous men in London, risking his life and amassing his fortune, leveraging every bit of power he could glean to grow his empire, it was deuced eerie to find himself investigating one of his own. He had always prided himself on the trustworthiness of his men. To think that one of them had been lying to him—even inadvertently, by keeping his true identity a secret—nettled.

To think he'd been too bloody stupid to realize Beast was far more than he had claimed to be…

That bloody well stung like the devil.

"Don't talk much," Hyde said. "A cold fish, that one. Capable of anything."

Nothing new there, and one of the reasons he was one of Archer's most-trusted mercenaries. He puffed on his cheroot again, contemplating.

"How long have you known him?" he asked.

Hyde scratched his head. "Ten years, I'd guess. Long time ago now. When we first met, 'e was raw-boned. Pale and gaunt. Little better than death's head upon a mop stick."

Ten years. There was something. A fine coincidence, indeed. And Beast hadn't been the strong, hale man he was now. That, too, was in keeping with what Stasia had told him of her brother. He had been near death, she'd said, after having been tortured and starved in her uncle's dungeons. But Archer needed to know for certain before he summoned Beast for another meeting with Stasia. She meant too much to him now, and he would be damned before he would do anything to cause her further hurt or disappointment.

He had to be sure.

Archer leaned forward, bracing his elbows on his rosewood desk. "How did you meet?"

"Staying in the rookeries, 'e was," Hyde offered. "We was both of us miserable rips. Stood by each other, made our way out of there soon as we could."

"Did he ever say anything about his past?"

"Not as I can recall. Said sommat about 'is mother and

father being dead, is all. Once, 'e was clear and told me that 'is uncle was a vicious bastard."

Clear.

In cant, that meant Beast had been soused. And likely more honest than he'd intended to be. Dead parents, an arrival in London ten years prior, and an uncle who was a vicious bastard. Add to that Stasia's belief that her brother was calling himself Beast...well, there was no question.

He had his man, and Stasia's brother was Beast. He hadn't a doubt of it.

Archer took another slow, steady pull of his cheroot, exhaling the smoke in a cloud overhead.

"Anything else, sir?" Hyde asked, the sheen of perspiration on his brow.

It was plain that the man didn't like this line of questioning.

"That will be all," Archer said, taking mercy on the poor chap. "Say nothing of this to Beast, do you understand?"

Hyde nodded vigorously. "Aye, sir."

"You may go."

Hyde tugged at his forelock and bowed before scuttling from the chamber, plainly happy to have been dismissed.

Archer finished his cheroot, mind churning with the latest round of facts he'd uncovered. Proceeding would require caution and care. Beast was a clever chap, and he had guarded his secrets well enough for ten years. Given his reaction to Archer's questions, he was determined to keep his past dead and buried. But that was too bloody bad. Because now there was a daring, beautiful princess who was depending upon Archer to make certain Beast could no longer hide in plain sight.

She had paid him a damned king's ransom to do so. But it wasn't the royal jewels worth a fortune that she had surrendered to him on their first meeting that was urging him on. It surprised him to realize that he cared far less for the value of the diamonds and emeralds and sapphires than he did for the plight of the woman who had paid him. Vastly unlike himself, and he wasn't certain what to make of it.

There was no doubt that Stasia's urgency spurred him. *I don't have much time*, she had said, such desperation in her sultry voice. *I need him found.*

He couldn't shake the suspicion that there was something she was keeping from him. That there was another reason behind her need to find her exiled brother and with such haste. It wasn't solely a reunion she was after. But just what that elusive reason was, he couldn't begin to guess. He couldn't deny it rankled that she would share so much of herself with him—her body, her passion, her innocence—and yet she would not reveal the full truth.

There was still so much of her that he didn't know. So much of her that he would never know. And that bitter realization settled like an ache in his gut.

Damn it, what was it about Stasia that held him so thoroughly in her thrall? He had shared his bed with women aplenty, but none of them had managed to pierce his protective shell the way she had. His past experiences had been about slaking mutual needs. A distraction from the grim world around him.

But Stasia...

There was no denying it. She felt like so much *more*. He didn't just want her in his bed. He wanted to know her. He wanted her hand in his, wanted her at his side, wanted to know every detail of her past, to understand what made her the woman she had become. He wanted to protect her and kiss her and sink inside her. To make her his forever.

He shook his head and rose from his desk, knowing it was bloody futile to both want her in a way he could never have her and attempt to complete any more work this evening. Ledgers could be tallied tomorrow. Correspondence could damn well wait. The time to meet with Stasia was growing near, and the need to see her again, to touch her, kiss her, breathe in her scent, supplanted all else.

Archer stalked from his study and into the hall. "Lucky?"

His butler appeared, looking customarily surly and unsmiling. "Sir?"

"Have the carriage brought round for me, will you?" he asked.

"Going to fetch your lady?" Lucky asked.

He sighed heavily. "She isn't mine, Lucky."

But God, how he wished she were. And that was bloody terrifying.

"Could make 'er yours," Lucky pointed out gruffly. "Never seen you this way over a set of petticoats before."

He shook his head. "If only it were that simple. The lady is promised to another."

And Christ, the way it felt to acknowledge that—like a vicious blow.

Lucky shrugged, unperturbed by the revelation. "Why let that stop you? If you want something enough, you take it. That's always been the way of things, eh?"

Yes, it most certainly had been the way of things in the past. Whatever Archer had wanted, he had ruthlessly worked to possess, whether by means fair or foul. Power, money, influence. This town house, the women in his bed. Hell, even his horseflesh. When he wanted something, he took it.

And he had never, in all his misbegotten life, wanted anything the way he wanted Princess Anastasia.

"I'm afraid, in this instance, the lady isn't mine to take," he explained carefully, thinking of the scars on her back, the danger inherent to her precarious position with her uncle and his guards. "She's suffered enough, and I'll not be the reason for more suffering in her life."

"Mayhap you ought to let the lady decide," Lucky suggested. "If she wants you enough in return, the risk may be worth the reward."

"I'll not have her put herself in jeopardy just because I want her," he countered. "I have scruples, Luck. Not many, but the few remaining tell me I can't just take without consequences this time."

"You could always have the other cove killed. Bang-up way to win a mort's affection."

He bit out a chuckle, shaking his head. "I can always count on you for a sally."

Lucky grunted. "Wasn't joking. Off to see the carriage brought round now."

With a tug at his forelock, the hulking butler disappeared, leaving Archer to ruminate upon his words. He had no intention of visiting any harm upon Stasia's betrothed. But Lucky had him thinking. Just who was the man Stasia was promised to marry?

∽

Stasia slipped from the gardens behind the town house, eagerness to see Archer Tierney again propelling her every step as she made her way to where she knew his carriage would be awaiting her. She had spent the day in her chamber, hiding from her uncle's guards, existing on tea and toast, the hours until she could be alone with Archer again looming like an eternity. One she had borne with little grace. She had paced the carpets until her feet ached. She had attempted to distract herself to no avail. Neither reading nor drawing nor needlework had offered sufficient diversion.

All she wanted was to see him again. And, to her shame, it was a selfish need along with the altruistic desire to find Theodoric before it was too late and her chance of seeing her brother restored to the throne was forever lost. She couldn't lie to herself. Despite the danger, despite the risk of discovery, despite the likelihood that she would incur the wrath of her future husband, she wanted Archer Tierney. Wanting him was a fire in her blood that she could not douse. He inhabited her thoughts, waking and sleeping.

The night before had been restless. She had dreamt of him, his clever mouth on her body, his lips and tongue reducing her to quivering mindlessness. And then she had awakened in her dark chamber, alone, her body throbbing with the need for release. One she had discovered reluctantly on her own, her fingers unerringly finding her pearl and stroking until she had gasped out his name into the night.

And still, it hadn't been sufficient. He had awakened her to desire. Had shown her pleasure unlike any she had ever known at her own hand. It was as if he had unlocked a door hidden within herself, one she hadn't realized existed previously. Now that it was open, she could not close it. She needed him. Needed more than the pleasure he had already given her.

She needed everything.

Tonight, she would give herself to him. Their time together was precious and growing shorter with each passing day. He could refuse her all he liked, but she was determined.

This would be the night that she gave her virginity to Archer Tierney.

The thought fanned the flames of need inside her ever higher, so that as she ventured through the shadows, each step exacerbated her hunger. She could feel her own wetness, an answering ache deep inside her core that could only be sated in one way.

His carriage was awaiting her as it had the night before. She increased her pace, her belly tensing as she wondered which version of the enigmatic man she would be treated to. Eager to see him. To hold him. To feel his lips against hers.

But before she could reach the carriage, a figure leapt toward her from the darkness, arm raised. In the low light of the streetlamps, she saw the unmistakable glint of metal on a vicious-looking blade. Everything next seemed to unfold with both agonizing torpor and terrifying speed. She cried out as the blade arced toward her, slashing her cloak. Pain seared her upper arm as she spun away from her attacker's path, racing for Tierney's carriage. From behind her came an animalistic snarl, followed by footsteps racing after her. Growing closer. Her boots were slippery on wet cobblestones.

"Archer!" she cried, no longer caring if they were seen or overheard, her need to survive supplanting all else. "Help!"

The door to his carriage was already thrown open, and he was rushing toward her, a pistol in hand. "Stasia!"

Everything happened in a blur of motion and sound. Archer pulled her behind him, using his body as a protective shield. The deafening report of a pistol echoed through the night. Her attacker stumbled backward, clutching his abdomen, falling to the damp alleyway. He had been shot, she realized numbly. Archer had shot him to save her. Was he dead?

Good, sweet Deus. There was a roaring in her ears followed by a high-pitched sound, her vision growing black around the edges. Shock had rendered her helpless. She listed to the right, nearly falling over, but caught herself at the last moment, stumbling to the side.

"Get in the carriage," Archer ordered her, his voice sounding eerily detached and cool.

Her heart was pounding hard, her mouth dry, but she hastened to obey his command, reaching to grasp her skirts in both hands so that she could alight into the carriage. More pain seared her, had her gasping as it radiated from her upper arm, then lower.

"Stasia?" He turned to her, his countenance a study in worry through the shadows. "What is it?"

"My...arm," she managed, feeling the world grow dizzied around her once more. She reached for the place where the blade had slashed through her cloak, warm liquid soaking her kid gloves.

"Holy Christ, Princess, you're bleeding."

Those were the last words she heard before her entire world went black.

CHAPTER 8

Stasia had been wounded.

And it was all his goddamned fault.

Archer paced the hall for what must have been the five hundredth time, feeling bloody helpless and furious and terrified all at once. Someone had dared to hurt her. Had spilled her blood. Her scream still echoed in his mind.

His name.

She'd called out his name.

He'd been in his carriage awaiting her, but she'd been early this evening. He hadn't expected her to leave the safety of the town house so soon. Despite that, he'd been checking for her, an eye to the partially opened Venetian blinds, when he spied movement. The night had been gloomy and darker than usual, rain having settled over, along with a thick fog.

He'd been trying to exercise extreme caution. Earlier in the day, he'd sent some of his men to investigate the perimeter of the town house and determine where her uncle's guards were stationed. He hadn't wanted to draw any undue attention, to alert the guards to his presence, and he had known they walked the mews every half hour. And so, he had hesitated before leaping from his carriage to her defense, a lapse in judgment he would eternally regret. He hadn't known it was her in the shadows. Not until she had cried out.

And she had called for *him*.

When he was the reason she was in a position to be in danger. The knowledge broke him. She'd been coming to him. He could have sent word to her instead. He could damn well pay anyone to do anything he liked. But he had been selfish and greedy. He had wanted to see her again.

There had been a great deal of blood on her arm. He'd tied his cravat around it in an effort to stay the bleeding. He'd kissed her, reassured her, but he'd been fucking terrified that he was about to lose her. He still didn't know how great the damage was that had been inflicted upon her. The bastard had taken a knife to her arm; Archer had been able to glean that much from the state of her cloak. He was no stranger to wounds; he'd been as calm as he'd been able, given the circumstances. Because he had never held a woman he cared for in his arms while she'd been bleeding and in pain before.

If he lost her...

No, he wouldn't think it.

Flesh wounds tended to bleed. She had a will forged in bloody steel. If anyone could survive what had happened this night, it would be her.

He had to believe it. Had to believe in her. Because he couldn't bear to contemplate the alternative. She had only been a part of his life for mere days, and already she had come to mean so very much to him.

Everything, whispered a voice within, and he couldn't deny it. She did bloody well mean everything to him, and the hell of it was, he had neither reason nor right to feel as he did about her. To feel so connected, as if she were a part of him.

Because that was how it felt, and he couldn't deny it. He felt as if he couldn't breathe without her.

Before he could contemplate that any further, the door to his bedchamber opened, the doctor he'd frantically summoned to tend to Stasia's wound stepping over the threshold. Archer rushed forward.

"How is she?" he demanded without preamble.

"The lady is resting now," Dr. Crisfield assured him. "Her wound was mercifully shallow. I feel confident that no permanent injury will result from it."

Relief hit him with so much force that a goddamn feather could have knocked him off his feet in that moment. Thank God. He'd never been a praying man, but he'd spent the entire carriage ride with Stasia in his arms, bleeding and in pain, silently begging the heavens above to spare her.

"You're certain?" he rasped, scarcely able to form words.

He'd never been in such a state. What had become of him? He didn't even recognize himself. His hands were trembling at his sides, balled into impotent fists.

The doctor nodded. "You'll need to keep a careful eye on her, however. If there's any sign of fever or infection, call for me immediately. The next few days are of the greatest import."

Fever. Infection. Those were words he didn't want to hear. Reminders of just how quickly any injury could become a mortal one. She wasn't safe yet, even if the wound hadn't been severe enough to cause her permanent harm.

Damn it, he had failed her.

Archer swallowed hard against another rush of guilt and worry. "What must I do to tend to her? Say the words, and it will be done."

"She will require rest," Dr. Crisfield said. "The bandage must be kept clean and dry as well. The lady is stubborn and strong, however. Her resilience is to be commended. The wound will likely cause her some pain, and she refused laudanum."

His princess was a bloody fighter. A warrior goddess who wasn't afraid to sacrifice herself for the good of her people. But she had almost sacrificed herself in coming to him tonight, and he could not allow her to take another chance like it. Something had to be done.

He managed a jerky nod for the doctor's benefit. "Thank you for coming so swiftly."

He had paid handsomely for the doctor's late-night call, but he would give every last ha'penny he possessed if it meant saving Stasia. He knew how to bring the best in the city running to his door, and he'd stopped at nothing to secure the finest doctor to be found.

Crisfield nodded. "Of course, Mr. Tierney. Send someone for me if necessary."

"Lucky will see you out," he said, nodding to his hovering butler and friend. "Lucky, give the good doctor something extra for his efforts this evening."

Lucky tugged at his forelock. "Aye, sir."

Archer didn't waste another second. He had to see Stasia. To touch her. To reassure himself that what the doctor had said was truth and that she would not suffer any long-lasting damage from the wound that bastard had inflicted upon her.

He burst into her chamber like a madman, not stopping until he was at her side. She was pale, her gown somehow mercifully intact because of its cap sleeves, though her cloak would need cleaning and mending. A bandage was wrapped around her upper left arm, visible beneath the short sleeves of her dress. The whoreson who had attacked Stasia had likely been aiming for her heart. Thank God the bastard was dead.

The realization was like ice in Archer's veins.

"How do you fare, Princess?" he asked, his voice rusty with pent-up emotion that he had no wish to reveal.

She gave him a wan smile. "Better now that your butcher is finished with my arm."

"He's a doctor, not a butcher," he corrected gently, as if the distinction mattered, settling his arse on the edge of his bed. "Are you in much pain, love? Dr. Crisfield said you refused laudanum."

"I cannot abide by it. My brother Reinald took it as a tonic, and it made him ill. I believe it is part of what killed him, along with my uncle."

The reminders of her past were as sharp as the dagger that had been used against her mere hours before.

"No laudanum, then," he agreed, wishing he could do something to take the pain from her. "What can I fetch you to help you, to make it better?"

The question was a weak and futile one, he knew. Nothing could make this precarious situation any better. She had always been in danger, but her association with him had heightened the risk.

"Some water, perhaps?" she asked. "My mouth is drier than the sandy beaches of Boritania in the heart of summer."

He rose, crossed the room to a pitcher and bowl, and poured some cool water into a glass. When he moved back to her side, she reached for it with her uninjured arm, their fingers brushing. The same powerful jolt snapped up his arm, awareness of her burning through him.

He tamped down the unwanted reaction. She had almost been killed tonight because of him. And he hated himself for that. He'd never forgive himself.

He watched as she drank thirstily, as if she hadn't had water in a week.

"Slowly," he cautioned gently. "You don't want to make yourself ill."

She lowered the drinking vessel at his words, her customary stubbornness notably absent. "Thank you."

He shook his head, feeling like the world's greatest beast. "The water is the least I can do."

"Not for the water," she said softly. "For coming to my rescue. If you hadn't been waiting for me, I shudder to think what would have happened."

More anger at himself rose. "If I hadn't told you to come to me again, you wouldn't have been out there in the night to be preyed upon. You would have been safe in your chamber where you bloody well belong, not putting yourself in danger by climbing trees and slipping about through the night. Make no mistake, Princess. What happened to you tonight was my fault."

"Archer."

His name spoken so tenderly was enough to incite a riot inside him. Everything within him was clamoring to take her in his arms. To hold her, feel her heart beating, to drink in her warmth and vitality. To never bloody well let her go.

But he couldn't.

"Someone tried to kill you tonight," he said baldly, hating those words. Hating what had happened to her.

"Why should anyone try to murder me?" she asked, confusion lacing her dulcet voice. "There is no reason for anyone to make an attempt on my life. It was likely a cutpurse, looking to avail himself of my valuables."

"No, Stasia." He sank back down on the bed, as close to her as he would allow himself to be. "Had it been a footpad, he wouldn't have attempted to stab you. He would have demanded your reticule or your jewels. This man lunged at you from the shadows. He was aiming to sink his blade into your heart."

The reminder left him colder than he had ever been.

Her lips parted, and he could see realization dawning in

her vibrant blue eyes. "It was my left arm, yes, but surely you are mistaken."

"I'm not, though I wish to God I were. My men dragged his carcass from the alley. His garments were far too fine for a common cutpurse."

"He is dead, then, the man who...the man," she finished, her voice uncharacteristically shaky.

He nodded grimly. "And damned fortunate he is, too. If my bullet hadn't ended him, I would have taken great pleasure in torturing him slowly for what he did to you. For what he intended to do."

"I wouldn't have wanted that," she said quietly.

He held her gaze. "Princess, for you, I would turn all London to ash. You're mine to protect, and I failed you tonight. For that, I am sorry. So fucking sorry."

"You didn't fail me. You saved me."

She was looking at him as if he were some sort of bloody hero instead of a lust-driven scoundrel who had put her in jeopardy. He couldn't bear the adulation, the tenderness he saw there. He didn't deserve it.

And that was why he had to put an end to this madness. Had to drive her away.

"I never should have allowed you to continue to flit about alone in the night. Bringing my carriage to you isn't sufficient to keep you from harm. From now on, you'll stay in the town house, in your bedchamber, where no one can pose you any threat. I'll find a way to deliver word to you. Perhaps through your lady-in-waiting."

Her chin jutted up, and even pale and weary and wounded, she was every inch the fiery princess, more regal than he had ever seen her. "You cannot *allow* me to do anything. I am my own woman."

Damn it, he might have known she would fight him on this. But he was every bit as stubborn as she was.

He clenched his jaw. "I'll not have you putting yourself in any more danger."

Her eyes flashed with blue fire. "The decision is not yours."

"Do you expect you can climb a bloody tree with a wounded arm? Because I can assure you that you cannot."

"How do you know about the tree?" she demanded.

"I followed you last night," he admitted. "I wanted to make certain you returned safely. This madness has to end, Stasia. You were nearly killed tonight."

"But instead, my assassin is dead. Because of you."

By God, they were going in bloody circles. "I'm not arguing with you about this. You are far too damned important to me."

His outburst hung between them. It was more than he had intended to reveal. More, too, than he wanted to feel for her, a woman who could never truly be his.

"You care for me," she said quietly, a hint of an emotion he couldn't define lacing her voice now.

Archer couldn't deny her charge; he was a fool for her. Since she had appeared at his town house, asking for his help in finding her brother, she had been haunting his waking and sleeping hours. He thought of her constantly. When he wasn't with her, he wanted to be with her. Teaching her the ways of pleasure had been the most intense form of sensual torture he'd ever experienced. Getting to know her in the small measure she had allowed and learning of her past had been humbling. What he felt for her was incredibly strong, the pull between them more potent a lure than any he'd ever known.

"Far more than I should," he conceded grudgingly.

"Then keep me here with you."

Stasia held her breath as she awaited Archer's response to her mad suggestion that he keep her here.

It was what she wanted, of course, more than anything else. What her heart was begging for. It was also a terribly dangerous risk, particularly since Tansy had just delivered such dire warnings to her concerning both Gustavson and King Maximilian. But she had no other options. Climbing into her bedchamber window was impossible, given the state of her arm, as Archer himself had just pointed out.

And aside from that inescapable fact, she couldn't deny that everything had changed between the two of them tonight. Nor could she deny the rightness of being with him.

The carriage ride to his town house had been a blur of pain and darkness and sound. But Archer had held her so carefully in his arms, whispering comforting words of reassurance in her ear, exerting every effort to make certain she wasn't jostled as the carriage raced over the streets. And his warmth and strength and scent had permeated the shock of everything that had happened. The sudden violence of the attack and the wound she had suffered, coupled with the loss of blood, had caused her to lose consciousness for a few moments.

But he had been there for her throughout. His tender caring and muscled body wrapped around her in an embrace that she never wanted to leave. She felt, for the first time in as long as she could recall, as if she belonged somewhere. Belonged with someone.

He had saved her life. Despite his protestations to the contrary, she would have taken the risks she had been taking since her arrival in London with or without knowing him. She had no other choice, for her freedom was limited and King Maximilian needed Theodoric to be found before their betrothal was announced. There was no doubt that if Archer hadn't been within the carriage, and if he hadn't been armed and leapt from the conveyance at just that moment, she would not be lying in his bed now, her upper arm throbbing.

"I can't keep you here, Princess."

His denial cut through her more viciously than the blade of her attacker earlier. Thank heavens the villain had possessed such abysmal aim. If he had struck her a few inches in the other direction, tonight would have ended differently.

"You can," she said, for he had no other choice, and neither did she. "Indeed, you must. If I remain with you, I risk discovery. But if I leave here tonight, I also risk discovery. As you said, I cannot climb a tree with one arm. All the doors to the town house are guarded. My sole means of escape was my bedchamber window, and that is lost to me until my arm is sufficiently healed."

A muscle in his jaw ticked. "If you don't return by morning, your woman will notice. She'll have no other choice, save to raise the alarm to your uncle's guards or face great peril herself."

She ran her tongue over her dry lips. "There is the possibility that she can persuade them that my illness has grown worse for a few days, just until I am recovered enough."

"How would she know to do so?" He shook his head. "This is futile, love."

He was calling her *love* again. The term of endearment hadn't escaped her. Did Englishmen use it without a care? She didn't know. But her foolish heart leapt at its every utterance, regardless of her practical mind's caution.

"You said you could send word to me," she pointed out. "Can you not send word to her as well?"

"Christ," he muttered, raking his long fingers through his dark hair.

In the low, flickering candlelight, she could see glints of

gold in the thick, lush strands. He was so handsome, so obviously torn, and she ached to touch him.

"She is loyal and trustworthy," Stasia added. "I have entrusted my life to her."

"What you're suggesting is damned unwise."

His green eyes burned into hers, and she didn't think she was mistaken in reading longing in their brilliant depths.

"One might argue that every action I've taken since arriving in London has been unwise," she said. "Why not one more?"

Particularly if that meant she could stay here with him, prolong their time together. Tansy could stave off her uncle's guards and hopefully King Maximilian as well. And Stasia would have Archer to herself for a few more blissful days.

He sighed, rubbing his jaw, looking quite torn. "Keeping you here is going to be difficult."

"Why?" she asked. "No one knows I am here with you except for Tansy."

But what if King Maximilian learned where she was? She wouldn't think about that now. Staying with Archer was the best course for her, given her injury.

"What of the man you're meant to marry?" he asked, almost as if he had read her thoughts.

Guilt pierced her, mingling with the same abiding dread that curdled her stomach whenever she contemplated her future as King Maximilian's unwilling bride. "He will never know. I am confident my lady-in-waiting will be able to keep everyone at bay for a few days."

In truth, if King Maximilian paid another unexpected visit, demanding to see her, Stasia couldn't be certain what would happen. Still, her other choices were impossible. Her arm ached, and any attempts at climbing the tree in the gardens would likely exacerbate her wound, in addition to being dreadfully painful.

"You must see that we have no other option save this one," she added when he remained silent, his countenance set in stone.

"I'll do my best to send word to your lady-in-waiting," he relented, still looking grim, his tone grudging. "She speaks English, yes?"

Relief washed over her. "Fluently."

"Good." His gaze searched her face, his expression softening. "Now get some rest. It's been a long night, and I expect you're weary."

He rose to his feet and turned on his heel, preparing to leave the chamber. Too soon. She didn't want him to leave. Not now, not ever.

"Archer?" she called after him.

He stopped, casting a glance over his shoulder.

"I care for you as well," Stasia confessed.

Archer was silent for a moment, his face unyielding, his stare harsh and hard, his sensual lips tightened in a forbidding line.

"You shouldn't, Princess," he said at last. "I'm not worthy of you."

Before she could protest, he was gone.

CHAPTER 9

Ordering one of his men to climb a tree in a Mayfair garden and steal into a lady's bedchamber was a new and unique black mark upon Archer's soul. Fortunately, the brazen feat had worked. His man had returned unscathed and unnoticed by the guards stationed on the periphery of the town house. Most importantly, he had managed to pass on the note Archer had written to Stasia's lady-in-waiting, in which he explained the circumstances of the night. He'd been as vague as possible, knowing that it was possible someone could intercept the note before it reached its intended audience.

His man had waited for a response before scaling back down the tree and disappearing into the night.

Archer stared down at the tersely written reply from the woman on his desk, reading it again.

My loyalty, as always, is to Her Royal Highness. I'll do my utmost to keep others from discovering her absence, but I recommend three days at most before suspicions rise, though sooner if at all practicable.

Respectfully,
T.
PS: I must insist that if an infection sets in, you notify me at once.

It wasn't the demand within the letter that had struck him most, nor the cool, almost condescending tone. Rather, it was the time allotment. Three days.

He closed his eyes. Every one of those days was going to be pure and utter torture, knowing how finite the hours were that he could have Stasia here with him, beneath his roof.

In his bed.

Which was where she was now, innocently sleeping and recovering from the vicious events of mere hours earlier. No, he couldn't lose sight of the reason she was here with him, the additional days they'd been given together having a far different purpose than what he so desperately yearned for.

Because someone wanted Stasia dead.

And he had no bloody notion of who it was or why. No idea of when or if the bastard would strike again. The suspects were obvious: her uncle or her betrothed. But why would her uncle send her to London for an official engagement only to have someone kill her? And if it had indeed been the king, why would he not have simply had one of his guards poison her or otherwise make an attempt within the town house? He felt reasonably certain that the man who had struck tonight had been watching her from the shadows for the past few days. He knew where to wait and lurk, prepared to strike. Was it the man she was meant to marry, then? She had certainly been adamant in her wish not to wed him.

But who was her betrothed? Did she fear him? Was he the sort of vicious monster who would hire an assassin to slay her? Her betrothed certainly knew what she was about—he had sent his carriage for her use. None of it made sense.

"Blast," he muttered, rising from his chair, the letter from Stasia's lady-in-waiting in hand.

He stalked to the fire and pitched the note into the grate, watching the elegant scrawl distort and then disappear entirely into ash. Best to remove all evidence, just as he had directed Lady Tansy to do in the note he had sent for her. The fewer connections that existed between himself and Stasia, the better.

For both of their sakes.

Her earlier words to him before he'd left his chamber returned, echoing in his mind. *I care for you as well.* She cared for him. And saints preserve him, he cared for her too. More than he had ever believed himself capable of.

He didn't like the feeling of helplessness holding him in its relentless grip just now. It had been many years since he had last felt so powerless, and he didn't like the place it took him in his mind.

Those were dark days he had no wish to revisit.

"You're still awake."

The husky, feminine voice behind him caught Archer by surprise. He turned to find Stasia at the threshold to his study, having opened the door without his hearing. Christ, another sign of how much she affected him. He had been a spy for the Crown, and not because he made such egregious errors.

"You were meant to be sleeping," he charged, summoning all his restraint to keep from crossing the room and going to her.

Her countenance was pale in contrast to her hair, which was unbound, hanging loosely over her shoulders. The gown she had been wearing earlier yet clung lovingly to her well-curved frame. The sight of the linen bandage wrapped around her arm hit him like a blow to the breadbasket, yet another reminder of why she was here and what had happened to her.

She gave him a sad smile. "I cannot. My arm aches."

Of course it did. By God, Archer despised the fact that she had been wounded. He wished he could resurrect the villain just so that he could put another bullet in him for daring to make her bleed.

He flexed his fingers at his sides, wishing he could touch her and yet not trusting himself to do so.

"Wine?" he suggested.

She drifted nearer, holding her injured arm stiffly. "Please."

He stalked to his sideboard and poured each of them a glass before turning back to her and offering one. She took it, their fingers brushing. Awareness blazed through him. He wanted to pull her into his arms, bury his face in her hair. Wanted to hold her and never let her go.

What a bloody fool he was.

How had she managed to burrow her way into his cold, dead heart with such intrepid ease?

"Take a seat," he told her curtly, vexed with himself for his uncontrollable reaction to her.

For wanting her so much when surrendering to that temptation was impossible.

For failing her.

"I don't wish to sit," she countered, watching him with a bright-eyed stare over the rim of her glass as she sipped from it. "I've been lying in bed for hours, and I've already grown tired of being an invalid."

Stubborn wench.

"Stand, then, if it pleases you." He took a long draught from his glass. "My man was able to send word to your lady-in-waiting without anyone discovering him."

Relief flared in her gaze. "Thank you."

"You needn't thank me. It's the least I can do after what transpired."

"Archer, you aren't to blame for what happened."

She was still looking at him as if he were some manner of knight who had gallantly protected her.

"Yes, I bloody well am, and I'll not argue the point with you any further." He tossed back some more wine, but he knew it wouldn't be sufficient to dull the twin aches of longing and guilt eating away at him.

She took another drink of her own wine as well. "That is because you know that if you continued arguing with me, you would only lose in the end."

Her arrogant response wrung a reluctant grin from him. "If that's what you want to believe, Princess."

"You'll not persuade me otherwise." Stasia tilted her head, considering him with a stare that saw far too much of him. "Do you want to know the real reason I couldn't sleep?"

He did, and he didn't. It was heaven and hell in one question, the burning desire for her to give voice to the simmering connection blazing between them and yet the fervent need to maintain distance. There were at least a dozen reasons why he shouldn't want Princess Anastasia St. George the way he did, and yet none of them seemed to matter one whit.

"Why?" he asked.

"Because I missed you."

Her softly voiced confession was too much. His reaction was visceral. He ground his molars with so much force, his jaw ached. Archer drained the rest of his wine and then stalked back to the sideboard, depositing his empty glass on the polished surface. He took a deep, steadying breath before he turned back to face her.

"You shouldn't tell me things like that," he managed.

She held his gaze, her lovely countenance far too solemn.

"It's the truth."

He swallowed hard. "You've had a shock tonight. It's only natural for you to feel unsettled and not want to be alone."

She closed the distance between them, not stopping until she was so near that the hem of her gown brushed the tops of his boots.

Stasia tipped her head back, her expression open and vulnerable. "The way I feel has nothing to do with what happened earlier and everything to do with you. I think I'm falling in love with you."

She was killing him. Slowly, painstakingly ruining him with every word she uttered, with the intensity of her stare. And he couldn't look away. Couldn't seem to break the spell she had cast over him.

"You lost rather a lot of blood before the doctor tended to your wound," he forced out. "You aren't thinking clearly."

"I'm thinking more clearly than I ever have."

"We should be discussing your brother," he said, attempting to change the subject. "I'm entirely convinced that Beast and Prince Theodoric are the same man."

"I don't want to talk about him just now."

He could see that she didn't. She had placed her half-empty wineglass on the sideboard along with his.

She isn't yours, he reminded himself sternly. *She can never be yours. She's a goddamned princess, and you're the bastard son of a marquess.*

But despite trying to cling to common sense, when her hand landed in his cravat, he found himself grasping her wrist in response. Not to pull her touch away. Rather, to hold it there.

"Stasia," he rasped. "What are you doing?"

"Kissing you," she said matter-of-factly as she rolled to her toes.

Bloody fucking hell.

"We shouldn't—"

The rest of his protest was effectively smothered as she aligned her lips to his. His resistance faded beneath the sensual onslaught of her lips. His hands found the sweet curve of her waist, their natural home. He pulled her body against his gently, keenly aware of the need to avoid jostling her wounded arm.

All the reasons why he shouldn't be kissing her fled his mind when her tongue tentatively sought entrance to his mouth.

∼

Archer tasted like wine and sin, and she wanted to lose herself in him. Wanted to forget about all the uncertainty of her future, to forget what had happened earlier, to distract herself from the burning pain in her arm. But most of all, she didn't want to waste a single second she had with this man.

He swiftly took control over the kiss, pulling her against him so that the tantalizing ridge of his cock prodded her stomach. And yet, he took great care with her, his touch tender, his movements slow. He was treating her as if she were as fragile as the finest Sèvres. She wanted to tell him he needn't take such care, that he wouldn't hurt her, but his mouth was having an astonishing effect upon her will to do anything other than continue kissing him.

It seemed as if she would perish if she stopped.

Her wounded arm remained immobile at her side, for she feared causing herself further injury if she took him entirely into her arms as she wished. Instead, with her uninjured arm, she slid her touch higher, leaving his simply tied linen cravat for his skin. She curled her hand around his nape, keeping him where she wanted him, urging him to continue feasting on her lips.

She had understood his intentions all too plainly—he was attempting to distance himself from her. But distance was the last thing she needed. She didn't wish him to be honorable, to play the gentleman, to worry over her. She wanted him to forget about everything except for their mutual desire.

When he groaned into her mouth, his tongue tangling with hers, a burst of triumph unfurled within her. She had never felt more alive than she did now, as if she had been given a new sense of purpose in the wake of the attack.

He broke the kiss but didn't retreat, instead keeping his lips a scant inch from hers, so close that his hot breath fell over her mouth. "We shouldn't be doing this. You've been hurt."

"Scarcely a scratch," she murmured. "I'll live."

He closed his eyes and leaned his forehead against hers, looking as if he waged a great inner battle. "Princess. Only you would call a knife wound a scratch."

She heard the reluctant admiration in his voice. She prided herself on her resilience; it was what had propelled her through the last ten years of terror. And it would be what carried her on to face what lay ahead. But she didn't want to think about marriage to King Maximilian now, nor did she want to think about what would happen if she couldn't persuade Theodoric to join in the plot against Gustavson. She didn't want to think about the danger her sisters faced or the fate of Boritania. She most certainly didn't want to think about the fact that someone was trying to have her killed.

All she desired was the man holding her close. The man who had prepared her a meal when she had been hungry, who had shot her attacker and saved her, who had shown her such exquisite pleasure. The man she wished could be forever hers.

"A cutpurse with dreadful aim isn't enough to keep me

from what I want," she told him, meaning those words to her marrow.

"We've discussed this. That was no cutpurse."

"Whoever he was, he's dead now, and I don't want to think about him for a moment longer. Kiss me again, Archer. Please."

He made a low sound, and then his mouth took hers once more, this time a bit more roughly, his teeth raking over the fullness of her bottom lip. She kissed him back with all the furor clamoring within her. Kissed him until she was breathless and her lips were swollen.

It was her turn to break the kiss, leaning back to drink in the sight of him, looking so furiously passionate that her knees threatened to give way.

"Come to bed with me," she whispered.

He licked his lips. "Your wound..."

"Is well bandaged by the doctor," she finished triumphantly.

"You've had enough pain for one night," he continued.

"Sweet Deus, cease being so gentlemanly." She shook her head, entreating him with her gaze, showing him that she was utterly certain of what she desired.

He raised a brow. "I'm the furthest one can get from a gentleman. But even I know the difference between right and wrong, and bedding you in this state is bloody wrong."

"What is wrong is you refusing us what we both want," Stasia countered, determined to stay her course. "Would you have me beg you?"

The question seemed to break the dam within him.

He muttered a curse she didn't understand, and then he scooped her into his arms, cradling her against his hard chest, taking them both from his study with long-legged strides that made short work of the distance to his bedchamber.

CHAPTER 10

Archer didn't stop until he reached his chamber. His heart was pounding, his breaths emerged in ragged gasps, and his cock was hard.

Perhaps he was going to loathe himself in the morning.

Certainly, he would regret what he was about to do.

But nearly losing her today had chipped away at his restraint. And her kisses in his study, coupled with her fiery determination, had driven him beyond rational thought. Beyond reason or honor.

He set her down as gently as possible on the carpet, careful to avoid her injured arm.

"This is your last chance to change your mind, Princess," he felt obliged to warn her. "Tell me to go to the devil."

"I'm not going to change my mind, and I don't want you to go anywhere other than into your bed, with me."

How was he to resist? The answer was plain: he couldn't. Surrender was his only option. He had known it from the second he had taken her into his arms. Hell, he had known it instinctively from their initial meeting. Had felt it to his bones, that there was something so very right about this woman.

Mine, mine, mine.

There went that errant thought again, the possessive desire surging forth. He had told himself that he kept his distance for her sake. But the truth was, he also had been trying to do so to protect himself. Because the way he felt for her was dangerous. He wanted more than she could give. Wanted everything.

"Is that a command, Your Royal Highness?" he asked, keeping his voice low.

She held his gaze, regal as ever, unflinching. "Yes."

But he had to be certain, for the sake of his conscience later, that not a modicum of doubt lingered in her mind.

"You're sure, Stasia?"

"The only thing in this world that I'm sure of is the way you make me feel," she told him quietly.

And he didn't doubt her, because it was the bloody same for him. Every touch, each kiss, stoked the fires higher. Introducing her to pleasure had been sweet torture. Knowing that she wanted far more of him than he had given her thus far had been no different. He had spent his days in an agony of pent-up desire.

"I'll be gentle," he promised, shedding his coat to the floor. "If anything hurts, if your arm begins to pain you more, say the word, and I'll stop."

She presented him with her back, sweeping her long hair over her shoulder in response. "Help me with my gown, if you please."

"With pleasure."

The garment could not be gone soon enough. His trembling hands flew over tapes, untying knots. He took great care in tugging her bodice down her arms, making certain the gown didn't cause pressure to her wound. Archer turned his attention to her petticoat and stays next, removing them with similar ease and attention to her injury.

Someone had removed her boots already, and she stood in her stockinged feet and chemise.

"Your boots," he ground out, jealousy lending a harsh edge to his voice. "Who took them off for you?"

"I did."

"Thank Christ," he muttered. "I didn't give Crisfield leave to go beneath your skirts. If he had…"

His words trailed off, for he supposed it was a moot point. He needn't tell her what his reaction would have been, and the good doctor would live to see another day.

Archer cleared his throat. "You ought to have asked me for help. I would have gladly aided you."

"I suspect I was rather dazed. I dripped blood all over the laces. I don't even know why I was so concerned with removing them. It's silly."

The reminder that her blood had been spilled today had him clenching his jaw. "You were suffering from shock. It's what happens to us when we are faced with sudden danger or injury. You needn't fret over them, love. I'll have them cleaned for you."

"You needn't do so."

Her soft, swift denial was not unexpected. He didn't know if it was her pride or her sense of independence that spurred her more. But she was going to have to accept his aid, damn it. She was here, beneath his roof and under his protection now, even if the arrangement was only temporary.

"Yes, I do need," he told her firmly. "I need to do far more than that, in truth. You're mine while you're here with me, and I take care of what is mine."

She was stubborn, his princess, but she also knew when to give in.

The fight fled her expression, replaced by gratitude. "Thank you, then."

If the tension between them—purely sexual in nature—weren't so heavy and strong, he might have teased her at her hasty capitulation and his victory. Instead, he kissed her. Slowly, deeply. Took her soft lips with his as he had been longing to do from the moment their mouths had parted before he had brought her to his bedchamber.

She made a heady sound deep in her throat, clutching his shoulder with one hand. He took the invitation to slide his tongue inside her mouth, to taste her again. She kissed him back every bit as passionately, as if she were drawing her life source from his lips, his tongue, his breath.

He dragged his mouth from hers, kissing along her delicate jaw, lips absorbing the fine bone structure beneath her silken skin. Inhaling her scent, his mouth traveling to her ear.

"I don't want your gratitude, Princess," he murmured softly. "I just want you."

She sighed, her breath coasting hot over his cheek. "I want you more."

He cupped her nape, took her mouth again.

After the shock they had both endured, after coming so close to losing her, all the danger swirling around them, his ability to rein himself in had waned.

It was wrong, and he didn't give a damn.

This woman—this princess—could never truly be his, and yet in this moment, it felt as if she could be. As if she *were* his, as if making love to her were inevitable. And if he couldn't have her for the rest of his days, at least he could have her now. Tonight. These fleeting hours of passion were all they could ever have. It would have to suffice.

Even if it never could.

Life wasn't fair. No one knew that better than he did, the bastard son of a marquess who had been betrayed by his own mother, forsaken by his father, and who had been forced to claw his way up from the depths of the hell to which he'd been sent as a young, naïve lad.

He dragged his lips down her throat to where her pulse beat fast and frantic. Cupped her breast and felt the hard bud of her nipple in his palm through her chemise. Reminded himself that her injury meant that removing her chemise would require more care than the rest of her clothing had.

He caught the fine linen in his grasp, giving it a light tug. "I want this off, love. But I have no wish to hurt you. Tell me if your arm pains you, and I'll stop at once."

She nodded, taking a step back to grant him better access. The garment was fitted differently to her form than her bodice had been. He saw that at once. Removing it would prove damned difficult without jostling her arm.

He was going to have to cut it off.

"Hell," he muttered, rubbing at his jaw in agitation. "I'm afraid there is no good way to take it off you without hurting you. I'm going to have to fetch a blade and cut it in two."

"Do it," she said, undeterred by the prospect of her undergarment being thoroughly ruined.

Archer stalked to the table at his bedside and released a lever that caused a hidden compartment to spring open, revealing the weapon. He kept it there for protection, but in this part of London, even with the enemies he had amassed over the years, it was no longer truly necessary. Gripping the hilt, he returned to where he had left her, taking the chemise in his free hand and holding it away from her as he used the blade to rend the fabric in two. He moved slowly and with extreme caution, cognizant of the sharpness of his dagger and its proximity to her skin.

When it was done, he peeled both halves easily down and then did away with her stockings and garters as well, until she wore nothing save a gold necklace at her throat. He couldn't resist a moment to admire her, his bold and brazen princess who climbed trees and flitted about London in the night and intended to sacrifice herself for the greater good of her people, who was brave and strong, who had been attacked and yet demonstrated such astounding resilience. Who was the most fearless and stubborn and beautiful woman he'd ever known.

"My God, Princess."

The words were torn from him, from the basest, deepest part of him where everything was dark and cruel. Where he'd forced the pain of his younger years. Because there she was like sunlight, shining into his night, banishing the shadows.

"Do you like what you see then, Tierney?" she asked, lips quirking in an arrogant smirk.

"There are no words," he rasped, closing the distance between them and wrapping an arm around her waist to pull her close. "No words sufficient to describe just how bloody much I like what I see."

A wicked glint entered her eyes, the smile still pulling at the corners of her kissable mouth. "Good. Because I also like what I see, but I want to see more of it."

Yes.

He was wearing far too much damned clothing, was he not?

His cock twitched. "You want me naked, Princess?"

Once again, she didn't hesitate. "I do."

Remaining clothed had helped to rein in his need for her during their previous encounters. But tonight, he wasn't playing the gentleman. Tonight, he was taking what she had been offering for days. Taking her. Making her his in every sense of the word, because almost losing her had brought him to the edge of reason.

"Then say the words," he said, his voice husky, betraying

his desire.

She held his gaze, unflinching. "I want you naked, Archer. I want you to fuck me and fill me, to make me yours."

Nothing could have prepared him for her declaration.

The lust that roared through him was almost dizzying.

"Where did you learn such wickedness, Princess?" he managed, though he already knew the answer, tossing his unneeded dagger to the floor, fingers flying over buttons.

"From you."

So she had.

He shucked his waistcoat. "I told you before, I'm a terrible influence, love."

"I don't mind if you corrupt me," she said.

His cock was harder than marble. He tore at the rest of his clothes, more eager to shed them than he had ever been. Desire made his fingers stupid, fumbling with stubborn buttons. His patience fled him, and the sound of rending fabric filled the air.

The last of the barriers between them fell away, and he took her mouth in another kiss as he guided them to the waiting bed. The counterpane was drawn back from when she had last left before coming to him in his study. Sheets that bore her delicate scent awaited—sweet orange and jasmine. He'd been surrounded by her last night, tormented at dawn by a bed that smelled of her, and yet alone. Nothing but his own hand for futile comfort. She was here with him now.

His while it lasted.

Possession burned through him, desire a rope that tightened on his chest, making his lungs ache. He realized he was holding his breath and released it in a gusty sigh of satisfaction as they lay down together in the bed, Stasia on her back and Archer atop her. She was all soft, warm womanly curves, and he wanted to lose himself in her. Her legs were parted, his cock pressed between them, burrowing into the supple yield of her belly.

Ever cognizant of her wound, he leveraged his weight on one forearm, trying to keep from unintentionally jostling her in any way. As he shifted, her hard nipples rubbed against his bare chest. A sharp arrow of lust winged through him.

She made a small sound.

"Are you comfortable?" he asked, instantly concerned that he had somehow caused her further pain.

Her uninjured hand settled on his shoulder, silken palm gliding over his hungry skin. "I told you, I'll not break."

As she said the words, she rolled her hips against his, seeking. His cock was aching and rigid. Desperate to be inside her.

"Tell me if it hurts," he ground out.

"It hurts," she said, her voice low and husky.

He was a beast, and this was wrong. He moved to disentangle himself, but she wrapped her legs around his hips, staying him.

"No, don't leave me," she said. "Stay."

He growled. "Princess, your wound is already hurting you. I'll not make it worse by—"

"It isn't my wound that pains me," she interrupted. "That isn't where I ache."

Fucking hell.

"Where?" he ground out. "Where does it hurt you?"

"Give me your hand."

What game was she playing? He had never been more agonizingly on edge before, desperation laced with all-encompassing need. He was helpless to do anything other than what she asked, giving her his hand. She took it, fingers wrapping around his wrist, and then brought it to her breast. The tight bud on the decadent swell greeted him like a salute. He instantly cupped his hand.

"Here," she whispered. "And other places too."

He rolled his thumb over her nipple. "Where else?"

"Lower."

Archer swallowed against another rush of desire and glided his touch down her stomach, following her lead, not stopping until he traced over the inviting mound between her legs. Wetness kissed his fingertips as he slid them over her seam and parted her folds. He found the swollen bud of her clitoris and strummed over it lightly, making her hips buck.

"Here?" he asked, teasing her by circling the bud.

"Mmm," was all she said in response.

Smiling, he lowered his head and sucked the pretty pink peak of one breast into his mouth, dancing over her cunny in light, teasing touches all the while. He wanted her desperate. Wanted to take her to the brink of spending and then slide inside her. But even as he knew he should take his time, his own need had been heightened to the point of almost pain.

He fluttered over her pearl, then sought her entrance where she was soaked, more than ready for him. He stroked her, unable to resist sliding his forefinger inside her tight heat all the way to the knuckle. Her inner muscles clenched in welcome, dragging him deeper as she tipped her hips toward him, chasing more. And he gave her what they both wanted, working deeper, finding the place that made her wild as he crooked his finger gently and pressed until she was panting, his thumb rubbing over her clitoris as he kissed the side of her breast.

She felt so good, so right, so bloody perfect. She felt like *his*, and he wanted to keep her here forever, even though he knew that sentiment for the impossibility it was. They had a few stolen days, no more. The futility of their situation spurred him on.

"I want you to remember this night," he murmured

against her sweetly scented skin. "To remember me. He may have you one day, but I'll always be your first."

"I'll never forget a single second of it," she told him, her voice throaty, her fingers sifting through his hair in a tender caress that took him straight to the edge of reason.

The way she touched him. The way she looked at him. It was like heaven and hell simultaneously. A torturous purgatory. Her body was pliant and soft beneath him, the pump of his fingers in her dripping cunny mingling with the sound of their ragged breathing. And suddenly, Archer couldn't wait any longer. He had to be inside her.

He withdrew his fingers from her and gripped his cock, gliding it along her folds and covering himself in wetness.

"Are you ready for me, Princess?" he asked, feeling almost light-headed, so strong was the fever in which he was gripped.

"Always," she said, lips still swollen from his kisses, her eyes glittering in the candlelight, her hair fanned out on his pillow like a chestnut cloud.

Every inch the regal princess. More beautiful than any woman had a right to be. Everything he'd never known he wanted and yet now couldn't fathom living without.

He shifted, leveraging himself higher so that he could take her mouth as he took her body. The head of his cock was poised. She sighed into his kiss, undulating beneath him with eager little lifts of her hips.

The friction was too much. It was not enough.

He moved, sinking inside her tight passage. She was so hot, so wet. Desire roared through him, urging him on. Another light thrust of his hips took him incrementally deeper. He had never bedded a virgin before, nor had he ever bedded a woman he cared for so much. He wanted this to be good for her. Better than good. He wanted to be not just her first lover, but her best.

Her only.

He couldn't have that, so he would settle for what he could have: making this night as memorable as possible. Making her come as many times as he could.

He gentled the kiss, lips parting from hers. "I don't want to hurt you. How does it feel, love?"

"It feels..." Her words trailed off, and she moved beneath him, impatient and bold as ever. "I need..."

Once again, her sentence went uncompleted. That was fine. He wanted her mindless and drunk on pleasure.

He moved again, stretching her, bringing himself deeper. "Is this what you need, Princess?"

She moaned and tightened on him, almost squeezing him out.

His fingers drifted over her clitoris, knowing how much pressure she liked there, how fast. "You want more of my cock?"

"Oh sweet Deus."

He had his answer in her body's reaction to him, in the way she writhed, seeking more, the way her body sucked him in. Another roll of his hips, and he was fully seated within her, her cunny clamping around him like a vise. He took her hand in his, guiding it to the place where they were joined.

"Feel us, Princess. Feel how perfectly we fit together." He withdrew slightly, allowing her questing fingers to travel over the base of his cock, to trail along the puffy, slick lips of her sex, to circle the place where he was rigid and thick, impaling her so deliciously.

"I love the way you feel inside me," she murmured, sounding breathy and drunk on desire.

He removed her hand, guiding it to his shoulder. "So do I, love. I'm going to make you mine properly now."

His words were met with the thrust of her hips and another rasped moan.

His control snapped. His body took over, hips chasing hers as he pumped his cock in and out of her cunny, filling and then withdrawing, finding the rhythm they both needed. Harder, faster, deeper, *more*. His careful seduction fell apart beneath the blazing furor of his ardor. He caressed her hip, her breasts. Tugged at her nipples. Dipped his head into the fragrant hollow of her neck and feasted like a starving man. Played with her clitoris until she was tightening on his cock. Drove into her with faster strokes, pinning her to the bed with his cock, the headboard clacking against the wall in rhythmic time to their frenzied fucking.

They were one, their bodies slick with sweat, working together for a common goal: fulfillment. Everything beyond the four walls of his bedchamber ceased to exist. They weren't princess and bastard but man and woman, Stasia and Archer, bound together by desire and the elemental need burning hotter than any flame between them. They were the most beautiful, raw, true versions of themselves.

And as he sank between her pretty thighs to the hilt, her cunny gripping at him as if her body wanted to hold him there forever and never let go, a most stunning realization blistered forth. It shot through him like fire. Painful, sudden, searing as any flame.

He had fallen in love with her.

He loved Princess Anastasia Augusta St. George.

Bloody fucking hell. When had it happened and why? How?

Questions, so many of them. But her nails dug into the tender flesh at his shoulder, and she arched her back, wrapping her legs around his hips as he continued pumping into her, finding her own pinnacle.

"Archer," she cried out, throwing her head back into the pillow, lips parted wide, eyes closed.

He felt as if he could conquer the whole damned world.

She was so beautiful like this, lost in ecstasy, breasts bouncing with the force of his thrusting hips, nipples tight points that begged for his mouth. His Boritanian goddess.

"Fuck yes, Princess," he gritted. "Come on my cock."

In answer, her cunny clenched hard, threatening to drain him dry.

"Good girl," he managed, the praise torn from him.

He thrust into her again, on the brink himself as he rode out the waves of her release. A few more strokes. He set his teeth on edge, staving off the inevitable. In and out, sinking deep into her soaking cunny. She was even wetter than before, her inner thighs smeared with her juices, a circle spreading on the bedclothes under her. Deep, hard, fast. Headboard banging. Skin slapping. He held his breath until his lungs ached from the pressure. So close, so bloody close.

It required every speck of control he had to withdraw from her at the last moment.

But he did, wrapping his hand around his cock in a poor replacement for her cunny, tightening his fist to jerk it up and down his shaft. He came in an instant, spurts of milky white jetting over her belly and breasts until there was nothing remaining, and he collapsed to the bed at her side, breathing as heavily as if he had just raced in circles about Hyde Park.

His heart was pounding, his mind incapable of coherent thought, his body humming with the force of his release. She was a soft and warm feminine presence at his side, pressed against him. A star that had been plucked from the midnight sky and delivered to him alone.

"Thank you," she said quietly, her hand finding his, their fingers lacing in the tousled bedclothes.

She was thanking *him*? Christ. She had no idea that she'd just brought him to his knees. That she had just ruined him forever. That after this, no other woman would ever do because none of them would be her.

He turned to Stasia. "I'm the one who should be grateful." Archer brought her hand to his lips for a reverent kiss. "You've given me a tremendous gift, one that is dearer than any riches I've ever sought."

It occurred to him that he should clean his spend from her. But he also liked the way she looked, covered in him. Marked by him in the most primitive sense.

She kissed his shoulder, the gesture making something deep in his gut tighten into a knot. "I liked it far more than I even supposed I would."

Her confession won a startled chuckle from him. "Careful, Princess. Your compliment will go to my head."

"I think you already know just how handsome you are," she countered, smiling back at him.

"Hearing you say it makes me happy." Happier, even, than he cared to admit. He forced himself not to dwell on the sensations teeming inside him, so many of them new and foreign, and reached out to rub his seed into her skin. "You look so bloody beautiful wearing nothing but me."

She shifted restlessly, arching into his touch. "How long before we can do that again?"

He'd thought it before, but saint's teeth, this woman was going to be the death of him. His cock twitched back to life with renewed interest. What a glorious death it would be.

"I don't want to make you sore," he said, struggling to fight his rampant lust and be a gentleman.

"You won't," she returned.

Then, his wicked princess took his hand in hers and brought his finger to her lips, licking the pearlescent drop of spend from his skin.

And all efforts at being a gentleman were promptly abandoned.

CHAPTER 11

*S*tasia woke with a possessive arm slung around her waist and a hot, hard male body pressed against hers.

The thick ridge of him prodded her hip, making her smile.

Very hard, indeed.

It was so perfect, the morning still and quiet, soft, gray light dancing around them, that for a moment, she was afraid she was dreaming. She didn't want to move and have the idyll come to an end. But the pain in her wounded arm reminded her that this was no dream. As did her surroundings. She was in a strange bed, in a room that didn't belong to her.

With a man who didn't belong to her.

Last night, Archer had made love to her twice over, and she would never be the same.

"How are you feeling this morning, love?"

The sleepy rasp of his voice had her turning her head on the pillow to find him watching her from beneath a hooded gaze. Yearning flared to life, hot and heavy, the place between her thighs throbbing both from their lovemaking last night and from fresh need. He made her feel flushed and achy, as if her skin was stretched too tightly over her body. As if she needed to be touched, and yet simultaneously as if she would shatter into a thousand tiny shards if he passed so much as a knowing hand over her greedy flesh.

It was disconcerting. So much of her existence had been ruled by repression and fear. Surrendering to this desire, to her body's needs, felt impossibly wicked and forbidden. Wrong and yet oh-so very right.

"I feel..." she began, only to allow her words to trail off.

For it was a confusing mass of emotions. She felt powerful and strong. She felt sated and yet eager for more. She felt perfect, as if she was where she had always been meant to be. And yet, that was nothing but a chimera, for their time together was finite. A few days, no more.

"You feel," he prompted, kissing her jaw, the rasp of his whiskers sending a shiver of delight through her.

"I feel wonderful, although my arm is aching like the very devil," she admitted.

"I should take a look at it, make certain infection isn't setting in."

She didn't want him to let her go or leave the bed. Ever.

"It will wait."

But he was already sliding from the bedclothes. Her eyes clung lovingly to his form. His back was all muscle and sinew, his shoulders wide and broad. But his arse...she'd never thought about a man's form in detail before, but Archer's was firm and delightfully tight. The urge to sink her fingers into that supple flesh rose.

Unfortunately, her lover was all business with the morning's light. He strode across the chamber and shrugged into a banyan, hiding his body from her avid study, much to her dismay. She would have preferred the opportunity to further gaze upon him.

As if he could read her thoughts, he cast a smug grin in her direction. "Like what you see, Princess?"

"Can you doubt it?" How she wished she'd had the opportunity to see the front of him more fully. Last night, there had been far too many shadows and, well, much of the time, her eyes had been closed as she had been lost to the sensations he was visiting upon her. "Of course I do. However, I would like to see more of you. Must you hide yourself from me? I want to...what is the English word...ogle?"

Her English was strong; both her parents and Gustavson had insisted upon the use of English at court. It was one of few tenets upon which they had ever agreed, the need to maintain a relationship with the far-more-powerful kingdom. But there were times when her mind couldn't quite seize the proper word. And as Archer had taught her, there were words she had yet to learn.

He chuckled as he reached her side. "You may ogle me later. First, I need to see that wound of yours."

He brought with him his scent of soap and musk and the undeniable undertone of their earlier lovemaking. His mahogany hair hung rakishly over his forehead as he seated himself on the bed. She reached out with her good hand and brushed it away, noticing for the first time the bump in the bridge of his nose, an imperfection in an otherwise flawless array of masculine beauty.

"Your nose," she murmured. "Was it broken?"

His green gaze slid from hers. "It was."

She waited, expecting him to elaborate, but he said nothing.

Instead, he gently began unraveling the linen bandage

that the doctor had pinned neatly in place the night before. "If it hurts, tell me. I'm trying to be as careful as I can."

"What happened?" she asked, knowing that he would do his utmost to make certain to move her arm as little as possible.

No man had ever touched her with as much tender care as Archer Tierney showed her.

His jaw clenched. "It was a long time ago."

It occurred to her how little she knew of him. She knew that he could cook. She knew that he had astounding power and connections in London and its underworld. She knew how he kissed, knew what he felt like deep inside her. But she knew nothing of his past, of what had made him the man he was. And she wanted very much—perhaps selfishly so—to know more. For him to give to her those secret parts of himself that he never gave to any other. Wanted to tuck those treasures into her heart for safekeeping.

"Will you not speak of it, then?" she pressed, hoping he would change his mind.

She had told him the truth about her scars, after all. An exchange seemed only fair.

He kept his attention carefully turned upon his task, continuing to unwind the bandage with torpid care. For a long moment, she thought he would refuse her request or ignore her question altogether. But then, at last, he spoke.

"It is a gift from my half brother, the Marquess of Granville," he said, his voice low and measured, as if he exerted great effort to keep all traces of emotion from his tone. "He is a vile bully who pushed our half sister into the lake at his country seat when she couldn't swim. She was nothing but a slip of a girl."

"Deus," she whispered, horrified at the revelation, fearful of what he would say next. "What happened to her?"

"I jumped in after her," he continued methodically,

"pulling her from the water. She was coughing and sputtering, but otherwise blessedly fine. I was furious with Granville. Even though I knew the difference in our stations—I was a mere bastard allowed to stay with the family as if I were truly a part of it—I pushed him. He was older than me and far stronger. He showed me what he thought of my anger with his fists."

"Thank heavens you were there to rescue her. What a despicable scoundrel."

"That is far too kind a description of him." Archer finished unraveling the last of the bandage, leaving her wound bare. "But never fear. In the end, I exacted the ultimate revenge upon him. He'll never hurt anyone again, my sister in particular, or he'll answer to me. And I'm a hell of a lot stronger than he is now, in every way. It won't go well for him should he choose to challenge me."

The ice-cold determination in his tone was so unlike the caring, considerate lover she had come to know.

"You've a sister," she said instead of further commenting on the half brother he loathed, a man who—given Archer's story about him—wasn't worth further discussion anyway.

Somehow, the knowledge that he had family surprised her. He seemed like such a fortress in some ways, a man alone.

"A legitimate half sister," he acknowledged. "Her name is Portia. The wound looks well enough to me, but Lucky has a poultice he swears by to ward off infection. I've used it myself in the past. I'll go and fetch it for you. Wait here."

A half sister named Portia who was the daughter of a marquess. Curiosity sparked inside her, but she would save it for later.

"Lucky," she repeated, thinking it vaguely amusing that he supposed she would venture anywhere when she wasn't wearing a stitch beneath the counterpane. "Your glowering butler?"

"That would be Lucky, yes. He's a good cove. Has had a difficult life. Far more so than my own, but I'd trust him with my life."

She wasn't certain she wanted anything that hulking, unsmiling fellow had to offer. But Archer trusted him, and she trusted Archer.

She nodded. "Go on, then. I'm hardly dressed to leave this room."

His gaze made an appreciative sweep over her form, concealed by the bedclothes. "This is how I prefer you, love. Naked in my bed."

She held his stare, longing for him cutting through her. "It's how I prefer myself as well."

Archer shot up from the bed as if she'd suddenly lit a fire beneath his bottom. "I'll be but a moment."

In his banyan and bare feet, he crossed the chamber with his signature long-limbed stride, leaving the room with quiet grace that belied his size and strength. When the door clicked closed at his back, she sighed, allowing her head to rest back on the pillow that smelled so deliciously of him. Her foolish heart was beating fast and hard, reminding her that the greatest threat to her welfare wasn't the cut on her upper arm growing infected, but rather the cruelly inconvenient feelings for Archer that wouldn't cease blossoming.

After last night, how could she consider herself anything other than in love with him? Helplessly, hopelessly so. He hadn't just changed her; he had changed the way she felt about him, the bonds between them so strong and true that she knew instinctively that cutting them would take a part of herself with them. A part of herself that she wasn't prepared to relinquish.

How had she imagined that she could give herself to him without wanting more? Without wanting everything?

He returned as promised, coming through the door as quietly and calmly as he had left, the poultice in hand.

The weight of her emotions was like a boulder on her chest, robbing her of the ability to breathe. She had to distract herself somehow. To think of anything other than the burgeoning love in her heart, the future that loomed without him in it.

"Did Lucky make this poultice himself?" she asked.

"Of course." Archer resumed his seat on the bed, the mattress dipping at her side.

"He didn't sprinkle poison in it?" Stasia pressed, attempting to bring some lightness to their conversation. To banish the pall that seemed to have settled over them now that their desires had been satisfied. "Or perhaps horse dung?"

That earned her the corner of Archer's lips quirking up. Just one.

"Not that I'm aware of." He paused, his eyes searing into hers. "It will sting a bit at first. Try to hold still if you can."

The scent of herbs, faintly medicinal, reached her. "It couldn't sting worse than the ointment Tansy applied to my back after the lashing. Do your worst."

"For you, only my best." He placed the poultice on her wound. "It's in place now. Have you any discomfort?"

She felt only a mild coldness, coupled with a slight sting. But as she had told him, Tansy's salve had been far less pleasant to endure.

"I'll live," she teased.

"Thank Christ," he muttered, frowning at her as his fingers went to work, restoring the bandage. "Don't joke about something like that. I could have lost you last night."

She waited for him to wind one length of the linen

around her arm before responding, unable to keep the bitterness from her voice. "You'll lose me anyway soon."

His jaw tightened, nostrils flaring. "Not like that. As long as you're safe, nothing else matters."

"Even if I'm married to someone else?"

The question left her before she could stop it. A futile, stupid question. One that had no good answer.

He stilled for a moment. "Yes, even if you're married to someone else."

And then he resumed wrapping the bandage around her arm, tightly enough to keep the poultice in place, but loosely enough to keep it from causing her further pain. She found herself feeling ridiculously irritated with him for that statement. What had she expected him to say? She never should have uttered those words.

However, she couldn't stop the surge of disappointment and frustration and hurt.

Couldn't stop wishing that he'd had a different answer. That he had told her he'd run away with her and make her his wife instead of King Maximilian's. That even for a heartbeat he had thought about making her his forever instead of surrendering her to someone else.

He finished with the bandage, securing it once more.

"Stasia," he said into the silence that had descended.

But his tone held a note of pity that she couldn't bear to hear. She was angry with herself, with her wounded pride. Resentful of the lack of control she had over her own life. If she hadn't been born a princess, she would have been able to marry any man of her choosing. She wouldn't have had to live a life of wretched sacrifice.

"I should dress," she told him coolly, attempting to hide her whirling emotions.

"I'll help you."

"I can do for myself."

"You're wounded. You've only the use of one arm."

Their gazes held, locked in a battle of wills.

"I don't need you to assist me," she countered.

"You're angry with me." He reached out, brushing a stray tendril of hair from her cheek in an intimate gesture she didn't wish melted her resolve so much.

"I'm angry with the circumstances."

His thumb lingered, his hand cupping her cheek. "What would you have had me say, Stasia? You're a princess, and I'm the bastard son of a marquess who was sold by his own mother. All we have are the next few days."

Part of that pronouncement was as true as it was grim. But there was another part of it that struck her every bit as much.

She frowned, searching his emerald gaze. "Your mother sold you?"

He nodded, the shadows of sadness passing through his eyes, making his jaw clench. "She did."

"When?" she asked, struggling to comprehend the full implications of what he had just revealed. "How?"

"It doesn't matter, love."

"It matters to me. I want to know. I want to know about you, about your past. I..."

She faltered, having been about to tell him that she loved him. And how gloriously ruinous such a confession would have been. She couldn't bear to say those words, for fear of his response.

"Tell me," she added quietly. "Please."

"It's not a burden for you to bear. It's mine." He rose from the bed, and it was as if he had closed a door inside himself.

One she was not welcome to trespass beyond.

She didn't want to press him, and yet she did. Learning about his past seemed somehow fundamental to understanding the complex man he had become. She threw back the bedclothes with her uninjured arm and rose from the bed, following him, uncaring of her nudity.

"What if I want to bear it with you?" she called to his retreating back.

He stopped, head going down, seemingly waging a war within himself.

"Stasia, you don't understand."

She went to him, laying her hand flat on the hard surface of his back. Muscle rippled beneath her touch, but he didn't jerk away.

"Make me understand, then. You've seen my scars. Show me yours."

He inhaled slowly and deeply, then exhaled. She felt the movement, the rasp of air in his lungs. For a moment, she feared he would leave her, leave the chamber. That he would decide he could no longer take the risk of hiding a wounded princess in his home. That she had pushed him too far.

But then he pivoted. Turned so that he faced her, her hand staying in place, until it was splayed over his heart instead of his shoulder blade. *Thump, thump, thump* went the steady rhythm, so vital and reassuring.

"You want to know?" he asked, his fingers circling her wrist in a grasp that was more caress than staying grip.

"Yes."

"I'll tell you," he relented at last, unsmiling, his visage seemingly honed from marble, "in return for you allowing me to assist you in dressing."

A neat checkmate. But had she expected anything less from him? Certainly not.

"Very well," she conceded. "I'll allow you to help me in return for you telling me about your past."

He shook his head. "Why should it matter so much?"

She held his gaze, opting this time for the truth. "Everything about you matters to me. That's simply the way of it."

Without waiting for his response, she moved past him, to the pile of their hastily discarded garments from the night before.

∽

Everything about you matters to me.

Holy God above. How was he to respond to those words, coming from her? They were words no one had spoken to him before. And she showed him care no lover ever had.

Archer swallowed hard against a stinging rush of emotion. Against the hot prick of something unfamiliar in the backs of his eyes. Not tears, surely. He didn't weep. Hadn't since he was a lad who'd been sold and sent away from the only home and family he'd ever known.

Stasia stormed past, distracting him, all womanly curves and decadent skin. Golden where she had lain in the sun, pale where she had been covered. Rounded everywhere she should be.

His woman.

She had taken up her chemise. He forced himself into motion, for she couldn't bloody well tell him she offered an even trade and then proceed with dressing herself anyway. If she wanted to hear the sordid secrets of his past, he would tell her. Perhaps it was for the best; she wouldn't look at him the same after she knew. He could resurrect the walls of defense she had blazed through. Put some much-needed distance between them.

Archer snatched the undergarment from her hand, then belatedly remembered its ruined state as he held it aloft, the two rent halves of the front panel flapping.

"I'll have to find you a replacement for this," he said, guilt lacing through him.

There'd been no easier method of removing it, but

neither had he thought about how he might procure a new chemise.

"I'll go without one," she said. "Now tell me, if you please."

He bent and retrieved her stays, still in one piece, and guided it slowly around her. "My mother was the Marquess of Granville's mistress. In her day, she was a celebrated actress, but her love of drink ruined her, and eventually, she became an opium eater as well." He began tightening the laces, beginning at the top, trying to keep old emotions reined in. "For some years, I was permitted to live with my half siblings. I was educated and treated as if I were a part of the family, in truth. But when my mother was no longer a favorite of the marquess, she became desperate. The marchioness didn't want her husband's by-blow underfoot. She offered my mother a tidy fortune to make me go away, and she accepted."

Stasia glanced at him over her shoulder, brow furrowed. "Oh, Archer."

He kept his attention firmly upon the lacing, tying a firm knot at the base. "That isn't the worst of it, I'm afraid. My mother took the sum from the marchioness and brought me to London, where she realized quickly that I could fetch another fortune for her. I was a comely lad, and there were brothels that traded in children."

He swallowed hard against the bile rising in his throat as old terror threatened to consume him. He preferred not to think about that part of his past, nor what had almost happened. What *had* happened to so many others just like him.

He finished his knot and bent to scoop up her petticoats.

"You needn't continue," she said softly.

And he didn't know whether it was for her benefit or his. But he'd already come this far. "I'll be as gentle as I'm able as I pull this over your head. Tell me if it hurts."

"Archer."

He ignored the pleading tone in her voice and resumed his twin tasks, helping her to dress and revealing his past. "She took the coin and left me. I was kept imprisoned in a room with another lad who had been stolen from the streets. The abbess who ran the brothel was a cruel witch set upon starving and drugging us into submission. We escaped through sheer will one night before anything worse could befall us, and then we spent the next few years surviving on our own by picking pockets and doing anything we could to keep alive."

The petticoat was draped over her now. He fastened a few buttons on each side.

"What became of the lad who escaped with you?" she asked.

"It was Lucky," he answered, reminded of how fortunate they were to have found each other and forged that brotherly bond. "He's been at my side ever since. Neither of us could have survived without the other. He's saved my life, and I've saved his."

The last of the buttons was tucked into its mooring, and she turned back to him. But the horror and disgust he thought he might find on her countenance—given the reaction he'd received in the past whenever he had spoken of his youth—was notably absent. In its stead, all he saw was compassion.

"I'm so glad you had each other," she told him. "How brave you both were. I cannot imagine how terrified you must have been."

"Not brave," he denied wryly. "Many nights, we cried like babes. But we made it through those trying times."

She reached for him with her uninjured hand, cradling his cheek, the warmth of her touch further weakening his resolve to resume a distance where she was concerned. "Thank you for telling me."

He took her wrist in a gentle grasp, bringing her palm to his mouth for a kiss. "I was bribed into doing so, if you recall."

The corners of her sensual lips turned down. "I'm sorry I forced you to speak of something you didn't wish to discuss."

He shrugged. "It's best you know the man you've allowed to bed you, Princess. I told you I'm no gentleman. I've done and seen things that would make even the most seasoned criminals flinch. I've begged and lied and stolen. I've been ruthless and heartless. I am the man my past made me. That will never change."

Archer was trying, in his own way, to force her to confront the truth. To stop looking at him with such tenderness in her eyes, as if he could save her from the future she didn't want. As if he could marry her himself. There had been a moment when the suggestion had hung, unspoken. He had known what she wanted to hear, but he'd told enough lies in his life. He wasn't going to deceive her.

"I like the man you are," she said, holding his gaze. "Just as you are. I wouldn't want you to change."

He had to swallow hard against a blinding rush of emotion and force himself to rescue her gown from the floor instead.

"You shouldn't say things like that to a man, Princess," he forced out.

She tilted her head, her expression turning inquisitive. "Why not?"

"Because it makes me want to do stupid things," he said. Things like tell her he loved her. Things like run away with her and marry her and keep her forever by his side, but he didn't say any of that either. "And neither one of us can afford that," he added.

He helped her back into the gown, taking great care with her wounded arm.

"No," she said with quiet, haunting sadness. "I suppose we cannot."

Archer tied the tapes on her bodice, hating how bloody futile the days that lay ahead of them suddenly seemed.

CHAPTER 12

"Who would want you dead?"

The grim question, issued by Archer from across the breakfast table, was one Stasia didn't want to contemplate. Because every answer was frightening, and the prospect of her own murder was not what she wanted to dwell upon when she was seated across from the brutally handsome man she would only have in her life for the span of a few more days.

She sighed. "We've been over this. I don't want to talk about it."

He made a low sound of dismissal. "Too bloody bad. You're damned lucky to be sitting here with only a wounded limb. If that bastard's aim had been any better…"

His words trailed off ominously.

She poked at the poached egg on her plate with her fork. "Fortunately for me, your aim was perfect."

"Yes, but the next time, I may not be there with a ready pistol."

Stasia didn't know which prospect alarmed her more,

that of another assassin coming for her, or Archer not being there for her as he had been last night.

"We cannot be certain he wasn't a footpad," she reminded him before shoveling a bite of egg into her mouth with a complete lack of grace and decorum.

The egg tasted like ash on her tongue. She swallowed it down with haste.

"Stasia, he wasn't a goddamn footpad."

The ire in his voice had her gaze shifting from her plate to his vibrant eyes. Even vexed as he was with her, he was beautiful to a fault. That chiseled jaw, those sensual lips that could work her body with such clever manipulation, turning her mindless. The bump on his nose, earned by saving his half sister. His slashing cheekbones. The column of his throat, the protrusion of his Adam's apple. His too-long hair that shimmered in the sunlight with hints of rich reds and gold.

He muttered a curse, dragging his hand along his jaw, bringing her attention to the long fingers that could pleasure her so well. "Stop looking at me like that, Princess."

Caught.

"Like what?" she asked, feigning innocence to needle him and—she hoped—sway him from his course.

"Like you're thinking about how good my cock felt inside you."

Thank heavens she hadn't taken another bite of egg, or else she would have choked on it. She took her time forming a response, making a show of sipping her tea, all whilst holding his gaze. She hoped that she appeared far calmer and more collected to him than she was. Because his wicked words had made her nipples go hard beneath her stays and had made an ache thrum to life between her thighs in exactly the place where his cock had been.

Where she wanted it to be again.

"That isn't what I was thinking of," she said at last, pleased with herself for summoning enough sangfroid to carry on her half of their conversation.

"Then what were you thinking? Don't try to persuade me you were thinking of the topic I'm attempting to discuss with you. I'll not believe it for a moment."

Even when he was being stern and harsh, he made her long for him. She pressed her thighs together to stave off the throbbing need and discovered that she was wet. Shamefully so.

"I was thinking about how handsome you are," she told him honestly.

In the absence of servants, they were free to speak plainly, and she was glad for the opportunity to be candid. And to study him as she wished. She couldn't seem to stop looking at him, thinking about everything that had passed between them.

Wanting more.

"My being handsome has nothing whatsoever to do with the fact that someone tried very hard to make great harm come to you last night," he countered. "Blast it, you're doing it again."

A smile twitched at her lips. "Doing what?"

"Looking at me that way. Stop it at once."

She raised a brow, feeling defiant. "Or?"

"Or I'll lift you onto the table here and now."

Her core clenched, her heart pounding hard.

"Is that meant to be a threat? Because it sounds more like a promise to me. One I would dearly like for you to keep."

Another blistering oath escaped him. "Your arm."

"You managed to avoid it well enough last night," she reminded him. "Twice."

He uttered a third curse, one she didn't comprehend,

which was likely for the best. "No more of your games, Princess. I want names, and I want them now."

Pity. She wanted *him*. But she wasn't entirely certain of the mechanics involved in making love on a table. Given the state of her arm, perhaps it was unwise.

She sighed, her body still wanting more, her mind knowing that he was right. "It could have been my uncle Gustavson. There is a possibility that one of the guards saw me leaving the town house and sent word back to him. If that is the case, I have no doubt he might simply wish me dead."

"We know he is ruthless enough to murder anyone who is in his way," Archer agreed. "What about the man you're meant to marry?"

"He is capable of it, I do not doubt. However, he needs me far too much to see me killed."

She was reasonably certain of that, for King Maximilian had been clear in his wish to overthrow Gustavson, a man he considered a threat to the peace he had worked hard to forge in his own kingdom. But to overthrow her uncle, the king needed her brother Theodoric. And for their best chance at persuading Theodoric to return to Boritania and regain the rightful throne, King Maximilian required her.

"In what way does he need you?" Archer asked sternly. "As his wife, you mean?"

It was on the tip of her tongue to make a complete confession to him. To explain everything. And yet, she couldn't shake the fear that if she told him who her betrothed truly was and what they had planned, Archer would decide the danger she presented to him wouldn't be worth the reward.

She couldn't bear to part with him sooner than necessary.

"Yes," she lied, glancing down at her plate, for she couldn't hold Archer's stare when she was deceiving him.

Guilt lanced her. After everything they had been through together, she should tell him.

"Who else?" he asked before she could say anything more on the matter. "Does your uncle have enemies in London?"

She thought for a moment, poking at the remainder of her egg. "None that I am aware of."

Aside from herself and King Maximilian, that was.

"What of your brother?"

His question had her jerking her head up in surprise. "Theodoric? Never. My brother would not harm me."

"Even if he believes you betrayed him ten years ago when he was exiled?" he pressed.

She didn't hesitate, for she knew her brother. "Not even then."

Theodoric was loyal and kindhearted. He had been something of a rake in his court days, it was true. But he had been so very young. And he had suffered greatly for his allegiance to their mother. He had nearly died for it. She had no doubt that he would have died for any of their siblings, had it been asked of him.

"Is there any other person you can think of who would wish harm to befall you?" Archer asked, dredging her from her thoughts of the past.

"No. In truth, my uncle seems the most likely." And the realization chilled her.

Because if Gustavson knew that she had been leaving the town house, it was possible that he also knew why.

"I'll have some of my men make inquiries in that vein," he said, his countenance bleak. "I'll also add some guards to the watch here at the town house whilst you're with me, in case he somehow discovers where you've gone."

She swallowed hard, new fear of Gustavson taking root in her heart. How had she imagined she would be beyond his reach in London? Or that his guards would be so easily fooled by her ruse? And what would become of Tansy? She couldn't place her loyal lady-in-waiting in further jeopardy. To do so would be wrong.

Which meant...

"I'll have to return to my uncle's town house sooner than we expected," she said. "If he is the one behind the attack on me yesterday, then word will reach him that he failed. He may have my lady-in-waiting arrested for being complicit."

"No," Archer said quickly, firmly. "You're in the most danger there. I won't allow it."

"It isn't your decision to make. I'll not put Tansy at risk. Besides, if my uncle wanted to have me killed, he had ample opportunity to do so before now. I expect he wants to make it look as if I were accosted by a cutpurse or some other such villain, outside the town house rather than within."

"Damn and blast." His fist cracked down on the table, startling her in this rare showing of anger, which she knew was not directed at her, but rather, their circumstances. "I'll find a better answer. Grant me some time."

But time was what they were running out of.

She sighed, devastation curdling all the hope of the morning. "How quickly can you summon Theodoric to see me? I'll need to speak with him as soon as possible."

"Today," Archer promised grimly.

They ate the rest of their breakfast in bleak silence.

~

"This is your library, then?" Stasia asked, walking the perimeter of the room, running her finger along the spines of books as she went.

Archer tamped down a feverish rush of longing and, with it, the need to be at her side. To be holding her, touching her. He had to remind himself that soon, she would be gone from his life forever. The note calling Stasia's brother to his town house had been sent. It was but a matter of waiting until he arrived. Thereafter, Stasia would return to her uncle's town house. And Archer would have to let her go, unless he could summon some means of keeping her with him for another day, another hour, another minute. He was greedy where she was concerned. He would take as much of her time as he could beg, borrow, or steal.

"It is *the* library, yes," he allowed, hands clasped behind his back as he stood by a bank of windows, half his attention upon the gray day beyond, a mirror for his thoughts. "Not truly mine, however. The books were left behind by the previous resident."

"Why would he leave them behind?" she asked, her voice curious. "So many books, shelves upon shelves of them."

"Because he owed me far more than what the house and all its contents were worth," he said mildly, looking away from her feminine form, hugged so deliciously by her purple gown.

Instead, he looked below, to the waterlogged street and impending gloom.

"How did he owe you such a sum?"

Her voice was near. She had wandered temptingly close in her perambulation.

Fucking hell.

He glanced away from the window, turning to find her within touching distance, unfairly beautiful.

Not mine, he told himself firmly. *Not mine.*

Meanwhile, his thudding heart had other ideas, as did his cock, which was twitching eagerly to life.

"I was a moneylender," he confessed, knowing all too well the dishonor inherent in such an occupation. "Still am one, if the opportunity arises and I'm sufficiently intrigued."

He was not ashamed of what he had done to earn his

bread. Moneylending had given him and Lucky a roof over their heads, had filled their bellies. Later, it had given him wealth beyond his ken. And after that, it had led him to other endeavors far more dangerous in nature, yet far more lucrative as well.

"A moneylender," she repeated, sounding thoughtful, those cool blue eyes of hers burning into him. "But the rest of what you do now, the services you offer, are they related?"

That she wanted to know more about him left him feeling strangely pleased. None of the women in his life had ever given a damn about how he'd earned his coin. They'd merely been pleased that he had enough to afford them whatever they wanted.

"Somewhat related, yes," he said simply, hoping that would satisfy her.

In truth, his past was complicated. He didn't regret a moment of what he had done to find himself here, standing with a beautiful princess in a Mayfair library filled with books he had neither chosen nor read.

"You are being deliberately vague, I think," she observed shrewdly, tilting her head and sending a stray tendril of hair over her cheek.

Her chignon was crude; he had gathered her hair into it himself after helping her dress. And whilst he was adept with a lady's undergarments and getting her in and out of them, his skill with a lady's toilette had proven decidedly in wont.

He reached out before he could think better of it, tucking the errant lock behind her ear, fingers lingering as they brushed over the plump, silken earlobe. Everything inside him screamed to cup her nape and haul her into him, to crash their mouths together and kiss her breathless whilst he still had the chance.

But if he did, he wouldn't be able to stop.

"Perhaps I wasn't certain how truly interested you were,

Princess," he suggested, striving to keep his tone light as he forced himself to cease touching her.

"I'm always interested where you're concerned," she said softly, sadly. "Far too much, I fear."

He understood. God, how he did.

Archer clasped his hands behind his back again in an effort to rein in his impulses. He wished he had a cheroot to smoke.

"What do you wish to know?" he found himself asking.

"All there is to know." She smiled, and he felt something in his chest tug.

"I had my start in moneylending," he said, trying to distract himself now. "It paid quite well. The education I received as a lad helped me. Lucky can't read or write. He was the muscle. I was the mind. Together, we were a team. We grew and grew. And then, another opportunity presented itself to us, one that was far more lucrative. We began working in secret for the Crown, using our eyes and ears to ferret out traitors and revolutionaries and see them arrested. Eventually, that led to the private services you availed yourself of. I've made it my life's aim to become more powerful and wealthier than those who hurt me, and I've done that."

"It's as if you've fashioned your own empire," she said, sounding impressed.

He shrugged, feeling uncomfortable, thinking of the dangers they had faced, of the men who had lost their lives. "Of criminals and thieves, I reckon. I've done everything I've had to do to survive, and I'm not ashamed of it. I'll never be welcomed in polite Society. I'll always be a marquess's byblow, a man who dirtied his hands in trade. A man desperately unfit for a princess. You never should have let me touch you, let alone bed you."

Stasia took a step closer, laid the hand on her uninjured

arm on his chest above his heart. "I don't regret a single moment of what has passed between us."

He swallowed hard. "You ought to, Princess. Hell, you shouldn't be here alone with me now. I can't control myself when you're near."

"Don't control yourself, then."

He slammed his eyes shut, trying to block out the sight of her, regal and gorgeous and looking at him as if he were someone worthy of her. "I have to, for your sake as well as mine."

"Why?" She cupped his jaw, the contact of her skin on his sending a jolt through him.

He hissed out a breath and opened his eyes, drinking in the sight of her. "Because I shouldn't have made love to you last night, and I sure as bloody hell shouldn't make love to you again."

"What if I want you to?" she murmured, giving him the same look she had earlier.

The one that had his cock rigid and straining against the fall of his trousers. The one that made him desperate to be inside her again, just one last time.

"Damn it, Princess," he growled, surrendering to temptation and settling his hands on the sweet curves of her waist. "I warned you earlier about looking at me that way."

A small smile graced her lips. She was the picture of seduction, a woman who understood all too well the effect she had upon a man, the power she wielded over him. He would do anything she asked of him, and the expression on her lovely face said she knew it. He was doomed.

He loved her.

He wanted her more than he wanted to live another day.

"I want you to fuck me, Archer," she said, her voice throaty, velvet and sin and everything wicked.

Holy.

Christ.

His body's reaction was instant, lust and the driving need to possess her raging through him. *Mine. Mine. Mine.*

He clenched his jaw. "I also told you not to use that word."

Her perfect lips drew together, her teeth catching the fullness of the lower. "Fuck?" she asked slowly, drawing out the word, the consonants.

Slaying his ability to resist her, one naughty word at a time.

"That's the one," he muttered. "Don't say it again."

"You never gave me a good reason I shouldn't." She caressed his jaw, then utterly destroyed him by using the satiny tip of her forefinger to trace the upper bow of his lips. "I don't want to be a princess or a lady right now. All I want to be is yours."

"Damn it, Stasia." His hands moved of their own volition, sliding down to cup her arse and grind her against his cock, showing her the effect she had on him. "Feel what you do to me."

She made a low hum of pleasure. "Please, Archer."

"Are you not sore?" he asked, mindful that last night had been her first and not wanting to hurt her.

"No," she reassured him. "I need you."

Those final words proved his undoing.

The rational part of his mind knew he shouldn't. But the rest of him knew he had to make love to Stasia once more before she was forever gone from his life.

He kissed her hard, a claiming, devouring kiss. "Come to my bedchamber."

CHAPTER 13

Stasia had spent the somber remnants of breakfast and the quiet tour of Archer's library telling herself that she should not initiate further intimacy with him. That if she did so, it would only make their inevitable parting that much more difficult for her. But the moment he had begun to reveal more of his past, standing by the window looking so brutally handsome and sad, she knew it would be impossible to maintain any sort of distance.

Because she loved him.

She longed for him.

She wanted him desperately.

And now, she was naked in his bedchamber again, kissing him as he helped her to remove the same gown and undergarments he had aided her in donning mere hours before. Her arm pained her less this morning, the wound bearing more of an acute ache deep inside the sliced flesh than anything else. Perhaps Lucky's poultice was doing its work. Or perhaps her body was far too consumed by other, far-more-pleasurable sensations to be bothered by the injury.

It hardly seemed to matter, because Archer was stringing a trail of kisses over her collarbone, his mouth hot and firm, his silken hair brushing her cheek. She clutched his shoulder with her good hand, newly grateful that it was her left arm that had been wounded instead of her right.

"You're wearing far too many clothes," she protested, noting that he had only shucked his coat thus far, whilst she was down to her petticoat and stays. "I want to feel you, to see you. To kiss you."

"Patience," he murmured against her skin, kissing the hollow of her throat. "I don't want to hurt your arm."

"To the devil with my arm," she said, frustrated. "It shall heal, but I only have you now."

He lifted his head, emerald gaze finding hers, his countenance solemn. "You have me always, Princess. Near or far, I'm yours. If you call me, I will come to you."

He was utterly serious, burning with an intensity she'd never seen in him before. Emotion swelled within her heart, love making her throat go thick and her eyes blur with tears.

"Thank you," she whispered, blindly finding his mouth and kissing him.

He cupped her nape, his lips ravishing and voracious, the salt of her tears mingling with the taste of him.

"No." Archer kissed the corner of her mouth, the tenderness in his voice alone enough to make her weep anew. "Don't cry, love. I don't want you sad. I want you burning for me."

As if in demonstration, he swept his hands over her eager body, bringing it back to life beneath his clever touch. What would she do without him? How would she possibly be able to walk away from him forever and marry another man?

He kissed her again, this one deeper than the last, his tongue sliding against hers, teasing her into a response. With a moan, she released his shoulder and moved her hand higher, grasping a handful of his hair. *I love you*, she told him with her lips and tongue, with the way her body twined around his. *I never want to let you go.*

She wouldn't think of that now.

Stasia banished all thoughts from her mind. She would only *feel*. Savor the man in her arms. Make certain that every moment would forever be emblazoned on her memory. Imprint upon her heart every touch, each breath, every kiss and caress. The scent of him, soap and musk and man and leather. The strength of him. The way he made her feel as if she were the only woman he would ever want, the one who was made for him alone.

Her tears stopped, and then he was taking her petticoat over her head with painstaking slowness, kissing every bare patch of skin his lips could find. She plucked at the buttons on his waistcoat, sliding them free and then drawing it down his shoulders and arms. His cravat was next, the knot more difficult to manage given her use of only one hand. He helped her, loosening it so that she could tug the linen aside.

Desperation and helplessness fell away like the layers of garments they shed. She would only live in the moment. Would forget that anything existed beyond this chamber. When his shirt was on the floor atop her discarded petticoat, she took her turn to admire him, kissing his broad chest, going on her toes to kiss his shoulder, his neck.

He made a low sound of approval, his fingers sinking into her hair and sending pins raining to the carpet. By the time her stays were gone and he had shed his trousers and smalls, she was burning for him, just as he had wanted her to be.

They made it to the bed, clinging to each other, kissing as if their mouths were the other's life source. As if they would cease to be if they stopped. Archer arranged her on her back, plumping pillows and placing them beneath her head and then bent to take a nipple in his mouth. The hot, wet suction made her moan and arch into his touch, and the light abrasion of his teeth made her gasp, wetness pooling between her thighs.

He flicked his tongue over her, his fingers dipping into her folds and giving her a single, light stroke. "You're soaked for me, aren't you, Princess?"

"Yes," she managed to hiss, hips pumping restlessly when he stilled, giving her no more.

He moved to her other breast, lightly biting the peak, taking her in his teeth and tugging before sucking hard. All the while, he kept the heel of his hand over her mound, the pressure heightening her need without giving her the required friction, his finger remaining maddeningly still. It was slow, subtle torture of the most sensual sort.

He released her nipple, the loud pop somehow sinfully erotic. "Do you know how beautiful you are in my bed, naked and ready for me?"

She writhed beneath him, wanting him to tell her. Wanting him to sink that finger deep. To rotate his palm over her throbbing clitoris.

"So damned beautiful." He kissed the valley between her breasts. "I could worship you forever and still never get enough. Kiss and lick every inch of you."

His finger made another tantalizing journey, sliding along her seam, painting her juices over her folds. But when he reached the demanding bud that wanted his attention the most, he stopped, removing his hand.

Deep inside, her muscles clenched, longing for him. Her breathing was already ragged, her nipples hard and aching. With her good hand, she palmed one of her breasts, pinching the taut bud and tugging.

"Show me how you touch yourself," he urged, his voice low—velvet and honey to her senses.

She had never touched her breasts before, at least not to give herself pleasure. She had never, in truth, paid them much attention until she had known the exquisite bliss of his mouth on them. Her attention had always been diverted elsewhere.

As if reading her mind, he took her hand in his and guided it between her legs. "Show me how you pleasure yourself here. Feel how wet you are. How hot and slick. I want to watch."

A little sound fled her involuntarily. His command made her clitoris pulse, and she wanted to please him. Wanted to please them both. Tentatively, she circled over the swollen bud, inhaling sharply at the first touch and then instantly needing more.

"That's it, love." He kissed her shoulder, her temple, watching her as she stroked between her thighs. "Get yourself ready to come."

She wasn't certain she could carry it through to the end. She felt bold and yet also shy. Needy and yet all too aware of his hooded gaze on her.

"This feels wicked," she said, but somehow, she couldn't seem to stop.

It also felt too good. Felt sinful and wrong and delicious. She applied more pressure, fingers moving with familiar ease, the wet sounds of her playing with herself filling the air.

"When you're close, I want you to tell me," he said, kissing her ear, then tonguing the hollow behind it and sending a liquid surge of pleasure straight to her toes. "Keep going until you're there."

He was sucking on her neck now, dragging his teeth lightly along the tender cord of muscle there. And she was working her sensitive flesh, pleasuring herself at his command.

Liking it.

But she also craved Archer's touch. Hers would be for the lonely years ahead of her, trapped as she would be in her loveless marriage to the king.

"I want you to touch me," she protested, frustrated and aching for him.

"You'll have me," he reassured her, kissing a path to her shoulder, biting the curve softly, as if she were a ripe apple he wanted to devour.

Her fingers seemed determined to disobey her, flying faster over her pearl and taking her ever closer to that delicious ledge.

"I want you now," she gasped, legs going taut as she inched nearer to reaching her pinnacle, her heart pounding, blood rushing in her ears.

"Soon," he promised, rubbing his whisker-stubbled jaw along the curve of one breast, making her shiver with more desire.

"When?" she asked, the question strangled.

He flicked at her nipple with his tongue. "Are you going to come soon, Princess?"

There was something about the way he called her princess in that low, decadent baritone, so knowing and sensual, that was her undoing. Her orgasm was there. She could feel it building, everything inside her tightening as if she were a knot.

"Almost," she gasped out.

"There's a good girl," he praised, and then he took her wrist in a gentle grasp and pulled her hand away. "You may stop now."

And then he took the finger she had been using to pleasure herself, the one that was glistening with her dew, and sucked and licked it clean, the hot wetness of his mouth taking her one step closer to the maddening place where everything exploded inside her.

Closer, but not close enough.

She hadn't come. Her cunny was fluttering, ready. She was holding her breath. It had been about to hit her like lightning arcing through a calm sky.

She exhaled. "But I haven't..."

"You haven't what, love?" He sounded amused as he moved down her body, kissing and licking and lightly nipping along the way. "Go on and say it. I thought you liked to tease me with vulgar words."

Fair enough. Her bravado had fled in the face of this all-encompassing lust. She forced herself to summon up some courage, to chase the desire-induced fog from her mind.

"I haven't come," she managed.

"You may come." He slanted her a wicked look, hands caressing her outer thighs as he kissed her hip bone. "But only when I tell you that you may."

A game, she realized. Archer was playing a game of seduction with her. Last night had been intense and frenzied and fervent and tender. But today was different. *He* was different. And so was she.

She wasn't a virgin any longer either. He had unlocked the secrets of her body. Now, it would seem, he intended to unlock even more. Secrets she hadn't known existed. Desires she hadn't known she wanted.

"What are you doing to me?" she asked, hand curling into the bedclothes at her side as he nudged her thighs apart even wider.

"Making certain you'll never forget that you'll always be mine." He bent his head lower, his lips almost grazing her sex but not quite, and blew a stream of hot air over her. His big hands were on her, keeping her spread open to his gaze. "Memorizing every part of you." He inhaled deeply. "Your scent." His tongue flicked over her folds once, in a tantalizing mimicry of what his finger had done earlier. "The way you taste." Softly, as if he were sampling the most delicate of sweets, he sipped at her, sending a jolt of molten desire straight through her and tearing a moan from Stasia's throat. "Mmm, the way you sound when you're desperate for my cock to fill you. I think that's the one I like best."

Deus, he meant to torture her. To keep her on the edge of spending until she was mad with need for him. And she was helpless to do anything but beg him for more. To plead for every touch, every loving swipe of his tongue, each kiss.

"I want you inside me," she said, writhing her hips and attempting to make contact with his handsome face hovering over her. Because that was how much she wanted more, how much she desired him. Not too proud to beg. "Please," she added.

"Hush, love. Let me enjoy this. Let me savor every moment. If it is to be our last, I want it to be enough to carry me to my deathbed and beyond, because I know to my black soul that I'll never want another the way I want you."

They stared at each other, gazes colliding and holding, emotion and desire becoming one. How she loved him. She should tell him now, while she had the chance, while she had the courage.

But then he lowered his head and kissed her sex. Kissed her openmouthed and hungry, the way he did her lips, and pleasure chased all thought from her mind. His tongue sank inside her cunny, probing deep and wet.

An old Boritanian oath fled her lips.

He licked into her again and again, his thumb swirling over her pearl. And that quickly, she was about to spend again, her body tensing, her breath catching in her lungs.

He lifted his head, his mouth glistening from her. "Not yet, Princess."

She groaned at the thwarted release, body painfully poised for another denied orgasm. "You mean to kill me."

"I mean to please you," he rasped, his voice low and deep and laden with sensual promise. "To please you so well. To ruin you for anyone else."

He already had, from the first time their lips had met. Perhaps even sooner.

"There is a word for you in English," she said, breathless. "It escapes me now."

"Handsome?" he suggested, flicking over her pearl with light little flutters that had her hips bucking beneath him.

"Yes, but not that one," she gasped out.

He sucked for a few seconds, no more, before releasing her throbbing flesh. "Wonderful?"

Her mind was failing her. She had read widely in English; it was what made her command of the language so easy. But she'd never had to think with Archer Tierney applying sensual torment to her before.

"Of course."

"The world's most extraordinary lover?" He blew another humid stream of air on her sex and then ran his forefinger through her folds, parting her, pausing at her entrance.

The word came to her. Miraculously, just as he slid inside.

"Machiavellian," she bit out, planting her feet on the mattress to give her leverage as she thrust against him, bringing that tantalizing digit deeper before he could withdraw.

He felt so good inside her, filling her, sliding deep to where she was so incredibly sensitive. Finding that place he had found before, the one that made her lose control.

"That one too, I reckon," he said softly, and then he plunged a second finger inside her, working the two in and out in a rhythm that had her rocking in time. "Are you close again, Princess?"

She'd never ceased being close. She was always almost

there. Ready to spend. Chasing his fingers, his tongue, anything he would give her.

"Yes," she said, writhing beneath him.

The wrong concession to make, as it happened. For he withdrew his fingers, leaving her empty and bereft, panting and unfulfilled.

"Not yet," that wicked voice murmured before he pressed a kiss to each of her inner thighs.

"Archer," she ground out.

"Princess." He kissed the rounded curve of her belly. "My princess."

"I need you," she tried again, hoping he would have mercy and give her what they both so obviously wanted.

He kissed her navel, his tongue gliding into the shallow dip and making her gasp again. "You have me."

"Inside me," she added.

"Soon." He kissed her rib cage, hands sweeping along her and leaving fire in their wake.

She grasped his shoulder with one hand, struggling to keep her injured arm immobile when all she wanted to do was move. Hold him. Drag him to where she longed for him most.

"Now," she demanded.

"Not yet."

Those two words again, a promise and a taunt in one.

He sucked a nipple into his mouth with a low rumble of pleasure, his hand cupping her sex in a possessive hold that stimulated as much as it denied.

Her body bowed from the bed, nails raking down his shoulder, a helpless whimper torn from her. It was excruciating in the very best way.

Archer released her nipple and cast a smoldering glance up at her. "So responsive. You love my mouth on you, don't you?"

He applied pressure with the heel of his palm before she could answer, giving her some relief, but not nearly what she craved.

"Mmm," she hummed. "I love everything you do."

I love you, she might have said, but it was too much and she didn't dare risk the revelation. Not when her mind wasn't properly functioning.

He lifted his hand, and then he lightly trailed a finger down her seam, bringing it up to her other breast and drawing a circle around the distended peak, slicking her wetness on her skin. He followed with his tongue, licking the glistening path he had just made.

"So sweet," he murmured against her breast. "Sweeter than honey."

He dipped his finger into her sex again, gathering more, this time bringing it to her own lips. "Taste how sweet you are."

She sucked his finger clean just as he had done, a fresh rush of wetness pooling between her legs at the shocking intimacy of the act, the forbidden nature of it. He pulled it free, then returned it to her, giving her a few featherlight strokes that were as maddening as they were delicious. He wasn't done with this game yet, but she was ravenous for him. Ruined, just as he had promised, for any other.

He returned to her breasts, licking and sucking the hard tips, continuing to tease the bud of her sex with delicate whorls and tiny strokes. Her cunny pulsed, and she arched her back, shamelessly pressing her body against his, eager for any connection of skin. They were both hot, a sheen of sweat on their skin, his hard, masculine body gliding against her soft, feminine curves. She felt feverish and light-headed, her breasts heavy and full, her sex throbbing beneath his tender touches.

Too much.

Not enough.

She never wanted it to end.

Never wanted him to stop.

He circled her entrance, the tip of his finger slipping inside her.

"You're fucking soaked," he groaned against her breast. "Your cunny is like a river."

She couldn't control her response, the wetness he was wringing from her. He smeared it all over her folds, on her pearl, showing her how wanton she was. The slippery sound of him playing with her sex mingled with their ragged breathing, with the needy moans she couldn't seem to contain. And then he was kissing her throat, his mouth open and hot and demanding, sucking so hard she knew there would be another bruise marking her skin there later. But she didn't care.

All she cared about was him.

Her entire world had shrunk to the size of the bedchamber they inhabited, to the beloved man atop her, his body's welcome weight pinning her to the mattress as he moved higher, sealing his lips over hers at last. His tongue tangled with hers, and she tasted herself on his mouth.

With her uninjured arm, she held tight to him, kissing him back as voraciously. He shifted himself, settling more firmly between her thighs. At long last, she felt the blunt tip of his cock probing her opening. Grasping himself, he slicked his rigid length up and down her folds, lingering over her painfully swollen clitoris in one final tease before he pressed against her cunny again.

"Ready for me, Princess?" he asked against her lips.

"Deus yes," she said, hips moving, seeking.

He entered her in one long thrust, filling her to the hilt. All his teasing had built her up inside so that she was already on the verge of spending. They sighed as one when he began to move, working in and out of her overly sensitized cunny.

"Bloody hell," he murmured. "You feel so good wrapped around my cock. So wet and hot and perfect."

He felt so good inside her. Hard, thick, and long. She would have told him, but he was kissing her again, that wicked mouth stealing her breath and taking all extraneous thought with it.

Their lovemaking turned almost frantic, bodies slapping together, breaths harsh, hearts pounding, mouths seeking. He found her hand and laced their fingers together, pinning her hand to the pillows by her head as he increased his pace. And when he moved his other hand to where they were joined, his thumb unerringly strumming over her pearl the way she craved, her body tightened.

"Come," he murmured against her lips.

Finally, his permission. His big cock stretching her, planted deep the way she wanted. She clenched on him, a thousand sparks bursting inside her, the pleasure even more intense than it had been the night before.

So intense that she threw her head back and gave a guttural cry. So, so good, the bliss flooding through her unlike anything else. She came long and hard, dark stars speckling the edges of her vision, her ears ringing, body thrumming.

"Ah, fuck," he muttered, riding her harder now, her body gliding across the bed as he sought his own completion. "Stasia."

His face was slack with pleasure, his eyes glittering, body so powerful and strong. He covered the top of her head with his hand, keeping it from striking the headboard as she slid higher beneath the delicious force of his thrusts. She was still glorying in the warm glow of her orgasm when he stiffened and withdrew, gripping his cock as he spent all over her sex, covering her in him.

She lay there in the aftermath of their explosive passion, wishing she had the courage to tell him she loved him before it was too late.

CHAPTER 14

He should tell her that he loved her.

It was the one regret that continued to nag Archer. Their time together was dwindling rapidly. Within mere hours, he would lose her. He should say those three terrifying words. Make the confession he had never supposed he would have to make. For before Stasia, no woman had ever mattered so much. More than his own life, more than his next breath. No woman had ever become the driving force of his every day, making him live for her rare smiles, making him long for her in ways that far transcended mere lust.

And yet, for those same reasons, every time he opened his mouth to tell her, his tongue would not comply.

They were back in the library, newly bathed and dressed once more, Stasia tucked against his side on a Grecian couch that was damned uncomfortable, but he was not inclined to move. He'd bloody well sit here until the devil claimed him, if it meant keeping her at his side.

"Tell me about your homeland, Princess," he said, trying

to distract them both from the inevitable—the wait for Beast to answer his summons.

The wait for her to leave him.

"Boritania is a beautiful country," she said quietly as he stroked her still-unbound hair.

He hadn't had the heart to make a second attempt at a chignon just yet, for he loved her hair. It was silken and long, its color rich and mesmerizing. Having it cascading down her back and shoulders buttressed the illusion that she was staying with him, that they had many hours and days and months and years together ahead of them.

That she truly was his, and not just for today, but for forever.

"What is beautiful about it?" he asked, his throat going tight with emotion.

"The beaches are one of my favorites," she said. "The August Palace is high on a bluff, overlooking them. There are wild horses there, and I adored watching them from my balcony, particularly in the spring when new foals were born. The climate is far more arid than England. We don't have nearly your rain, and in the summer, the sky is the clearest shade of blue you'll ever behold."

He kissed her crown. "It couldn't compare to your eyes."

The sentiment was maudlin, but he didn't give a damn. The man he'd been before she had whirled into his life would have laughed at the domesticated, love-sick puppy he'd become. And he didn't care about that either.

"Why, Mr. Tierney, have you been admiring my eyes?" she teased, tilting her head back to glance up at him, her air equal parts sultry and coquettish.

She was a bloody Siren.

He had to remind his rampant cock to stand down, for he couldn't risk fucking her here in the library when her brother was set to arrive at any moment.

Even if he wanted to do so more than anything.

"Your eyes and every other part of you," he said solemnly.

"I don't want to leave," she whispered, sadness haunting her eyes.

"Then don't." He sought her mouth, kissing her slowly, deeply, telling her everything he dared with his lips that he could not seem to with words, before lifting his head again. "Stay with me. At least for another day."

"I wish I could." Tears glittered in the blue depths of her eyes. "It's too dangerous for everyone. I need to return."

"So that your bastard of an uncle can have you killed properly this time?" he demanded, unable to keep the harsh edge from his voice.

The very thought of her uncle hiring someone to murder her filled him with protective rage. The scars on her back made him long to beat that bastard to within an inch of his life, making him suffer as he had forced Stasia and her family to suffer. The wound on her arm would leave another mark upon her, yet one more symptom of the violence that she never should have faced. He hated the danger lurking for her in the shadows. Hated that he was powerless to protect her.

"He won't make any attempts from within the town house," she said, but her tone was hardly reassuring. "He would have done so before now, otherwise. He'll not wish to make it obvious, for questions to be raised. As long as I stay in my chamber until my betrothal is announced, I will be safe, and so will my lady-in-waiting."

Her answer was predictable. She was stubborn and selfless, and she would always put the needs of others before her own, particularly her own countrymen and women. But it wasn't what he wanted to hear, damn it. Archer had grown accustomed to the power he wielded. Money and influence were formidable forces, and he'd had both for years. No one

HER WICKED ROGUE

questioned him. No one denied him what he wanted. He simply took it.

Having his hands tied where Stasia was concerned was utter torture.

"I want to help you," he said grimly. "I have some powerful connections. Perhaps some of them might make inquiries. Make certain that your uncle is made aware that should harm befall you in London, it will be a criminal matter, one for which Boritania and its king will be held responsible."

"No." She shook her head, mournful. "The less Gustavson knows of all this, the better. He's a very dangerous man and particularly vengeful when he feels he has been betrayed in any manner. Please promise me that you won't approach anyone on my behalf."

Blast it, why was she so determined to resist his aid?

"If anything happens to you, I'll never forgive myself," he told her, needing her to understand how much she meant to him, the lengths he would go to in order to protect her. "Put yourself first, before the needs of your people, your lady-in-waiting."

Her expression softened. "I cannot do that. My mother was a wonderful queen. She cared for the people deeply. She felt it was not just her duty to rule with my father, but her great honor as well. She told me once that a worthy ruler must always place the good of the people before herself, and I've never forgotten it. That has been my driving principle over the last ten years. I've never wavered from that except over the past few days, with you."

"You haven't put yourself before your people by being with me, Stasia," he countered, moved by her selflessness, nonetheless. "What we've shared together has harmed no one."

She worried her plump lower lip with her teeth, a sign of

177

agitation he had come to recognize from her. "It could harm them, however. The risks I've taken in spending time with you, in giving you myself...if my betrothed were to discover them, or my uncle, there is no telling what the repercussions would be. Those were actions I took in pure selfishness, solely for me."

"Damn it," he ground out, hating this bloody hopeless situation. "You told me when you first offered this arrangement to me that you wanted something that was your choice alone, something that was purely for you. But that is a rudimentary right, Stasia, and one you wholeheartedly deserve, not just as a princess but as a woman."

"Women haven't many choices in this life, and princesses have even less," she said sadly, her bleak tone of acceptance cutting into his heart.

"What if you had one?" He cupped her cheek, stroking the delicate bone structure with his thumb. "What if I could help you?"

She turned, pressing a kiss to his palm. "You can't, Archer. No one can. My fate is as grim as it is certain. I haven't had a choice from the moment I was born a St. George."

She had fought and prevailed through her uncle's tyranny and vile abuse, had brazenly waltzed into Archer's study and asked him to take her virginity, and her calm surrender was deuced maddening. He wanted her to fight her uncle. To fight against this unwanted marriage.

He wanted her for himself.

Sweet Christ, he wanted to make her his wife.

The realization was as astounding as it was impossible. Even if he could use his connections to help save her from her uncle, he had no way of keeping her from the marriage she would be forced to make. And a princess would never align herself with the bastard son of a marquess, regardless of how well he mastered her body and how much pleasure he showed her.

All he could do was try to keep her with him for a few more days. To allay the fears she had concerning her lady-in-waiting. And at that thought, a new plan began to form. One that was daring and not without its risks, but one that would most certainly be worth its reward. But he couldn't tell her that, not if he wanted his plan to work.

Archer kissed her instead, wanting to take the sadness from her eyes. She kissed him back with equal fervor. It wouldn't be their last.

This, he vowed to himself and to Stasia both.

⁓

STASIA LINGERED by the fire in Archer's study, a tangled mess of worries and hopes and fears. Hours had passed since he had summoned her brother, many of which had been spent happily lost in Archer's arms. But the hour was growing later, the day darker, and they had moved to the room where he conducted business in anticipation.

Lucky knocked at the door, signaling that Theodoric had arrived. She jumped at the sound, feeling suddenly as if she were about to leap from a great height with no promise of safety below. Archer turned to her, a question in his gaze.

"Ready, Princess?"

"As ready as I shall ever be." She closed her eyes for a moment, gathering her strength and composure.

"Come," Archer called, his voice meant to carry.

And then the door opened, and so did her eyes, because she had spent ten long, agonizing years dreaming of this day. Even so, nothing could have prepared her for the sight of her brother.

Because the man crossing the threshold into Archer's

study was, without doubt, Theodoric. He was older, broader, his form having filled in over the years. A man now instead of a boy. His hair and clothing were damp, likely from the merciless rains that had been lashing London all day. He looked harder, different than she remembered. But he had their mother's hazel eyes, and on his forefinger, the gleam of a gold band that had belonged to their mother gave him away.

Theodoric stopped when he saw her, their stares clashing. He looked so much like their mother and father that memories rose, bittersweet and sad, bringing tears to sting her eyes. She blinked them away furiously.

Her brother was pale and still, looking at her as if she were a ghost risen from the dead. And indeed, perhaps that was what she was to him. She knew instinctively that she would have to be the first to make a move in this unexpected chess game of theirs.

"Theodoric," she said, striding toward him, watching as his eyes widened when he saw the gold necklace she had fastened at her throat yesterday, before she had gone to meet Archer.

It was a piece of jewelry that she had kept in secret. One she couldn't wear in Boritania, for it bore the coat of arms their mother had been given at her marriage to the king. A coat of arms that had been banished and outlawed by their father's deathbed decree so that anyone caught wearing it would be punished by death on the gallows. It was her sign to him that she wasn't afraid to show her loyalty to their mother, to their family.

To him.

She prayed he understood the meaning, the significance.

Theodoric looked away from her, turning to Archer, who stood with a hip propped against his rosewood desk.

"What is she doing here?" her brother ground out, as if she weren't present.

Or as if he couldn't bear to communicate with her. And how could she blame him? He had spent all these years in exile, while she had been allowed to remain in their homeland, in the August Palace. He couldn't know what she had suffered under Gustavson's watchful eye.

"You may speak to me directly, brother," she told him, determined to change his mind. To make him see the necessity of King Maximilian's plan.

But her brother was glaring at Archer instead of looking at her, almost as if it hurt him to gaze upon her.

Archer shrugged, looking markedly calm. "I delivered your message. The princess is deuced persistent."

Theodoric turned back to Stasia at last. "You should have listened to Tierney when he told you that your brother is dead. You've wasted your time in seeking out a man who doesn't exist."

The coldness in his voice shook her. He was angry, and she didn't blame him.

"But I can see you, living and breathing before me," she countered, refusing to waver, deciding that she must be stern with him, to show him the stark necessity of his returning to Boritania. "How do you dare to lie to my face, after everything I've endured to find you?"

"I never asked anyone to find me," he snarled, apparently unmoved.

"Well, Christ, does this mean you *are* a Boritanian prince, Beast?" Archer drawled, arms crossed over his chest now as he watched.

"No," Theodoric said.

"Yes," Stasia answered simultaneously.

Because she wouldn't allow him to deny it. He was her brother. Her blood.

Boritania's last hope for salvation.

"I shudder to think what the rest of your siblings are like," Archer said then, humor lacing his voice, as if he sought to lighten the heaviness of their exchange.

"I haven't any family." Theodoric shook his head. "No siblings."

"That's a lie." She tipped her chin up, daring him to defy her now. "His name is not Beast. He is Theodoric Augustus St. George and the true and rightful king of Boritania."

He jolted, as if her words had struck him with a physical blow. For a long moment that stretched on like an eternity, he said nothing. Merely stared at her. And then he blinked.

"Reinald is the true and rightful king of Boritania," he said.

"That is why I've come looking for you," she told him.

"Because Reinald has demanded my return?" Theodoric snorted. "The only way I'll go back to Boritania is as a dead man. Or perhaps, sister, that's why you've come."

His accusation stung, even if he couldn't know just how much without merit it was. She would give her life to save him. And gladly, too.

"Now you acknowledge me, when you accuse me of plotting your murder?" she asked, staring at him hard.

Archer pressed a glass into her brother's hand. "Gin? Go on, old chap. I know you don't ordinarily imbibe, but you look as if you need it."

Her brother curled his fingers around the drink. Stasia was suddenly tired and in need of fortification. It hadn't escaped her notice, however, that Archer hadn't poured a gin for her.

"Am I not to be offered any?" she asked him, raising a brow.

His green gaze burned into hers, and for a heartbeat, she

thought he might refuse. Or tell her that a lady ought not to drink gin. Either might have been his prerogative.

But then he bowed. "Whatever Her Royal Highness desires."

The formality didn't sit well with her. She was accustomed to him calling her Princess as if it were a term of endearment rather than a title. Or Stasia or simply *love*. They had an audience, however, and this meeting served as a pointed reminder of the fact that all too soon they would be strangers once more.

When Archer brought her the gin, she accepted it, raising her glass in Boritanian tradition toward her brother.

"*Saluté*," she said, using the traditional Boritanian toast, and then she took a large pull from the glass.

It burned and tasted dreadful, but she managed to choke it down. She wasn't about to allow her reaction to be mirrored on her face. Instead, she kept her countenance a carefully schooled mask of indifference.

"There," she said triumphantly. "Now we will speak."

"Stasia," her brother protested, as if he wanted to stay her further words.

But if he believed that she had managed to find herself here with him against all odds and would allow him to flee with such ease, he was wrong.

"Reinald is missing, and Gustavson has assumed the throne," she said in Boritanian, switching to their native tongue so that Archer wouldn't understand the revelations she was about to make.

Her brother's mouth fell open, shock evident in every line on his familiar-yet-changed visage. "Missing?" he repeated in their mother tongue.

She wondered if he had lost some of his fluency. Ten years abroad with likely few to no others who spoke the language would have surely rendered him rusty. She could only hope that he would remember well enough to comprehend everything she was about to tell him.

"Yes." She cast a glance in Archer's direction, feeling guilty for speaking in a different language before him, and yet knowing it was necessary.

She wouldn't make Archer vulnerable to any danger, and knowing the full extent of what she had planned with King Maximilian could well be deadly. Her uncle was not a forgiving man. Beyond that, she knew Archer was not the sort of man to sit idly by. He would want to help, just as he wished to try to use his influence on her behalf where her uncle was concerned. No, she would not bring harm to the man she loved. She would sacrifice herself a thousand times over first.

"I believe he was killed by Gustavson," she continued, "although I have no proof. Our uncle has been reigning in his absence, having proclaimed himself king. That's the reason I've come to find you. Our kingdom needs you. Our people need you."

Theodoric shook his head, as if he were just waking from a long sleep. "This has naught to do with me. There is nothing I can offer to help Boritania or her people."

How wrong he was. If only he would allow her to explain.

"But there is, brother," she insisted, entreating. "If you will listen."

"I'm sorry for what happened to Reinald," he told her, his Boritanian as smooth as if he had last spoken it yesterday. "Despite our differences and everything that occurred ten years ago, I wish him no ill. I wish none of you ill."

"You have every right to be angry with us," she reassured him. "To hate us, even. Everything was taken from you. You were stripped of your homeland, your kingdom, your birthright. Even your family."

Tears gathered in her eyes at the last, because she mourned their mother, mourned all they had lost.

"Don't weep, Stasia," he said gruffly, still speaking in their native tongue.

"Perhaps the two of you would like a moment alone," Archer suggested wryly then.

She turned to him, hating the secrets she kept, the lies of omission between them. "I am sorry," she apologized, reverting to English. "It feels more natural to converse with my brother in our language."

Another lie.

His brow quirked, telling her plainly that he didn't believe her excuse. But he said nothing of it, instead extracting a handkerchief from his coat and extending it to her. "Perhaps Your Royal Highness wishes to dry her eyes."

She accepted the offering, noting that the thin square of linen retained the warmth from his body. It required all the restraint she had to keep from bringing it to her nose and inhaling deeply of his scent. But just like revealing her plans to Archer was impossible, so too was allowing her brother to see that there was an intimate bond between herself and Tierney.

She dabbed at her eyes. "Thank you, Mr. Tierney."

How strange it felt to speak to him thus, as formally as if they were mere acquaintances instead of lovers. It was, she realized with dread, how she would soon be forced to carry on with him always, for what little time she had remaining in London.

Not enough, whispered her heart. *Not nearly enough.*

He offered her a courtly bow. "I am, as ever, your servant, Princess."

His tone was so cool and formal, her heated, demanding lover of earlier that morning bearing scarcely any resemblance to the perfect gentleman he seemed now.

It is for the best, she reminded herself. There could be no future for them.

"You needn't leave us alone," Theodoric said, cutting through her tumultuous thoughts. "I've heard enough for this evening. I must return to my post."

His pronouncement brought shock and dismay colliding inside her. She had yet to even present him with King Maximilian's plan, and now, he wished to leave.

"Brother, please," she entreated, turning back to him. "Do not go just yet."

But Theodoric remained impervious to her plea.

"I must, Stasia," he said quietly, unsmiling.

Their gazes held, and in that moment, she knew that the brother she remembered, the one she had known and loved ten years ago, was indeed dead, just as he had said. In his place was a stranger.

And in his hands, he held the last hope for Boritania.

CHAPTER 15

"Interesting way of getting a set of petticoats to stay with you," Lucky remarked.

He and Archer were alone in his study, a distraught Stasia having excused herself in the wake of her brother's abrupt departure. She had said she wished for a moment alone, and he had granted her that. And whilst everything within him urged him to follow and do his utmost to banish the sadness and disappointment in her eyes, he had known he didn't have any choice but to take advantage of the fleeting opportunity to speak with Lucky alone.

He pinned his old friend with a narrow-eyed look. "Saint's teeth, I'm not drugging her so that she stays in my bed. Do you think me that incapable of finding a woman to tup?"

"Not incapable," Lucky said with a shrug. "Been a time since you tried, 'owever."

He wasn't wrong about that. Archer had been far too occupied in recent times, first with his missions for the Crown and then with running his own business. As it happened, fixing problems for a select, wealthy clientele brought even more coin than spying had. It was also more work. Particularly when clients such as a Boritanian princess appeared, offering him royal jewels and an even more priceless manner of recompense: his use of her delectable body.

"I've been busy," he countered, still glowering at Lucky, for he had no wish to admit to his friend just how helpless he was. Just how in love and trapped beneath the dainty thumb of that same glorious princess.

"Too busy for quim." Lucky chuckled. "No such thing, Avery."

The use of his former name surprised him; no one knew him as Avery except for Lucky, his sister Portia, and the Marquess of Granville. He had rather a lot in common with Beast, it would seem. For both of them had forged new identities out of the ashes of the old. From the night Archer and Lucky had escaped the clutches of the vile bawd and her clients who would have ill-used them, he had been Archer. The choice had been purposeful: a hunter equipped with a bow and a quiver of sharp, deadly arrows, his aim deliberate and unyielding.

He passed a hand over his jaw, feeling the bristles of a beard beginning. Hell, when had he last shaved? Stasia was distracting him from everything and everyone.

"You haven't called me Avery in years," he observed, wondering what it meant.

If there was anything he knew about Lucky, it was that the man didn't make a single move that wasn't entirely calculated. That was the irony in his own chosen name; he hadn't had a single stroke of luck. He'd made it for himself where there was none.

"Seemed a fitting way to remind you of who you are," Lucky said. "I don't know who the lady is, but seems as if she could be the sort to bring danger neither of us needs darkening our door."

"I know who I am." He would never forget, for he had come a long way from the lad who had been smaller and outmuscled by his half brother. Who had been sold by his mother. Who had been abandoned and betrayed. "I don't require the reminder," he added.

"What are you planning for tonight, then?" Lucky asked, his gaze searching.

"I need the lady to sleep," he said simply, holding up the small vial Lucky had reluctantly given him. "For her own sake. There is a delicate matter that needs attending to, and she'll give me a great deal of trouble if she knows I am going. I'll give her your tonic, she'll fall asleep, and when she wakes, she'll be locked in my chamber. Have a man guard every window and door. She's incredibly adept at escaping."

Lucky's lip curled. "You know I never ask questions—"

"Then don't start now, old friend," Archer said pointedly. "Treat her as if she is more priceless than all the royal jewels combined."

Because she is, damn it.

Because I love her.

Because I'd fight the devil himself to make her my wife, even if I know it for the impossibility it is.

But he didn't say any of that aloud, because he wasn't a complete fool. Lucky wouldn't approve of how deeply he'd fallen in love with Stasia, nor how quickly. And if he had any inkling that she was a royal princess who appeared to have a price on her head… Hellfire, he couldn't begin to imagine the tongue-lashing his old friend would deliver him.

"I know she's been sharing your bed, but this sounds like trouble," Lucky said, crossing his arms over his broad chest in a gesture of disapproval Archer hadn't seen since he had told Lucky they were going to start working for the Crown.

The coin had changed his mind then.

Archer wasn't sure if anything could change Lucky's mind this time.

"She's a lady," Archer said firmly. "One for whom I harbor immense respect."

"Thinking with your prick is more like," Lucky grumbled.

"I'm thinking with my head," he bit out, nettled at his friend's insistence that his feelings for Stasia were rooted in lust.

To be sure, he desired her more than he had any woman before her, and he knew without doubt more than he would any who would have the misfortune to come after her. But he also loved her. The way he felt for her transcended desire. It was stronger, fiercer, more potent than a hundred thousand storms raging over the vast sea at once. And Lucky was damned fortunate that Archer considered him a brother. Else, he would have had a fist slamming into his nose in short order.

Lucky just raised a brow, unimpressed. "The wrong one, if you ask me."

Archer tucked the vial inside his waistcoat before he threw it at his friend's vexing head. "What I feel for her is far more than base lust. It's deeper, truer. However, the lady has found herself at the mercy of some ruthless bastards. One she's set to wed, and another her uncle. The uncle is trying to murder her. But she's too goddamned selfless to see that if she returns to her uncle's town house, she is signing her own death writ."

"Bleeding 'ell," Lucky swore. "You're in love, ain't you?"

For the first time in his life, Archer experienced the novel sensation of heat creeping up his throat, past his cravat and to the tips of his ears. "Fuck yourself, Lucky."

"I do." Lucky raised a hand and wiggled his fingers, planting a suggestive leer on his face. "The five sisters and Lady Palm stand me in good stead quite regular-like."

"Christ," he muttered. "That's best kept between you and your hand."

His friend remained unperturbed. "You're the one wot told me to fuck m'self."

"As well I should have done," he countered. "You're sticking that long beak of yours in my business where it doesn't belong, aye? All I need from you tonight is your promise that you'll not let the lady out of my chamber, no matter how prettily she asks or how rudely she demands. And that you keep the guards at every window and door. I'll do what I must and return as quickly as I'm able."

"Would feel better if I knew wot you was up to," Lucky grumbled, scowling at him.

He felt a stab of guilt at keeping the full truth from his oldest and most-trusted friend, the man who had been like a brother to him, the lad who had helped him flee that hellhole they'd been sent to, and who had saved his own life on more than one occasion. But it couldn't be helped. He had to protect Stasia first. And to do that, he needed her safely locked away in his chamber, no one else the wiser of what he was about to do.

Because if no one knew, they couldn't bloody well attempt to talk him out of it.

He clapped his friend on the shoulder. "I'll not be telling you, brother. It's best if you don't know. Now, if you please, you promise the tonic won't harm her in any way? It will only make her sleep, no ill effects?"

He didn't know what the devil was in the liquid Lucky had given him. It didn't matter, as long as it didn't hurt Stasia and produced the desired effect.

"She'll be tired, is all," Lucky reassured him. "Dry mouth, perhaps. Like as if she's groggy. It'll wear off in time, and she'll be none the worse for wear. Won't be none too 'appy with you, though, when she realizes wot you've done."

"It's for her own good, Lucky." He said it to reassure himself as much as his friend.

In truth, he knew that Stasia would be utterly furious with him when she realized he was gone and she was a prisoner in his bedchamber. He could only hope that his plan worked and that she would forgive him.

"As you say," Lucky said in a tone that suggested he didn't believe Archer one whit.

It hardly mattered. His course was set. He had to damn well do something for Stasia. Everyone else in her life—even her bloody brother—had abandoned her to her fate.

Archer patted his waistcoat, above where the vial was secreted. "Thank you, old friend. I'll be slipping this into the lady's wine posthaste."

He turned to leave the study in search of Stasia but then thought better of his departure and paused, glancing over his shoulder to where his trusted friend stood, frowning mightily, looking as worried as he'd ever seen him.

"Oh, and Lucky?" he added, having had an afterthought.

"Aye, sir?" Lucky responded, his customary insolence firmly in place now, the show of concern hastily disappearing.

"If I don't return by morning, I'm a dead man."

With that morose pronouncement, he took his leave.

~

Stasia hovered near the crackling fire in the library, trying in vain to warm herself. The damp and chill of the day had settled into her bones. Her brother's denial to hear her request had left her equally numbed.

She had failed.

Ten long and terrible years, the frantic struggle to find him in the vast sea of London, and now that she knew where her brother was, he was every bit as lost to her as he had been before. He didn't want to return to Boritania. He'd made that abundantly clear. Could she change his mind?

She had to try.

She had to make him see that he was the only hope for their people, for their kingdom. That if he didn't seize this opportunity to overthrow Gustavson, the land they had loved and all its innocent inhabitants would be forever destroyed.

The door to the library opened, and she turned to find Archer striding over the threshold in that bold, masculine way of his.

She longed to meet him halfway across the room and throw herself into his arms, but she also knew she needed to keep her wits about her. To put Boritania before her own wicked wants.

"Stasia," he greeted, looking grim and unsmiling as he approached. "I thought I might find you here."

"I've always had a fondness for libraries," she admitted, thinking of the cavernous two-story chamber in the August Palace that had been her mother's pride. "We had a beautiful library in the palace, one my mother worked diligently to build. My uncle has been systematically seeking to destroy it, much as he has everything else in Boritania."

Archer stopped before her, tall and strong and tempting. So very tempting.

"I'm sorry for what you've lost," he said softly, the aching tenderness in his voice piercing her heart.

"Others have lost far more than I have. I can only hope…" She had been about to reveal too much, and she stopped herself, shaking her head. "It was good to see my brother today, for him to acknowledge who he is. But he is so very changed."

"As are you, I would imagine." Archer reached for her,

nothing more than the stroke of his forefinger along her jaw, and yet it melted her inside.

Her traitorous body took a step nearer, seeking his warmth, seeking him. "I suppose I have. I was a foolish girl when he was exiled."

And now she was a foolish woman, falling for a man who could never be hers. Unable to stay away, even when she knew she must.

"I cannot believe you were ever foolish, love." His arms came around her, drawing her against him in a comforting embrace that she very much needed.

She pressed her cheek to his chest, inhaling deeply of his scent, her uninjured arm winding around him with a will all its own. "I still am."

Because I've fallen in love with you, she thought.

But the words remained where they belonged, written upon her heart. Her secret to keep.

Archer kissed the top of her head. "Was the reunion with your brother what you hoped for?"

"No," she admitted. "Far from it."

"I expected as much, though I couldn't understand what the two of you were saying to each other." His voice rumbled beneath her ear, deep and steady and strong, one of his hands stroking up her spine in a comforting caress.

"I am sorry for speaking Boritanian," she said, guilt cutting away at her anew.

"You needn't apologize, love. The two of you are family. You deserve your privacy after all these years spent apart."

His calm understanding only served to double her misery. He was being so kind, so compassionate, so caring. No one had ever shown her as much devotion, and it terrified her to know that these fleeting moments with him were the only tenderness and caring she could ever have before she retreated to her cold, loveless marriage.

"You are too good to me," she murmured into his coat. "I'll miss you."

And with that admission came the bitter sting of tears, scalding hot.

"Princess."

She was perilously near to sobbing again.

She glanced up at him.

"Don't weep," he said softly. "I can't bear it."

She blinked, her vision blurring, tears gathering on her lashes. And then he lowered his head, taking her lips in a kiss that was sweet and gentle, consoling her without words.

Sweet Deus, she didn't deserve this man.

Too soon, he ended the kiss, staring down at her with such affection that she thought she might begin crying anew.

She swallowed hard against a rising lump of emotion threatening to clog her throat. "Now that I've finally been able to speak with my brother, I ought to return to my uncle's town house. Every hour that I'm gone heightens the risk to Tansy, and I would never forgive myself should anything happen to her because of me."

Archer's jaw tightened. "Will you not stay a bit longer, just for dinner? I don't like the thought of you going hungry, and I find myself unwilling to say farewell just yet."

Yes, she thought frantically. *Keep me here with you. Never let me go.*

But that was more nonsensical thinking. A wish that could never come to fruition.

Did she dare linger?

"I don't know if I should," she said, hesitating.

Tempted. So very tempted.

"Another hour," he said. "What can be the harm?"

To her heart? Only utter devastation when inevitably they had to part after that additional hour. Her mind and her conscience both told her that her answer must be a resounding *no*. However, the rest of her, that vulnerable organ thumping in her breast most specifically, had other ideas.

"Perhaps I might stay for dinner," she allowed.

A small half smile kicked up the corner of his sensual mouth. "I was beginning to fear I'd have to beg."

"And would you have done?" she asked stupidly. "Begged me, I mean."

His smile deepened, making the corners of his eyes crinkle, and yet it was a sad smile, one laden with regret. "On my knees, Princess."

Oh, her poor heart. It could not withstand such torture, such raw, vivid agony. How would she leave him? How would she force herself to do what she must over the coming hours and days?

He released her and offered her his arm, as if they were at court together instead of standing alone in his library with no one as witness save the fire crackling in the grate and the hundreds of spines of books that had once belonged to another. She took it, allowing him to escort her from the chamber.

But to her surprise, he didn't take her to the dining room as she had expected. Instead, they made their way to the staircase.

"Where are you taking me?" she asked, half hoping that he intended to seduce her all over again.

"To my bedroom," he said, adding, "I thought we might enjoy a more intimate meal there without the formality of the dining room. If this is to be the last meal we share, I'd prefer not to be sitting at a bloody table, presided over by servants."

The last meal.

How final it sounded. How terrible.

She sniffed, trying to hold back those stubborn tears that

still threatened to fall, struggling to maintain a composure that was increasingly more elusive. "That sounds lovely."

"There's also something there that I want to give you before you leave," he added, his voice low to keep from carrying. "A few somethings, actually."

Presents? For her? But she had nothing for him.

"You need not give me anything," she protested, for he had already given her so much. "I'm indebted to you enough as it is."

He had cared for her in a way no one had in years. He had opened her eyes to new, unimagined pleasures. And he had shown her what love felt like. Had given her a brief, wonderful piece of happiness where there otherwise would have been none. But beyond that, he had also given her the use of his carriage, had fed her, tended to her, bathed her, kept her safe.

"You owe me nothing, Stasia," he told her quietly as they reached his bedroom door, gesturing for her to precede him.

When they were within, she saw that a tray of delicacies had already been laid out on a blanket spread on the floor in the manner of a picnic. There were plates, goblets of wine and serviettes, a candelabra blazing from above to illuminate the intimate dinner.

She moved toward the tableau, drawn by the charm as much as by the sudden, corresponding rumble in her stomach. "You've gone to such trouble on my account."

"It's not every day that a man is fortunate enough to dine with a princess." His hand settled on the small of her back, fitting there as naturally as if her form had been fashioned with him in mind. "Besides that, it was the servants who went to the trouble."

"Perhaps, but you arranged all this."

He shrugged. "It's nothing. How is your arm feeling?"

"Well enough. Lucky's poultice is doing its work."

They stared at each other for a heated moment, and she wondered if he was thinking about everything they had shared in this room the way she was.

But he nodded, his countenance betraying nothing. "I am glad to hear it." He turned away from her then, moving in leonine strides across the chamber to retrieve something before returning to her side, his hands full. "A new chemise," he said, "and the jewels you paid me to find your brother."

"I can't accept that," she demurred. "You found my brother for me, just as you promised you would. The jewels are yours."

"You told me when you paid me with them at our first meeting that they belonged to your mother the queen," he said softly. "They should remain with you. I have no need of them."

"Archer," she protested.

"They're yours, Stasia." He extended his hand, the pouch containing the gems atop the neatly folded chemise. "Take them."

"I hardly expect you to offer me your services without recompense."

"I know that." He took the hand of her unwounded arm in his and pressed the chemise and pouch into it. "But I would do anything for you, Princess. *Anything.* And I bloody well won't take a single ha'penny for it."

He was being stubborn. It ought not to surprise her, nor should the gesture. But somehow, she hadn't expected him to return what she had paid him. The jewels were worth a hefty sum, and she had known that his services were not to be cheaply had. She had secreted them in a pocket she had sewn into one of her gowns for just such a purpose, since Gustavson made certain she neither had funds of her own nor access to the royal coffers.

"I don't know what to say," she admitted.

"Say you'll keep the jewels." He curled her fingers around the pouch, and she felt the familiar heavy weight of the stones within. "Keep them for me, if not for yourself. They belong to you. You've already had enough taken from you. I'll not be another who takes without giving in return."

"Very well," she relented. "I'll keep the jewels."

He nodded, apparently satisfied. "Now sit and eat, love. You must be hungry."

Her stomach gave a distinctive and embarrassing rumble, proof she was famished. They had only eaten a small repast since breakfast as they awaited Theodoric's imminent arrival. And having eaten so little before coming to Archer, coupled with all their adventurous lovemaking, she was ravenous even as her stomach was tied in knots.

He helped her to sit and then seated himself as well on the spread coverlet, wordlessly filling a plate for her that was brimming with a deliciously scented array of offerings. She took the plate, their fingers brushing, a renewed spark of heat burning hot and quick between them.

But they couldn't indulge in it now. All they had left was this meal. And after it…

No, she wouldn't think of what would come after. She would pretend as if she could stay here in this room with Archer forever.

Determined to distract herself, she bit into a flaky tart that appeared to be filled with fruit. The forkful in her mouth was pure heaven, citrus coupled with the sweetness of apple. "What is this called?" she asked when she had chewed and swallowed.

The look he cast in her direction was intent, but there was something different about his regard, and she couldn't quite place it.

"Apple pudding."

"It's lovely," she said lamely, before noticing he had yet to fill a plate for himself. "Will you not eat as well?"

"Of course." The smile he gave her felt forced as he scooped up a goblet of wine and held it out to her. "Wine?"

She took it, thinking she required the fortification. "Thank you."

The meal carried on in a miserable blur for Stasia. She hated each passing second for bringing her closer to the time when she would have to leave Archer. And although the fare was undeniably pleasant, by the time she finished her plate, the contents may as well have been mud. She drained the remnants of her wine, seeking a way to drown out the pain of what was to come.

When she lowered the empty goblet to the blanket, it fell on its side.

"Pray forgive me," she apologized, the words emerging with unusual torpor. Her tongue felt as if it were suddenly two times its size. "I'm not ordinarily graceless so."

That didn't make sense.

In her upset, she had confused the proper order of the words in English.

She shook her head, the walls around them momentarily looking as if they had tilted, and blinked, struggling to keep her suddenly heavy eyes open.

"So graceless," she corrected, feeling odd.

Something was amiss. Her vision was blurred. Archer's face was lacking in definition, and her head felt as if it were filled with air. She felt too light for her body. It made no sense.

"Is something wrong?"

His voice pierced through the strange fog crowding her mind.

Yes, something was wrong. She couldn't quite seem to grasp what, however. Had she drunk too much wine?

Perhaps she was...what was the word in English? It escaped her now.

"I am too much wine, I think," she managed, struggling into a standing position with the thought that perhaps she might clear her head if she weren't sitting. "A shot cup."

"Cup-shot," Archer corrected, somehow at her side, steadying her with a calming touch on her elbow. "Perhaps you should lie down in the bed. You look weary."

"I'm not tired," she argued, still making her best effort to keep her drooping eyes open. "I need to...go. I'll not you or Tansy endanger. This is...battle mine, and I'll myself fight."

Once again, the words were in the wrong order. She heard them fall strangely in her own ear, finding it miraculous that she had spoken them. What was happening to her mind? She didn't understand.

But Archer was before her, and he was so tall and so handsome.

And so tall.

And handsome.

Had she already thought that? Well, he was. She wished she had more ways to describe him. She was certain she did, but they were beyond her ken at the moment.

"I'm so sorry, love," he said.

She listed on her feet, the world seeming to tip and swirl around her. "No, it is I who must be...I am..." She ended with a sigh. Words were elusive. Stasia muttered something in Boritanian, tripping over her own feet.

But Archer was there.

Archer was always there.

Catching her.

Holding her.

Holding her in his strong, big arms.

His arms bigstrong.

No, that wasn't right.

She frowned, reaching for his face. Why were there two of him? What was happening? There couldn't be two when there was only one.

"Archer?" she asked, her tongue feeling fatter and heavier, her eyelids drooping until she could no longer see.

Eyes closed now. That better felt. No, *felt better*. The world was spinning faster, faster around her.

Lips at her ear, a voice she loved. "Forgive me, my darling."

And then, nothing but blackness.

CHAPTER 16

Archer was going to hell for many sins. Of that, he had no doubt. But of all the sins he'd committed in his thirty years, the worst had been drugging the woman he loved.

His motive had been pure enough. He wanted to help her. But the guilt gnawing at his gut ever since he had caught her in his arms when Lucky's potion had finally managed to take its full intended effect…

That would rot him to his core.

He had left her peacefully sleeping in his bed, after checking her wound for any sign of infection and tucking the bedclothes carefully around her. He had stopped at the door and doubled back to make certain she was still breathing evenly, her chest rising and falling in rhythmic motion. Because he trusted Lucky with his own life, Christ yes. But he wasn't entirely sure he trusted him with hers. Stasia was more important than anyone had ever been.

And more important than anyone would ever be.

It hadn't a bloody goddamned thing to do with her title. He didn't care if she was a princess. Hell, he wished that she were anyone *but* a princess. Because if she were Miss Stasia St. George from some filthy rookeries street instead of Her Royal Highness Princess Anastasia Augustina St. George of Boritania, he would have made her his wife yesterday.

His carriage clattered on through the night, taking him to the town house where her uncle's guards were lying in wait. He rested his head against the Morocco leather squabs and exhaled a long sigh. He had a pistol secreted on his person and three knives. The night was either going to go very poorly, or very well indeed.

Clearly, he hoped for the latter.

But he was also prepared for the former.

In any event, Lucky would know what to do with Stasia. Protecting her was of the gravest import. Archer would happily sacrifice himself if it meant that she could be safe. And to be safe, she needed to be far from the town house her uncle controlled. Archer knew he couldn't keep her away from it, given her loyalty to her lady-in-waiting. His princess was selfless to a fault. So he was going to liberate her lady-in-waiting.

By force.

He'd sent his men to investigate the perimeter again earlier on his behalf. There were a total of six guards that he knew of. Not impossible. Likely, there were more within the home. He would deal with them if necessary.

If all went as planned, not a single guard would spy him. No pistols would be shot. No blades would be bloodied.

If all didn't go well…

He would face that later, when and if it should happen.

He felt the carriage drawing to a halt and leaned forward to part the Venetian blinds. The darkened street beyond gave away precious few of its secrets, but he knew where he was. Knew the way to the town house. To the window. To the guards.

All he had to do was keep his wits about him. Stay cool and calm. Not allow emotion or fear to guide him. Stasia's very life was in danger, and he meant to do everything in his power to keep her safe. Even if it meant sacrificing his own.

Archer left the carriage, giving his coachman directions to return to his own town house without him and inform Lucky if he didn't return within two hours' time. With that accomplished, he slipped into the night. He had provided careful instructions to his coachman to leave him a short enough distance from the town house that he wouldn't need to walk far, and yet he wouldn't risk being seen by the guards.

It was his hope that he could infiltrate the town house without having to kill a soul. However, he was prepared for the worst and to do what he must in order to accomplish the goal of liberating Stasia's lady-in-waiting from the residence.

He hadn't traveled far when a carriage rumbled around a corner, slowing as it approached him. A tremor of unease slid down his spine. The unmarked vehicle was instantly familiar; he recalled it from the night he had told Stasia she would have the use of his own carriage whilst he helped her.

It belonged to her betrothed.

Archer reached for the pistol inside his coat, at the ready, curling his fingers around the smooth wood of the stock lest he require it.

The door to the carriage opened, revealing a harsh, angular face in the lamplight's glow and a massive form clad all in black.

"Get in," the man within said, a distinct accent flavoring those two curt words.

"Not in need of a ride this evening, old chap," Archer returned. "Thank you all the same."

Hoping to avoid further altercation, for he had a mission

to accomplish this night, Archer moved to skirt the conveyance and carry on his way.

The grim-looking specter within the carriage whistled. Another man leapt down from the rear of the carriage, stopping on the pavements before him, pistol pointed at Archer's head.

"Halt," the second cove ordered coldly, his voice similarly accented.

Christ. This wasn't what he needed. What in the hell was this about? Archer's fingers clenched instinctively on the gun concealed in his greatcoat.

"There seems to be some sort of mistake afoot," he said patiently, all too aware that he couldn't risk shooting now, lest he raise the suspicions of the guards. "I don't want any trouble."

This was a fine neighborhood, and the report of a pistol would not go unnoticed.

"Take your hand from your coat," ordered the man in the carriage, ignoring Archer's protest. "Slowly."

The pistol was his only good chance of defending himself. And bloody hell, he would use it if he had to, even at the risk of alerting the guards. When it came down to his life, he had no choice. He couldn't help Stasia if he was dead.

"Who the bloody hell are you?" he demanded instead of complying.

"I'm King Maximilian of Varros," the man inside the carriage drawled coldly, his accent more pronounced. "Tell me, just what have you been doing with my future queen, Mr. Tierney?"

All the blood in his head felt as if it drained away.

Fucking hell.

Stasia's betrothed was a goddamned king.

Someone could have knocked him over with a bloody feather, so great was Archer's shock. In all their conversations, she'd never called her betrothed by name. He knew little of Varros other than that it was a small island kingdom near Boritania. The need for the marriage suddenly made sense; as the queen, she would be uniquely positioned to aid her uncle's greedy ambitions.

The thought of Stasia becoming this massive man's wife made Archer's throat go tight, every protective instinct he possessed raging against her being anyone's other than his.

"What is this about?" he asked hoarsely, finding his voice.

"Get in the carriage, and we'll talk," King Maximilian said.

"Hand out of your coat," the wiry guard who continued to point his weapon at Archer growled.

Still, he didn't move, his mind whirling with possibilities. Means of escape. Did he dare draw his pistol and shoot a king? The answer was a swift and resounding no. Even if the man before him was slower to fire, assassinating a monarch would only end in his own imprisonment and execution.

He hadn't a choice. Not truly.

"Do you want to die today, Tierney?" the king asked.

"I reckon not." Swallowing hard, he released his pistol and withdrew his hand from his greatcoat, raising both arms, palms outward, to show his lack of armament.

"Excellent choice." The king turned his attention to the pistol-toting guard. "Felix, disarm him."

Archer clenched his jaw as the smaller man stepped forward, neatly removing his secreted pistol and two of the three blades from his person. At least he would still be armed with the third, then.

But any comfort he felt at maintaining a weapon for himself should he require it was banished when the guard knelt and swiftly withdrew the blade from its sheath secreted in Archer's boot.

Damn it.

He had nothing save his fists now, and they would have to be sufficient.

The guard stood, satisfied that he had removed every last weapon from Archer's person, and nodded toward the waiting carriage. "Get in."

The longer they lingered in the street, the greater the chance that they would attract unwanted attention. Blast. He hadn't any other choice.

An ominous sense of dread settled low in his gut, heavy as a boulder.

Archer stepped up and into the carriage, the door slamming shut behind him.

∼

Stasia woke with a dry mouth and an aching head, bleary and confused. The bed she was in was familiar by now—Archer's. There was no light in the room save the flickering glow coming from the fire in the grate. The counterpane was tucked painstakingly around her.

Had she somehow fallen asleep? Why would she have done so, when she needed to return to the town house? What time was it?

Her sluggish mind swirled with questions, none of which she had a ready answer to. Emitting a yawn that would not be suppressed, she reached for Archer with her uninjured arm, but her hand met with the cool softness of an empty pillow.

She blinked the sleepiness from her eyes, casting a glance around the chamber. "Archer?"

They had been eating a final repast together, she remembered now. After her brother's heartrending refusal to listen to Maximilian's plan to overthrow Gustavson, she had no more reason to remain at Archer's town house. Particularly not when doing so could potentially place Tansy in a position of grave danger now that Stasia realized that her uncle was likely having her watched by others. And that he was trying to have her killed.

She had outlived her use to him. Had taken too many risks in the name of finding Theodoric. And in being selfish enough to seek out Archer for herself, as well.

But where was Archer now? And why was she in his bed alone, fully dressed except for her boots?

Stasia sat up slowly, her head still spinning, feeling sluggish and strange. Almost as if her body refused to cooperate with her mind. Something was wrong.

She struggled to remember more. She had been feeling strangely, she recalled. Archer's voice echoed in her mind. *I'm so sorry, love*, he had said. But what had he been apologizing for?

Eerie suspicion rose, making the back of her neck prickle. There had been the wine he had been encouraging her to drink. By the time she had finished her goblet, she'd been feeling quite odd. But surely Archer would not have—could not have—placed something in her wine. Would he?

Could he?

She recalled him catching her in his arms, his voice near her ear murmuring *forgive me, my darling*.

And then, nothing else.

No.

No, no, *no.*

He wouldn't drug her. She refused to believe the man she loved would betray her in such cruel fashion. She threw back the bedclothes and made her way through the shadows, across the Aubusson to the door.

Her hand on the latch found it, quite undeniably, locked.

She was *locked* inside Archer's chamber.

Alone.

Which meant...

"Archer?" she called out again, alarm rising along with the pitch of her voice. High, almost shrill as desperation set in. "Archer, where are you?"

"Ain't 'ere, m'lady," said another familiar voice from the hall.

"Lucky," she said, struggling with the latch again. "The door seems to be locked. Would you please help me?"

"Sorry, m'lady," the butler said. "You're to stay right where you are, Tierney's orders."

His orders?

Her heart plummeted.

She tried the door with greater insistence, but it was firmly latched, and with her other arm wounded, she only had half the strength she ordinarily would to put toward the effort. Outrage and panic rose within her, making her throat constrict.

"Why would he wish me to be locked inside this room?" she demanded.

"Couldn't say, m'lady."

"You couldn't say, or you won't?" she asked, giving the door another ineffectual rattle.

No use. She was trapped. Trapped in Archer's chamber by his own decree. How could he have betrayed her so thoroughly? And how foolish had she been to fall neatly into his ploy?

"Didn't ask," came Lucky's terse reply. "Wouldn't tell you if I knew. Ain't my place to do so."

Desperation surged.

She released the door, slamming her palm on it in frustration. "Where has Mr. Tierney gone? I wish to speak with him."

There was silence, and for a prolonged moment, Stasia

feared that the formidable butler had left the hall beyond the chamber.

"Didn't say, madam," Lucky said at last.

Heaving a sigh of frustration, she pressed her forehead to the door, her head aching worse than when she had blearily woken from sleep. "You cannot mean to keep me prisoner here, Lucky."

"None of this is my concern, m'lady. You've drink and food aplenty. Ring if you need aught else."

His voice was already fading in time with his footfalls in the hall as he walked away.

"Lucky!" she cried out. "Please don't go! I need to get out of here!"

She needed to get back to Tansy. To warn her lady-in-waiting of the danger. A flurry of curses fled her lips, old Boritanian oaths that were certainly not befitting a lady, let alone a princess.

"Lucky?" she tried again.

But this time, there was no answer.

She was alone.

"Of all the arrogant, self-important…" she grumbled, whirling away from the door.

The room was so dark that she could scarcely see. Surely she could turn something into a weapon to help her out of the door. She made her way through the murkiness to the spills on the mantel above the fireplace. Holding one into the low flames, she waited until it lit and then used it to illuminate a nearby candelabra one wick at a time.

The effort produced a meager amount of light. Just enough for her to make a thorough examination of Archer's chamber. Nothing leapt out at her as being of potential use. Throwing back the window dressing revealed no convenient tree, nor gardens below, quite unlike her chamber at her uncle's town house.

What was she going to do?

~

ARCHER FOUND himself seated on the squabs opposite King Maximilian as the carriage swayed down the street. The man was immense, easily taking up half the carriage with his tremendous size. He wasn't just tall, but broad of shoulder. Decidedly not the sort of chap anyone would want to meet alone in a darkened alley.

Nor face in an enclosed carriage, nary a weapon left upon him for defense, as it happened.

"What do you want from me?" Archer asked guardedly, his past misdeeds as a spy returning to him too late, his senses finally awakened.

Earlier, he had been too bloody caught up in the task that lay ahead of him. He'd been fretting over Gustavson's guards when he should have been watching his surroundings more thoroughly. If he had, he'd have noticed the king's carriage before it was too late and he was staring down the barrel of a pistol, losing his gun and blades to some wet-behind-the-ears Varrosian whelp.

"I want to know where my betrothed is," his opponent said. "Her lady-in-waiting told me that you have her."

Blast. He should have known that someone would get to the lady-in-waiting. If not Gustavson's guards, then Stasia's betrothed, the unsmiling king before him.

"She is safe," he said simply, trying to quell a sharp spear of guilt threatening to rise within him as he thought of the means by which he had achieved her safety.

Later, he would pay for locking her in his chamber and drugging her with one of Lucky's potions. Of that, he was more than certain.

Supposing he didn't meet a grisly fate at the hands of the behemoth before him first, that was.

"And what of her brother?" the king asked next, surprising Archer with the query.

But then, he supposed it made sense; this man had been giving her the use of his carriage as she wandered in the night, meeting Archer.

"You know about her brother?" he returned, not certain what, if anything, he should reveal.

He knew that Stasia's position was dreadfully precarious. Her welfare was of the utmost importance, taking precedence over his own.

"Of course I do," the other man said coolly. "I learned from Gustavson himself that the lost prince was in London."

"You call him the lost prince," he observed, taking great care in the phrasing of his every word, not knowing how much King Maximilian knew, whether he could truly be trusted. "I understand he was exiled."

The king shrugged. "The means matter not. Have you found him?"

Understanding dawned. "*You're* the reason she sought me out to find her brother."

The other man's lip curled. "I was told you were the best. Clearly, I was misadvised."

The slight wasn't lost on Archer, but he cared far less about any insult paid him and his abilities than he did for what would happen to Stasia.

"I've found him," he said evenly. "However, he's made it more than apparent that he had no wish to be found."

"Tell me." The king's eyes glittered in the carriage lamp's glow, so dark that they were almost black. "Where is Princess Anastasia?"

"She's safe," Archer repeated.

In my bed, where she belongs, he thought, even as he knew

he couldn't keep her there. He'd give everything he had to do so, but he had unfortunately come across the first instance in his life where coin didn't rule all else.

"According to whom?" Again, the king's lip curled into a derisive sneer. "*You*, Tierney?"

"Why were you following me?" he countered with a question of his own. "What do you want?"

"I want Theodoric St. George. You've been paid a handsome sum to deliver him to me."

Through Stasia, he realized.

"The gems belonged to the princess's mother, not to you," Archer said, "and moreover, they've been returned to her. I'll accept no payment for my services."

The king raised a brow, his sneer still firmly in place. "And why would that be, I wonder? Could it also have something to do with the reason the princess failed to return to her bedchamber last night?"

"If you are insinuating that something untoward has happened between the princess and me, you're wrong," Archer lied, for it wasn't any of the king's business what had transpired between Stasia and himself. She wasn't his wife. At least, not yet, damn it. "She was wounded. That is the reason she didn't return. Did her lady-in-waiting not tell you that?"

"I'll ask you the same question I asked her," the king said coldly. "Do you think me stupid?"

He shrugged. "I'm sure I couldn't say."

The king pinned him with a glare. "I wasn't in favor of having you killed as Felix wanted, but I may change my mind yet."

"I invite him to try," Archer said, refusing to retreat from a fight.

He never had. And he never would. He'd been fighting since the day he'd been born.

"Felix is my most highly trained assassin," the king returned. "No one can slit a man's throat as quickly and quietly."

"If your intention is to kill me, then have done with it," he bit out. "As we speak, the princess's uncle is conspiring to have her murdered. He tried once, but fortunately I was there to shoot the bastard dead before he could do more than wound her arm. If you want a *living* wife, you may wish to consider that."

The word *wife* in conjunction with Stasia and the man before him sat as bitterly on Archer's tongue as any poison. He hated the utterance. Hated the thought of her bound to another. In another man's life, in another man's bed.

He ground his jaw to stave off a stinging wave of possession. This wasn't about what he wanted. This was about protecting the woman he loved.

"How do you know Gustavson was behind the attack?" King Maximilian demanded, eyes narrowed.

"I can't be certain," he admitted. "But when my men gathered the body, they found Boritanian coins on him. He wasn't known to me or my men. Nor was he a common footpad. He didn't attempt to steal anything. His intent was to wound the princess, and his blade was mere inches from her heart. There is only one Boritanian with the motive and the means to assassinate the princess in London, and it's her uncle."

The king's expression shifted, his gloved hands balling into fists. "I don't disagree."

"The princess was escaping from her uncle's town house using her bedchamber window," he added, "by climbing a tree. A physician tended to her wound, but I feared she would cause further harm if she tried to exert herself too soon after the injury occurred. I sent word to her lady-in-waiting that the princess would remain with me in the hopes that her wound would heal well enough that she could safely return. However, given the fact that her uncle wishes her dead, there is ample reason for her to remain where she is, beyond her uncle's reach."

"If all this is true, then what were you doing this evening?" the king asked sharply.

"You had me followed," he said baldly, still furious that he hadn't realized sooner.

That he hadn't been more aware. By God, he had once been one of the Crown's most-trusted spies, and now he was so lost in Stasia that he hadn't the prescience to suspect he would be watched.

"Naturally," King Maximilian admitted. "Princess Anastasia's lady-in-waiting is loyal to a fault, and I wasn't certain I could trust her. I had to see for myself what you were about. Why were you going to the town house tonight, armed as you were?"

"The princess was deeply concerned for her lady-in-waiting's welfare. My intent was to liberate Lady Tansy and bring her to my home, where she would be far more protected than in her current location."

"You intended to kidnap a princess and her lady-in-waiting."

The king's grim assessment of Archer's bold plan sounded every bit as mad as he'd known it was. But he had taken many risks in his life without hesitation.

"Not the princess," he said. "But her lady-in-waiting, perhaps. Only if she resisted."

"You're an idiot, Mr. Tierney."

"So it would seem, considering I've been captured by you," he acknowledged, unable to keep the taunt from his voice.

They stared at each other, unspeaking, taking each other's mettle. The king's dislike of him was plain. Archer made no effort to hide his mutual enmity. He didn't give a damn about the title or throne of the man before him. Varros was but a tiny island, a veritable speck in the sea.

"I don't like you, Tierney," the king growled. "You're an insolent Englishman, and I ought to have Felix slit you from gut to gullet."

"Felix isn't in this carriage," Archer countered. "I could kill you with my bare hands before he even knew anything was amiss."

A muscle in the king's wide jaw ticked. "I fear you underestimate me, English puppy. I'd snap you like a twig and use your bones to pick my teeth."

Archer laughed at the affront, not intimidated in the least. "If it pleases you to imagine you could best me, then by all means, do so."

More silence descended, their glares clashing as the carriage swayed on, bouncing over a rut in the road.

"I've a bargain to offer if you wish to hear it," Archer ventured, thinking it likely best to gain the king's support.

For Stasia's sake.

The king's eyes narrowed.

Another tense silence passed until he nodded. "Go on, then Englishman. Say it."

Archer took a deep breath. "You want Theodoric St. George, do you not? I believe I can deliver him."

CHAPTER 17

If Archer Tierney believed Princess Anastasia Augusta St. George was going to sit quietly and await his return after he had deceived her and drugged her wine, he didn't know her at all.

Stasia had that thought to bolster her flagging spirits as she worked to secure her freedom. And with each passing moment, her agitation and her determination had increased in equal measures.

Stasia had fashioned the bedclothes into a long, knotted rope, and she was securing one end to the leg of the sturdy wardrobe she had managed to muscle halfway across the chamber using nothing more than her own body weight and fierce determination. Already, she had determined that her rope would take her near enough to the ground that a short jump would land her safely below. All she had to do was lower herself with the power of her uninjured arm and pray that the rope held in the bedchamber above as she scaled down.

Giving it a sound one-armed tug, she opened the window, hoping she could support herself sufficiently without her wounded arm. She was halfway over the window casement, her body sliding into the dark, cold, and damp night air, when she realized her idea had been a very, very bad one.

Because there was no way she could propel herself safely down the rope hampered by the use of one arm. Moreover, the wardrobe was beginning to tilt toward the leg she'd tied the rope to, and she hadn't the strength to pull herself back inside to safety.

Terror clawed at her throat.

She was going to fall.

Instinct kicked in, and she clung to the bedclothes rope with both arms, fingers clawing at the casement, as pain shot through her wounded arm.

In the next instant, the door to Archer's bedchamber opened, the draft from the opened window propelling it into the wall. And there he was, calling her name, rushing to her.

"Stasia, what in the hell are you doing?" he demanded as she struggled to keep from falling to her imminent doom below.

"Trying...not...to fall," she gritted through the pain, her breaths ragged, thanks to the effort it required to hold on to the makeshift rope.

He reached her in a rush of wind and a comforting pair of arms swooping around her. And despite her outrage with him, Stasia instantly knew she was safe, that Archer would never allow harm to come to her. Muscled arms banded about her waist, hauling her over the casement and back inside his chamber.

She held tightly to him, fear rendering it impossible for her to let go, shivering as the chill of the night whirled around them both, coming in through the open window. She hadn't fallen. Archer's warmth and muscled strength surrounded her, never more life-affirming than in that moment, the very real fear of dropping to her death still holding her in its grip.

"Are you hurt?" he asked, his voice low at her ear.

The wound in her arm ached like the very devil, and she was sure she had managed to undo whatever meager healing had thus far begun when she'd grappled with the bedclothes rope to keep from landing on the ground below.

"I'm fine," she managed to say, still struggling with the fear that had gripped her when she had believed she was going to plummet to earth.

Somehow, it had been even more frightening than when she had been attacked. The assailant had come at her so quickly, and then Archer had saved her. But the time she'd spent hanging from the bedclothes rope had felt like a lifetime in comparison.

Archer jerked back to look down at her, frowning mightily. "Christ, Princess. You're bleeding."

She followed his gaze, realizing belatedly that, yes, she was. A red stain marred the linen bandage Archer himself had wrapped for her earlier. She had torn open her wound then, just as she had suspected.

The sight of the blood made her go light-headed, and if he hadn't still been holding her, she had no doubt she would have withered to the Aubusson.

"It must have happened when I had to hold tight to the rope to keep from falling." The words slipped past her numb lips, her teeth chattering as another gust of cold night air burst through the still-open window.

"You're shivering," he observed grimly.

"It's c-cold," she offered lamely, all her earlier ire having been banished by her scrape with death.

"Come." Gently, he led her to a chair positioned by the glowing hearth, all that remained of the pleasant fire that had been roaring earlier when they had shared their picnic dinner.

"I'll n-never grow accustomed to the w-weather in England," she said through teeth that continued to clack involuntarily.

But then, she didn't suppose it would matter for much longer. Soon, she would be in sun-drenched Varros as another man's wife.

"Sit," Archer ordered, tenderness creeping into his tone.

She did as he asked, still thoroughly put out with him for what he had done and yet too stunned to summon her outrage just yet.

He strode across the chamber, pulling up what remained of her escape, throwing the knotted bedclothes to the floor before closing the window and blocking off the night air. He passed the wardrobe she had painstakingly forced to its current placement, shaking his head.

"Did you push the wardrobe there yourself?"

Her chin went up, some of her defiance making a resurgence. "Did you think your ruffian Lucky would have aided me? Of course I d-did."

How that last chattering of her teeth vexed her. She was summoning her fury now that the danger had passed and a hint of warmth was creeping back over her. The fire, however, was far too low for her comfort.

"Little wonder you've torn open your wound." He dropped to his knees at her side, taking her injured arm in a firm-but-gentle grasp. "Let me see the damage you've done to yourself, love."

Love.

How the term of endearment rankled now, after what he had done.

"I don't require your assistance," she told him coolly. "I can tend to myself perfectly well."

"Clearly not, else you wouldn't have been hanging out the damned window about to fall to your death," he countered, unwinding the bandage despite her protest. "You could have broken your neck if you'd fallen from such a height, you know. I haven't any accommodating trees to break your fall or help you down."

"The rope would have sufficed, if not for my arm," she grumbled, still nettled to have failed at her escape.

And worse, to have been saved by him. She was thankful and irritated all at once.

"I should have tied you to the bloody bed," he said as the last of the bandage came undone.

She had to avert her gaze hastily from the sight of the ugly wound, her puckered flesh torn anew from her adventures, the blood oozing from the gash enough to make her dizzied again.

"You drugged me," she accused.

"I am sorry, Princess." There was a true mournful note of contrition in his deep voice as he rose to his feet and left her side. "Stay where you are. I want to cleanse the wound and see if I can stay the bleeding."

"I told you that you needn't attend me," she said, making the mistake of peering at her wound out of the corner of her eye and growing unsteady, her throat tightening.

"Don't look at it," he commanded softly, returning to her, a damp cloth in hand, as if he could read her thoughts.

As if he knew her so very well.

How was it possible to love someone and hate him at the same time?

"This may sting a bit," he added.

She kept her gaze turned toward the warmth of the fire, watching the flickering coals and wishing he wasn't being so kind and concerned.

"Do you not have an explanation for why you drugged me

and locked me inside your bedchamber?" she asked, wincing and inhaling on a sharp hiss as he made contact with the sensitive flesh surrounding her wound.

"Did I hurt you, love?" His tone was solicitous, chipping away at the defenses she had newly resurrected around her foolish heart.

"It would hurt less if you answered me."

"For your own good," he answered, giving her arm a few more gentle dabs to cleanse the rest of the blood. "You were intending to place yourself in grave danger, all for the sake of your lady-in-waiting."

"Tansy is like another sister to me," she defended. "I cannot abandon her."

"You needn't worry about her now. She will be looked after."

Disbelief shot through her as she turned to him, forgetting about her wound and then catching a glimpse of blood.

She looked quickly away. "What do you mean, she will be looked after? What have you done? Where is she now?"

Archer began winding the bandage around her arm once more, blessedly covering the blood and ooze.

"I intended to steal into your uncle's town house so that I could bring her here to safety," he said conversationally, as if they were not speaking of grave matters but instead something innocuous, like what he preferred to have on his plate at breakfast.

"I cannot believe you would take such a reckless risk," she said, head swiveling back to him now that her wound was no longer visible. "Why would you do such a thing?"

"To protect you," he said simply, pinning the bandage back in place.

She struggled to understand. Had he gone mad? He was yet on his knees at her side, looking up at her with that vibrant green gaze that never failed to melt an insidious part of her. Heat and longing suffused her against her will. She was still cross with him, damn the man. He had no right to look so handsome after what he had done. To have a mouth that invited kisses and wicked thoughts.

"How could you think that kidnapping my lady-in-waiting and drugging me would protect me?" she demanded, forcing herself to tamp down those traitorous yearnings.

"Because, Princess, you were hell-bent upon returning to that den of vipers created by your vile uncle, all to protect your lady-in-waiting. And while I admire your constancy, there was no goddamned way I was going to allow you to put yourself in such needless danger. You're too precious to me to allow it."

Too precious to him.

Those words had all the hard edges inside her softening.

But no, she had to cling to her anger. He had deceived her. Had imperiously conceived of this plot without informing her or inquiring after her opinion. The arrogance of the man was still astounding and infuriating. And moreover, he had yet to tell her what he had done with Tansy and where she was.

"You look as if you could use a fortifying drink," he said, rising to his feet. "You're pale. Brandy?"

He was distracting her, of course. Delaying his response. She didn't like it, nor did she trust his motives at present.

"Forgive me if I don't feel like accepting any food or drink from the man who has just drugged me and lied to me," she snapped, leaving her chair because being seated whilst he stood felt somehow as if it gave him power over her.

Power she didn't want to relinquish.

He had moved to a cabinet across the chamber. She followed him, careful to keep a discreet distance between them, stopping beyond arm's reach as she watched him open the cabinet and extract a bottle and glass.

"I promise you that this is untainted," he said, pouring a measure of the red-gold liquid into a glass and turning to offer it to her.

"And now I should trust you, after you have betrayed me?" She shook her head. "After you lied to me? I think not."

"Fair enough. I'll show you, then." He held her gaze, bringing the glass to his lips and taking a long sip.

And curse her, but she couldn't help but admire the strong, masculine lines of his throat, the dip in his Adam's apple as he swallowed. Couldn't help but want to place her lips there. To absorb his heat and inhale deeply of his scent.

He offered her the glass again, his tongue passing over his lower lip as he did so. "There you are, Princess. Untainted, just as I promised."

She jerked her eyes away from his mouth. "I'm well enough without it."

"Stubborn wench." He stepped nearer, closing the distance separating them. "Take the drink. It will help to calm you. You've just had a fright, nearly falling from the window like that."

His jaw hardened as he said the last, the only indication that he was anything other than calm. She *had* nearly fallen, and he had saved her. If he hadn't arrived when he had... She shivered again.

"You're still cold." He frowned, taking her hand in his and pressing the glass into her palm. "Drink. It will warm you as well."

She curled her fingers around the glass to keep it from dropping when he released it, the amber spirits within swishing lazily.

"Your lady-in-waiting is safe," he added. "She is now under the protection of your betrothed, King Maximilian of Varros. He is sending his men to the town house to guard your chamber as a condition of the betrothal."

The revelation sent a new wave of shock washing over her.

Archer knew.

And Tansy, poor, sweet Tansy. She was under the protection of King Maximilian now? What, precisely, would that entail?

Stasia raised the glass to her lips and took a long swig, swallowing it down with a wince. The taste of the stuff was smoother than the gin she had drunk with Theodoric, but it was dreadful, nonetheless. She preferred wine. But Archer's gaze was on her, hard and scrutinizing, and she didn't know what to make of this stunning new turn of events, so she took another lengthy sip. And then another.

"Easy, love," he cautioned, plucking the glass from her fingers. "It's meant to be savored, not to drown in."

There was a new edge in his words, and she suspected she knew the reason.

"Why is my lady-in-waiting going to be under the protection of King Maximilian?" she asked instead of addressing the fact that he had discovered she was promised to marry the king of Varros.

Tansy's words came back to her.

He kissed me.

Stasia didn't trust King Maximilian with her friend. Didn't trust him at all. The only reason she had conceded to his plan was that there had been no other choice. Aiding him in finding Theodoric and plotting to overthrow Gustavson was the last, best hope for Boritania and its people and what remained of her family.

"Because there is no better option for her at the moment," Archer said, his stare hard and searching and intense on hers. "When did you intend to tell me?"

She knew what he was asking, but she didn't want to discuss it. Not now. Perhaps not ever. Because doing so acknowledged the painful truth of the grim future awaiting her, one she had been seeking to avoid by losing herself in the present.

And look at where that had landed her.

"I didn't intend to tell you," she admitted.

He took a long drink from the brandy as well, leaving her with no choice but to watch him in the heavy silence. When the brandy was gone, he crudely wiped his mouth with the back of his hand.

"You didn't intend to tell me you're marrying a *bloody king*," he repeated, his emphasis on the last two words as stinging as a slap.

Guilt was a tangled knot inside her, one that she couldn't seem to undo.

"Why should it have mattered?" she asked, summoning her defiance.

"I had a right to know, Stasia," he said quietly.

And somehow, his lack of anger sliced her more deeply than any show of fury could have.

"You didn't ask," she offered lamely.

"My mistake," he said bitterly, before returning to the cabinet and splashing another measure of brandy into the empty glass.

She watched his broad back, the silence charged, and wondered how he had so neatly turned the tables on her. He was the one who had lied to her, who had imprisoned her in his bedchamber against her will, and now he dared to act as if he were the injured party between the two of them because she hadn't told him she was marrying King Maximilian.

"I didn't think my future marriage was any concern of yours," she said, feeling suddenly weary after everything that had happened.

Twice, she had come alarmingly close to death. She had been drugged, she had been lied to, and she had nearly been stabbed and dropped to her doom from a great height. Her uncle wanted her dead, she was set to marry a man who terrified her, and the man she loved had turned into a cool stranger. What more could happen?

"Your marriage became my concern when you gave yourself to me," Archer said harshly. "I took the maidenhead of the future queen to a bloodthirsty madman, Stasia. It matters not that I didn't know it. The deed is done. Tonight, he threatened to kill me, and he should have done for my stupidity in allowing myself to be caught. I was only spared because of my usefulness to him."

The breath fled her at his words.

"Forgive me," she murmured, the apology ineffectual. "It would seem I am a poison to all who know me."

Perhaps she was cursed. Her family had been largely destroyed, and now it seemed that everyone she touched, everyone whose life she entered, was at risk. Tansy and Archer. Who else?

"You're not a poison, Princess." Archer stood before her again, looming and tall and grim in the low, flickering candlelight. "You're a panacea."

"A panacea," she repeated, the English word unfamiliar to her, trying to understand. "What does that mean?"

"A cure," he said tenderly. "One that heals all. Because that's what you've done to me. You've changed me, healed the broken pieces inside me and brought them together again. I would give my life for yours a hundred times over, and do it gladly, too."

Sweet Deus, he was doing it again.

Being so agonizingly gentle, looking at her as if he revered her. Telling her everything she wanted and needed to hear. But he had been wrong to do what he had tonight, even if his intentions had been pure.

"But I don't want you to give your life for mine," she told

him. "Nor do I want to be locked away as if I'm incapable of choosing my own risks."

"Would you have stayed if I had asked you?"

"No."

His jaw hardened. "And you would have returned to that town house, to your death. I'm sorry I deceived you, but I'm not sorry you're here with me. I'm bloody well not sorry you aren't lying in your lonely bed in that house like an innocent lamb awaiting her slaughter."

"I can't stay with you for long," she said. "Whatever you've done tonight, you have only delayed the inevitable. I'll still need to return as soon as I'm able. I must marry King Maximilian, or my sisters will be in grave danger."

He worked his jaw and then tossed back the contents of his glass. "You're not going anywhere until I say you are, Princess."

"You intend to keep me here as your prisoner?"

"Aye, love. I'm afraid so." The smile he gave her didn't reach his eyes. "Until we can deliver your brother to King Maximilian, you're mine."

CHAPTER 18

"Not bleeding, I see. Thought the she-cat might've laid you low for locking 'er in a room like that."

Lucky's taunting observation rankled.

Archer pierced his oldest friend with a glare. The hour was nearing dawn, and he hadn't slept. Stasia was locked in his bedchamber with a guard posted below her window lest she take any more stupid risks with her lovely neck. And Archer was sitting in his study before a dying fire, drinking himself into oblivion.

Tomorrow—strike that, *today*—could bloody well go to the devil where it belonged as far as he was concerned.

"What are you doing in here?" he asked Lucky grimly. "Shouldn't you be off somewhere sleeping or plotting the vicious murders of all your enemies?"

"Already plotted those," Lucky said brightly, kicking the leg of the empty chair at Archer's side. "Mind if I rest these old bones?"

"Sit." He waved with his glass, sending brandy splashing over the edge and onto the back of his hand, but he didn't give a proper goddamn about the mess, nor the droplets that went raining to the Aubusson at his feet. "And Christ, if your bones are old, what are mine?"

"Old," Lucky grunted as he folded himself into the chair. "We're of an age, ain't we?"

Archer sighed heavily, feeling old. And dejected. And helpless. And foolish. And so many other emotions, his drink-addled mind couldn't identify them all.

"We are," he said instead, taking another hearty pull of brandy from his glass, gratified when it didn't dribble down his shirt. "I feel it tonight, old friend."

"This morning, you mean."

"Morning." Another sip. "Whatever the bloody fuck time of day it is."

"You're clipping the King's English, you are," Lucky said. "Any more brandy, and you'll be shooting the cat in a few hours."

"Would serve me right," he muttered, staring morosely into the dying fire. "I'm bloody miserable, Luck."

"On account of the wench?"

He nodded, lifting his glass to his lips despite his friend's warning that he'd imbibed far too much. "She's not a wench."

"All wenches are wenches."

"Not this one." He wanted to elaborate, to explain to Lucky just how incredible Stasia was, the princess who placed all others before herself, who climbed trees and took flesh wounds with aplomb, who moved mountainous furniture and attempted to escape by improvising her own rope through a window.

But all that emerged was a hiccup instead.

"This one is different," he added imprecisely, before hiccupping again.

Likely for the best. He couldn't begin to express just how

different and wonderful she was. Lucky would laugh him into the next century.

"Different," his friend repeated, a knowing tone entering his voice.

A tone that irritated Archer in the extreme.

Hiccup.

"I've got a remedy for those," Lucky said politely.

Of course he did. Lucky had a remedy for everything, and his remedies always worked. The man was a bloody glowering, walking enigma.

Hiccup.

"They'll go away on their own." Archer drank some more brandy in an effort to drown the maddening reaction happening somewhere in his throat.

And to quell the equally maddening effect taking place somewhere in his stupid heart.

"If you insist," Lucky said, sounding considerably less confident.

Hiccup.

"Would you fetch it for me?" he asked dejectedly.

With another grunt, Lucky rose from his chair, the sound of his footfalls leaving the room of precious little comfort to Archer. Stasia was angry with him. He was about to lose her. And to a damned king, at that. Another ungodly hiccup escaped him as he glared into the dwindling flames, waiting for Lucky to come back with his miracle potion.

By the time his old friend returned, his brandy glass had been drained, and the blasted affliction was still racking his frame with vexing persistence.

Lucky offered him a cup of something that wasn't precisely foul-smelling but wasn't entirely appealing either.

"Drink it," his friend ordered gruffly, seating himself once more.

HER WICKED ROGUE

Archer took a sip of the oddly scented drink, and it was bitter on his tongue. With great effort, he swallowed it down, coughing when he had finished.

"What the hell is it, Luck?" he demanded, sputtering.

"Take another sip," Lucky told him. "You need more than one for it to do its work proper-like."

Holding his breath, Archer did as his friend advised, taking another sip.

"It's horse piss," Lucky announced, grinning at him from his chair.

Archer immediately spat the stuff everywhere. On his shirt, his lap, into the fire, which hissed as if in protest.

"Joking," the bastard said. "But it's my secret just the same."

"I don't know if I dare trust you." He pinned his friend with a glare and then hiccupped again.

Lucky raised a dark, shaggy brow. "Because I've given you something to drink and you don't know wot is in it? A bit familiar-sounding, ain't it?"

Fucking hell. Was he being upbraided by his own friend now, too?

Archer held his breath and poured some more of the unpleasant liquid down his throat, hoping it would finally do its work and prove a point as well. "It was for her own good."

"Aye, try telling a wench that and see where it gets you."

He gave Lucky a narrow-eyed glare. "What do you know about wenches, anyway?"

His friend's countenance turned wry. "More than I'd like to, I reckon. I know that when you've one wot's precious to you, you do everything you can to keep 'er yours. You don't sit by a fire at dawn, pouring brandy down your throat."

"Hmm," Archer said, wondering at the faint edge of regret he heard in Lucky's voice.

He hadn't ever known Lucky to chase petticoats. But then, their spy work had become so all-consuming before it had come to an end that he hadn't truly been spending a great deal of time with Lucky. For all he knew, his friend had a woman at every rookery tavern.

But Archer couldn't deny that Stasia was precious to him. More precious than he ever could have imagined one woman could be. The thought of her marrying the brutal, massive, cold-eyed king he'd met hours earlier left him longing to slam his fists into something. Preferably that king's nose. But the bastard son of a marquess couldn't attack a king without consequences, regardless of how much he longed to. Hell, he couldn't even save the woman he loved from having to marry the king. Nor could he earn her forgiveness for doing everything he could to save her life.

An utter failure was what he bloody well was.

At least his hiccups were finally gone.

He held his empty cup to Lucky in mock salute. "Your horse piss worked its magic on me. I'm cured."

"Cured of the 'iccups, perhaps, but not of what truly ails you."

His friend was far too perceptive.

"What do you propose I do, Luck?" he asked, aware that Lucky didn't know the full extent of the story.

No one knew Stasia was a royal princess in his household except for Archer. The omission was for her protection and at her request, not because Archer didn't trust his friend. He would entrust his own life to Lucky any day without hesitation.

"Get off your arse and go to your wench," his friend suggested gruffly. "Tell 'er you're sorry and that you love 'er."

He might have denied that he was in love with Stasia for the sake of his pride, but what was the sense? It was true, and Lucky was no fool.

"I've never loved a woman before," he admitted, settling his empty glass on the Aubusson.

Lucky was not wrong. Archer ought to stop hiding in his study and drowning himself in drink. He wasn't solving any problems by doing either.

"But you love this one, aye?"

"Christ yes." He laughed, the sound not carrying any mirth. Laughed at himself for his own foolishness. Of all the women in the world, he had found the one who could never be his to love. "It's bloody terrifying, Luck."

"I know it is, old friend." Lucky clapped him on the back. "But don't let your pride get in the fucking way, eh? You'll lose 'er for good if you do. Lesson I learned the rough way."

Did he dare to tell Stasia he loved her?

Could he?

Would it matter? She was betrothed to a bloody king.

"If you don't say the words, you'll always regret it," Lucky said. "Go to your wench."

Perhaps his friend was right.

"I think I will," he conceded, rising on unsteady feet, more proof he'd drained far too much of his brandy stores this night.

And morning.

"Thank you for the horse piss and the advice, old chum," he called over his shoulder as he made his painstaking way from the study.

∽

A GENTLE HAND cupping her cheek.

That was what stole Stasia from the bowels of a sleep fractured by unwanted dreams that had all been the same. In every instance, she had been torn away from Archer, trying in vain to find her way back to him. It was fitting then, that she opened her eyes to find him lying at her side in his bed, fully clothed, watching her with an unguarded expression of such tenderness that her breath caught.

"Archer." Her first instinct was to reach for him, to reassure herself that he was here, that she could touch him.

The last dream had been particularly dreadful. They had been on a ship together in a vast sea when a storm had suddenly set upon them. The boat had begun to sink, and she had found herself adrift in the waves, calling for him. Unable to find him.

"I'm sorry, Princess," he said.

Brazen morning light was seeping around the edges of the curtains, dancing over the floor beyond, but he was mostly enshrouded in shadow. His voice was mournful, and there was the unmistakable, faint scent of spirits on his breath.

She remembered the reason she was still here. The reason he was apologizing. All the reasons why she should cling to her fury. He had told her that she was his prisoner, only to return in such a state at this early hour.

"You're soused," she returned, but without heat.

Because despite the overbearingness of his actions, she knew he was only doing what he believed in her best interest. Even if it was quite wrongheaded of him.

"Perhaps a trifle disguised," he acknowledged.

A sad smile played at his lips.

Lips she very much wanted to kiss, despite everything.

"Why are you here?" she forced herself to ask, recalling how he had locked her inside his bedchamber again after they had argued in the depths of the night.

"It's my bedchamber, is it not?" He shifted his hand, using his knuckles to caress her jaw, his touch light, almost as if he feared to touch her too firmly.

As if doing so would break her or send her from him.

In truth, there was no other place she would rather be than here with him, by his side.

"Did you sleep all night in your clothing?" she asked next, glancing down at yesterday's trousers and shirt.

His cravat was missing, as was his waistcoat. His boots, however, remained on his feet, resting atop the fresh counterpane as if they belonged there.

"I haven't slept," he said softly.

"Why not?"

His knuckle trailed down her throat. She was still wearing her gown as well. She had been too furious with him to allow him to aid her in disrobing, and by the time she had realized that she couldn't remove her garments on her own with the use of one good arm alone, she had simply lain on his bed, surrounded by his scent, and dreamt of him.

"Because I hate that you're angry with me." His voice was a low, decadent rumble that landed, as always, as something molten and forbidden lodged deep inside her. "I hate that I'm going to lose you."

His quiet confession shouldn't affect her the way it did.

He was in his cups. He had locked her inside a room against her will, and more than once. Had drugged her wine! She ought to be better equipped to resist him.

And yet, this was the man she loved. This strong, fearless by-blow of a marquess with a bump in his nose from defending his half sister and beautiful green cat's eyes that saw all the parts of her no one else had seen before. He brought her to life with his touch, showed her passion and pleasure, and tended her wounds, bathed her, fed her when she was hungry. Caught her when she was about to fall.

Saved her life.

Yes, he had done that, too.

How could she stay angry at him? The arrogant man had been trying to protect her, even if he had gone about the entire affair all wrong.

"I'm angry that you didn't consult me." She swallowed as his traveling hand moved to her nape, his fingers gliding over her skin to cup the base of her head, kneading the taut muscles there. "I'm angry that you locked me away in here and placed yourself in danger without warning me of what you had intended. You could have been gravely injured or worse."

And to think that he had somehow met with King Maximilian. That the king had threatened Archer's life, and all because of her... She couldn't bear to imagine what might have happened. Nor what manner of bargain the two men had struck.

"I was wrong, Princess," he conceded, surprising her as he continued to massage the tension from her neck and scalp. "I should have talked with you first. I should have told you of my intentions."

Her uninjured arm came up, her hand finding his beloved face with a will of its own. She trailed her touch over that arrogant slash of jaw, his whiskers prickling her palm deliciously. How could she resist him? From the first moment she had met him, entering his study to find him standing by the mantel, idly smoking a cheroot, she hadn't been able. Why should it be any different now that she knew him, now that he had held her in his arms.

Now that he had been inside her.

"What would you have done if I had disagreed with you?" she asked, even though she knew it didn't matter. She would soon be another man's wife, and her time in his bed would be naught but a distant memory.

A slow, confident smile curved his lips. "I would have

done it anyway." He kissed her palm reverently. "Someone has to protect you, Princess. Christ knows you don't know how to protect yourself."

He wasn't entirely wrong, and it rather rankled that he was right and that he knew it. That he knew *her* as well as he did, from such a short acquaintance.

"You took the choice from me," she reminded him. "And you kept me here like a prisoner."

He caught her wrist with his other hand and removed hers from his jaw, laying it over his heart. She couldn't help but wonder at the placement, but then he did another odd thing and laced their fingers together, keeping her hand trapped over the steady thrumming beats.

His eyelids drooped sleepily, his gaze growing hooded. "Because you are so bloody stubborn and strong that I knew you would follow me or refuse altogether."

No sense in arguing. If he had confided in her, she would have stopped him. She never would have allowed him to go to the town house without her.

"This bargain you've struck with King Maximilian," she said instead, studying his features, committing them to memory. Wishing she could stitch the sight of him to the insides of her eyelids, so that years from now, she could close them and see him still. "Tell me about it. Tell me why."

"Was my idea, not your betrothed's."

His eyes were closed now, the fingers kneading her nape moving more slowly, the pressure lessening. Was it her imagination, or had he spoken the word betrothed with great bitterness, as if the word cost him some essential part of himself that he could never recover?

Jealousy, then?

"You know why I must marry him."

"That doesn't mean I don't hate it, Princess. Nor that the

thought of you in another man's arms, in his bed, doesn't make me want to kill that man with my bare hands."

It was a vicious thing to say. Violent and bloodthirsty and wholly uncivilized. And yet she couldn't deny that hearing it from him made her own heart give an answering pang of longing deep in her breast. A physical ache resided there that had nothing to do with lust and everything to do with the love she had for him.

"You should sleep," she murmured, feeling guilty that he had been awake all night long.

Knowing she was the source of his unrest. Likely the source of his drinking as well.

"You want to know about the bargain," he said, eyes closed now, his voice taking on a drowsy quality so that it was lower and almost mellifluous. "Your betrothed knows you were wounded. I told him about the attempt on your life, the assassin hired by your uncle." He paused, yawning quietly before continuing. "In exchange for you remaining here with me, and the use of his guards to watch over your lady-in-waiting, I'm to deliver your brother to him. It was either that, or take my chances with the king's assassin."

More guilt washed over Stasia. "I am so very sorry that you found yourself in danger because of me. But I'm not certain Tansy will be any safer with the king's guards watching over her."

"Your betrothed assures me she will be protected."

His chest was rising in more even breaths now, and it was clear that he was losing the battle against the slumber that wanted to claim him.

"You took his word?" Her alarm grew as she thought again of what Tansy had said.

The kiss hadn't been forced, she had told her. But what if the king demanded more as his price for guarding Tansy?

"Not much choice in the matter." Archer's eyes remained

closed, his every word seeming to grow more difficult. "Besides, I have the two things he wants most just now: you and your brother. Your king wants to meet with the lost prince."

The knot in her stomach tightened, for her brother had made it clear that he didn't want any part of returning to Boritania.

"What if Theodoric doesn't agree to it?"

Archer's eyes opened a crack. "Don't worry, love. All will be well."

"Don't worry?" A bitter laugh tore from her. "How dare you tell me not to worry and fall asleep on me?"

His eyes had already fluttered closed. "Rest, Princess. You'll need it."

In that moment, she could have boxed his ears, so great was her vexation with his plotting and his half answers. Instead, she moved to disentangle herself from him, regardless of the comfort of his body aligned with hers, his hands on her, his heart beating steadily beneath her palm.

But his arm snaked around her waist, keeping her from moving. "Don't leave me. Please."

The plea from him was unexpected. As was the show of vulnerability. She bit her lip, staring at him, his handsome features relaxed and poised for sleep. She ought to slip away from him. Sleep in a chair. Pace the floor until he woke and released her from her prison.

Instead, she found herself softening toward him, gliding incrementally closer on the mattress, their fully clothed bodies connecting. Her hip to his, his arm banded around her in a possessive hold. It wasn't passion sparking between them in this moment of weariness and mutual need. Rather, it was something far deeper. It was taking solace, finding comfort, and yes, for Stasia, it was *love*. So much love that it welled inside her chest, as if she were holding her breath, painful and burning, needing to expand and be released.

He sighed, kissing her brow, her temple, his breath a hot benediction over her greedy skin. "Thank you, Princess."

Tears stung her eyes, and she screwed them tightly closed, refusing to allow them to fall. How could she ever part from him when she could not bear to leave his side?

CHAPTER 19

Archer woke with a jolt to an aching head and a mouth as dry as the ashes in a fireplace. Blinking blearily against the unforgiving light shining through the windows, he realized he was alone in his bed. The curtains had been hauled back to illuminate his bedchamber in what he could only presume was midday light. Unlike most days of late, the sky beyond wasn't cast with grim, gray portent. Instead, the sun was awake, burning with recrimination.

"Arsehole," he muttered at the sun for daring to rise with such irreverence for the fact that he had overindulged in brandy.

His arm shot out, reaching for the familiar warmth and curves of the woman he'd fallen asleep beside. But his hand met with nothing but a perfectly smoothed counterpane, the bed made around him as if she had never been there.

Stasia was gone.

He sat up, rubbing the sleep from his eyes, head thumping.

Where was she?

Last night—Christ, *this morning*—when he had wandered

to his chamber, he had left the door unlocked. Buoyed by Lucky's advice, he had been determined to make amends and to tell her that he loved her. Instead, he'd fallen asleep in his goddamn boots.

And now, she had taken advantage of his stupidity, and she had fled.

Served him right for falling into a bottle of brandy. Ordinarily, he never imbibed too much. He had seen the ruin that had befallen his own mother—blue ruin, opium, anything she could find. Last night had been a failure in nearly all ways.

He rose, still wearing yesterday's clothes. At least his irresponsibility was proving convenient in one sense. He could make haste in trying to decipher where Stasia had gone without bothering to dress.

He swung his legs to the floor, boots landing with a loud thump, head still pounding, and wished he had a cup of cool water to pour down his dry gullet. No time for that, however. He had an errant princess to find.

With a groan, he forced himself up, feeling for a moment like a foal on new legs as he availed himself of a chamber pot to relieve himself of the dregs of his brandy. A hasty wash of his hands and face was all he allowed before striding toward the door.

The door that opened suddenly to reveal the very woman he was looking for. Behind her and towering over her, bearing a tray laden with coffee and toast and eggs, stood Lucky.

"You're awake, then," Stasia pronounced, her gaze flicking over him as she conducted an unsmiling assessment of his person.

No doubt finding him wanting.

He was, after all, wearing the same trousers and shirt he'd fallen asleep in.

He raked his fingers through his hair, sure it was also dreadfully unkempt. "If that's what one wishes to call it."

He certainly didn't feel awake. Indeed, he felt as if he might fall back into bed and sleep for another day to cure himself of this terrible affliction. He felt like the devil's own arsehole. But she was here, and that was something. She hadn't run.

"Morning," Lucky greeted him, hefting the tray onto a nearby table. "There's a cure for wot ails you on the tray."

"Not more horse piss, I hope," he grumbled, strangely nettled by the sight of his friend and Stasia working together. "You could have sent a footman with the tray, you know."

"And lose the opportunity to see you cropsick and looking like a puppy wot lost its way?" He had the audacity to wink in a show of good humor that was exceedingly rare. "Don't worry, I assured the wench you ain't a swill tub."

Fucking Lucky.

"I'm indebted," he drawled, raising a brow, and even this slight action made the ache in his head increase twofold.

"You've been indebted for years," Lucky said with a half grin. "Maybe one of these days I'll collect."

With a slightly mocking bow, Lucky made his exit, leaving Archer and Stasia alone. For the first time, he realized she was wearing a different gown, this one a light, becoming blue that rendered her cool eyes all the more intense.

"You look beautiful," he blurted stupidly, love and elation and primitive possession welling up inside him. "Where did you get that gown?"

"You look dreadful," she said conversationally, turning to the tray to pour coffee into a cup. "The gown was delivered this morning. Apparently from a Madame Beauchamp. I gathered it was for my use. Presuming I am your only female prisoner, that is."

He might have winced at the word *prisoner* and the way she said it, but his head was aching enough. Archer searched his mind for the name Beauchamp, his old knowledge box vexingly blank for a moment until it came to him.

Ah, yes. The sought-after modiste who had provided him with the chemise. He had inquired after a gown as well, hoping she might have a garment close enough to Stasia's size. The woman had said she would send over something suitable after making a few alterations. He had quite forgotten in all the upheaval. Kings and danger and brandy, et cetera.

"Who helped you to dress?" he asked, rubbing his jaw and feeling all the whiskers that told him he likely looked like a barbarian in desperate need of a shave.

"One of your maids," Stasia answered, finishing her flawless one-handed pour and returning the coffeepot to its tray. "A girl named Abigail. She was eager to be of assistance. Here is your coffee, then. It appears as if you need a restorative of some sort."

She moved toward him, the gown fluttering around her, the saucer and its cup extended rather like an olive branch. Dare he hope that it was? That her presence in his bedchamber this morning of her own free will meant something? He had never felt more like an abject failure than last night, and the feeling remained, damned unpleasant.

Archer accepted the offering, their fingers brushing, heat and awareness striking him like lightning bolting down from the heavens above. "Thank you."

The rich scent of coffee wafted to him, beckoning. He took a sip, watching her over the cup. She watched him in return, her countenance shuttered.

"Who is Madame Beauchamp?" she asked.

He swallowed hard. The coffee was bloody hot, and it

scorched his throat on its way down. No doubt deserved. The cup landed in its saucer with an unmannerly clatter.

"A modiste," he answered hoarsely. "Why do you ask?"

A faint color spread over her high cheekbones, and it occurred to him that perhaps she had been jealous of Madame Beauchamp.

"I merely wondered if she was a…consort of yours. I wouldn't wish to wear the gown if she were."

"And yet you donned it this morning," he pointed out.

Her brow wrinkled. "My gown was beginning to stink. I would have worn the drawing room curtains had they been offered to me."

He took a much smaller sip of his coffee, grateful for something to occupy him, to keep him from taking her in his arms as he so desperately longed. "You must forgive me for my lapse in hospitality, Your Royal Highness. It isn't every day that I imprison a Boritanian princess, have my life threatened by the king she's meant to marry, and rescue her from falling to her death out a window."

Her lips pursed. "I wouldn't have been climbing out the window if it weren't for you, and you've neglected to mention drowning yourself in brandy until dawn."

Her waspish comment stirred something inside him. He loved her ice every bit as much as he loved her fire.

"You disapprove of me," he commented lightly.

"I disapprove of some of your actions." She sighed, drawing his attention to the hollow at the base of her throat, the glint of her golden necklace nestled there, a place he desperately longed to press his lips. "I disapprove of you keeping me your prisoner here without my permission."

He couldn't hide his smile. "Princess, being a prisoner, by definition, doesn't involve permission."

Her brows drew together. "You are being deliberately obtuse."

He wondered if he should tell her that he loved her now? Blurt it like a fool. Swallow his pride along with his hot coffee. He reckoned the sting would be the same.

"I'm trying to make you smile," he countered instead. "I hate being the cause of your distress."

She sighed heavily. "It is these dreadful circumstances that cause my discontent. Will you not sit and eat? Your breakfast grows cold."

And thankfully the scent of it—buttered toast, poached eggs, and gammon—didn't make his stomach threaten to cast up its contents in protest. In his misbegotten life, he'd certainly had far more to drink than he had the night before.

Morning before.

He frowned. "Have you eaten?"

"I took breakfast with Lucky."

His frown deepened. He wasn't sure he liked the thought of his oldest friend and Stasia dining together.

But he took another sip of his coffee before he responded. "I've never known Lucky to dine anywhere other than below stairs. I've begged him to eat with me in the dining room on numerous occasions."

Yes, he knew that it wasn't done for a butler to dine with his employer. But Lucky was far more than a butler, and the only reason he held that position was at his own insistence. Besides, Archer wasn't a part of Society, despite his town house amongst the lords and ladies of the *ton*.

Stasia shrugged. "Much like other circumstances, perhaps you should have asked nicely."

Her barb was a direct hit, reminding him that he wasn't entirely forgiven, even if she had remained here.

"Touché, Princess," he said quietly. "I'd like to say I've learned my lesson."

Her lips pinched together in a regal moue of disapproval. "But you haven't, have you?"

"Given the chance, I'd do it again if it meant keeping you safe from that bastard uncle of yours and his bloody assassins," he said this without hesitation, for it was true.

A man could be wrong and yet harbor no regret. His was solely in denying Stasia the right to tell him *no*. He would have carried on with his plan anyway.

She stared at him, her glacial eyes assessing, and then she presented him with the elegant lines of her back as she turned to the waiting breakfast tray. "Sit."

There was a sharp command in her voice that he hadn't often heard. One his manly instincts balked at.

"I'm not a hound," he grumbled to her elaborately constructed chignon rounded with braids.

Also, he reckoned, a result of Abigail the maid and not, he prayed, Lucky the glowering butler and sometime best chum.

She glanced over her shoulder, treating him to an arch look that reminded him, in case he dared forget, that she was Princess Anastasia Augusta St. George and he was a lowly marquess's bastard.

"Sit," she repeated sternly.

And though it aggrieved him mightily to be ordered about, Archer reluctantly did as his woman pleased, folding himself into a stuffed armchair by the fireplace.

Stasia seemed to keep her back presented to him for an eternity, making small movements over the large tray, an occasional clink echoing in the stillness of the chamber before turning back to him, holding a much smaller tray which must have been secreted within the larger, balancing it with one hand.

"Damn it, you shouldn't be carrying anything," he protested, gripping the arms of his chair and making to rise.

"Stay," she ordered firmly, reaching him and extending the silver tray in his direction.

He accepted it with haste but not without muttering, "Next, I expect you'll ask me to bark."

That earned him a small smile. "And would you?"

"Woof," he replied instantly, and he couldn't say why.

There was something inherent within him that desired to please the woman hovering over him, whatever the cost to his heart, pride, or mortal soul.

"Fitting." Her lips twitched. "You are rather resembling a mongrel this morning."

"I need to dress," he agreed, "but I need to eat more, I think. A change of trousers can wait."

The plate awaiting him promised excellent fortification.

"It is everything you prefer," she said quietly. "I took the liberty of asking Lucky for your favorites."

This was her doing, then. He might have known, except she had been so frightfully angry with him last night.

And this morning, he thought with a grimace.

"I hope you don't mind," she added.

He took up his utensils, glancing at her. Christ, she was lovely. He wanted to touch every inch of her golden skin and then find all the places she was pale and pink and lick and kiss her there until she was writhing and desperate for more.

As it turned out, cockstands weren't deterred by getting despicably cup-shot the night before.

"Of course I don't mind," he told her, his voice thick with emotion and suppressed need. "But you should not have done this, Princess. You are wounded, and I've been an ass. Necessarily in some instances, I might add, but an ass, nonetheless."

She was staring at him, looming over him, the scent of her, floral and crisp, teasing his senses along with the scent of the breakfast she had procured on his behalf.

"Will you sit?" he asked her, gesturing to the chair flanking his, realizing for the first time that this chamber had been decorated once with a mind to a couple who might settle here, talking by the fireside into the late night hours.

How strange he'd never noticed before. In many ways, he felt a stranger in this home. The furniture, like the books in the library, had all come secondhand.

Stasia seated herself primly, her dainty hand smoothing her skirts. He drank in the sight of her here, thinking how domestic it was, and how he would give his eyeteeth to sit here thus with her every morning for the rest of their lives. A stupid, futile thought, for that could never be.

"Word came a half an hour ago from King Maximilian," she said, the mentioning of her betrothed swiftly killing any further foolish imaginings of a future in which the two of them could be together.

He was probably still half sotted.

"I trust you read the missive," he said, cutting into his gammon so viciously that his silverware made a wretched screeching sound on the plate. "Since it came from your betrothed."

The hated word was like a blade in his heart, cutting it to bits.

"He reports that his guards are installed in my uncle's town house for the protection of my lady-in-waiting," Stasia added.

Relief replaced his bitterness.

"Well, thank Christ for that," he said. "Now there is the matter of keeping anyone from discovering where you are and persuading your brother to meet with King Maximilian."

"What will happen if we can't convince Theodoric to do so?" she asked, concern lacing her dulcet voice.

King Maximilian would likely set his vicious little Varrosian assassin upon him. The king's ominous words echoed in Archer's mind. *No one can slit a man's throat as quickly and quietly.*

"We'll worry about that later," he said smoothly.

No need to cause her further distress. Besides, he was fully prepared to compel her brother to speak with King Maximilian using whatever means required.

"I wish to worry about it now," Stasia protested. "Tell me."

He sighed, then shoved a bite of egg into his mouth so that he would have an excuse not to immediately form an answer. He didn't want to worry Stasia unnecessarily, but he was also keenly aware that he owed her the truth. He'd kept enough from her the day before.

He finished chewing, then washed it down with more coffee, which had mercifully cooled. "Suffice it to say that your betrothed intends to turn me over to his bloodthirsty minions."

"No," she whispered, going pale. "He cannot mean to do that."

He wondered if she knew just how vicious and unyielding the man she was going to marry was. But then, he suspected she did and that was part of the reason behind her reticence.

"Don't fret, love," he told her with his most devil-may-care smile. "It wouldn't be the first time a madman wanted me dead, and I strongly doubt it shall be the last."

"How can you joke about this?" she asked, the color still leached from her lovely face.

"Simple. As in most matters in life, it is laugh or cry. No sense in the latter. I always choose the former." He turned his attention back to his plate, cutting another bite of pork. "You forget that my own mother sold me to whoremongers and I spent years in the rookeries before becoming a spy. There have always been people wanting me dead at any given moment. And yet, here I sit."

"You speak of your own life so flippantly," she countered. "As if it is of no import."

"It isn't when compared to yours." He glanced up at her,

meeting her gaze, allowing all the feigned levity to drain from his own countenance. "You are what matters most to me, Princess. As I told you, I would give my life for yours a hundred times over, and do it gladly, too."

Her eyes were glistening with unshed tears. "It was never my intention to bring danger to you."

"I know that, and trust me when I say I don't regret a single second you've been in my life." The smile he gave her was neither careless nor false. "I would do everything again, just as I have done, all for the chance to have you in my arms again."

She pressed a hand over her lips, making a soft sound that made his gut clench, not in rebellion over his breakfast, but over any pain she endured, whether emotional or physical. Damn it, he hated to see her hurt.

"I'll send word to your brother again today," he forced himself to say.

Stasia took a moment, clearly gathering her composure, before moving her hand away. There was still a sheen in her icy-blue eyes, but her shoulders had straightened with renewed determination.

There she was, his warrior princess.

"No," she said. "This time, I'll go to him. I've placed you in peril, and I need to remedy that. Theodoric is *my* brother. You need but tell me where to find him."

His response was instant and instinctive. "You can't. The possibility of you being seen is a risk we can't afford when you are meant to be ill in your bedchamber."

"I want to do this for myself." She held his stare, unflinching. "Alone."

He wanted to argue. But he knew that he owed her this chance.

He nodded. "You'll have my carriage and three of my men as guards. I'm not taking any chances with you, Princess."

"Thank you." She rose from her chair abruptly, as if she couldn't bear to remain another moment. "I should allow you to finish your breakfast in peace."

Archer doubted very much that he would ever have peace again. But he didn't bother to correct her. He ate the remainder of his breakfast alone, in a grim silence.

CHAPTER 20

Seated in Archer's carriage opposite her brother as it rocked along the street, Stasia surrendered her every attempt at persuading him with ration and reason. He had remained steadfast in his refusal, despite her determination to win him over to her cause. To what ought to be *their* cause.

And now, she had another cause to fight for entirely—the life of the man she loved. Archer might be willing to surrender his life for her, but she wasn't about to allow that to happen.

She had exhausted her logical arguments and explanations with Theodoric. She had no recourse remaining save one. It was time to plead.

"Please," she implored. "I beg of you."

"There's nothing I can do, Stasia," Theodoric said flatly, apparently unmoved.

Ever mindful of the possibility that the coachman might be able to overhear pieces of their conversation, she switched to Boritanian.

"You can come home," she said. "You can come home to Boritania, where you belong."

"I don't have a home," he answered, likewise in Boritanian, "and nor do I belong anywhere."

So stubborn. But then, they were brother and sister, were they not? It stood to reason that despite the time and distance, he was not so different than she was. They were both St. Georges, after all.

"Lies." She shook her head, equally determined. "You belong in Boritania. You are a prince of the blood."

"I've been banished," he reminded her. "My return is punishable by death. If you don't think Gustavson would have me arrested, imprisoned, and send me to the gallows as quickly as you can blink an eye, you're deluding yourself."

That was indeed true, but she was still a princess in her own right. She had neither been exiled nor repudiated, and her royal blood enabled her to make decrees that others could not.

"You know that your exile can be renounced by someone of royal blood," she argued. "I could revoke it now, here, in this moment."

Surely he knew the old law, one that Gustavson lacked the power to rescind, for it was one of the founding principles of the kingdom's royal line. He had managed to manipulate the monarchy in every other way, but the old laws remained sacred. This was the one way in which she could help her brother.

But Theodoric was shaking his head. "Renouncing my exile would be dangerous for you. Our uncle would have you imprisoned and tortured, just as he did to me."

She would already have to lose Archer, regardless of the decision Theodoric made. Sacrificing her life for the good of Boritania was her duty and her honor. And she needed him to agree to King Maximilian's plans now more than she ever had, because Archer's life was at stake.

"I'm not concerned with what our uncle would do to me," she said. "Saving our kingdom is far more important than saving myself could ever be."

"You *should* be concerned," her brother said, his voice harsh.

And then suddenly, his demeanor changed, taking on a pallor that made him appear ill. At his sides, his hands were clenched in fists. His entire bearing was stiff, as if he were fashioned of marble. And the haunted look in his eyes terrified her.

"Theodoric," she said quietly, concern making her stomach feel as if it were twisted in knots.

She reached for him with her unwounded arm, her hand on his coat, intending to soothe him. To chase whatever demons yet haunted him from his time of imprisonment and torture.

He flinched and caught her wrist. "Don't."

"Brother." She withdrew her touch, for he seemed like a trapped animal in that moment, backed into a corner and terrified. "What is wrong?"

His response was delayed, as if the words were sharp and painful on his tongue. "What they did to me in the dungeon…I wouldn't wish it upon my mortal enemy, and most certainly not upon you, Stasia. I'll not allow you to renounce my exile at your own expense."

Sweet Deus, what had they done to him? She couldn't bear to guess.

"I know they hurt you badly." Her voice broke, betraying her as she tried to remain poised and calm for her brother's sake. "Reinald said you were near death when they removed you to the ship's hold that day."

Tears prickled, pooling and falling down her cheeks, beyond her control.

Her brother's eyes closed for a moment, almost as if he couldn't stomach seeing the evidence of her grief, before he opened them again, a new resolve etched on his countenance.

A muscle ticked in his jaw. "I survived."

"But did you, truly?" she demanded, wishing she could somehow take on the burden of his pain for him. That she could have done something to help him ten years ago. "I scarcely recognize you as my brother. Indeed, I wouldn't have known it but for your ring and Mother's eyes."

"You see me before you," he said. "I'm alive."

"But a part of you died in that dungeon," she whispered, knowing the truth as she spoke it. "I can see it, and I hate him for it. Do you not despise Gustavson too, for everything he has done to us, to our family? To our mother, our brother?"

"I loathe him with the fires of a thousand burning hells," he said, his voice dark and damning.

There was the brother she remembered. The man who had refused to disavow their mother, almost to the death.

"Then return home," she urged him, sensing the Theodoric she remembered there beneath this stranger's harsh exterior. "You can fight him and win."

"I won't place you or our sisters in that kind of danger. I'd sooner go back into the dungeon myself."

He was being protective. Of course he was. She might have known it. But she didn't need his protection. Indeed, she was beyond it now.

"I am marrying a monarch far more powerful than he is," she said, hating those words as they left her, the unwanted future they held, "and Gustavson would not dare to imprison me. He needs my marriage to King Maximilian far too much."

"Our uncle would never honor your renouncement," Theodoric countered. "Gustavson won't allow anyone to take the power from him. He was planning to overthrow Father before you and I had even been born, and when Father died, it spared him the trouble. He'll stop at nothing to keep the power he's seized for himself. He'll have my head if I return, and then he'll have yours."

"What if I promised you his head instead?"

Those were words she hadn't dared to utter aloud before. Words that had once made her go numb with fear. But they were necessary words. Because King Maximilian's plan to overthrow Gustavson would lead to nothing less than her uncle's death. And if anyone deserved to die for his sins, it was Gustavson.

"You can't promise me that, Stasia," Theodoric denied quietly. "I'm sorry you've risked so much in search of me during your stay in London, only to find disappointment. But I'll not return to Boritania. When I left there, I was nearly dead, and I promised myself I would never go back."

"I've already set the plans in motion."

His gaze, so like their mother's, was searching. "You've made a plot against him, Stasia?"

"I'm not the only one who wishes Gustavson dead," she said calmly. "There are many of us, united for a common goal. Our kingdom has suffered under his tyrannical rule. His soldiers plunder villages and bring the spoils back to him. The farmers can no longer bear the taxes being levied upon them. Our people are poor and hungry and mistreated, and Gustavson has turned the capital into a haven for prostitution and other vices. He has killed nearly everyone close to him. Those who are alive have been tortured in his dungeon. He has almost certainly killed Reinald. If I don't marry as he has chosen and follow his demands, he will kill me as well, and then he will do the same to our younger sisters."

"This plot of yours," he began, his voice thickened by emotion, her first sign that he was perhaps relenting. "What is it?"

"It isn't my plot alone," Stasia said quietly. "King Maximilian has offered me his aid. I've accepted on behalf of our sisters and our people, but we need you, Theodoric. When Gustavson is killed, the rightful heir must ascend to the throne, or the kingdom will be plunged into chaos. I'm not sacrificing myself and my future to a union that I do not want merely so that Boritania can descend into civil war. I would have explained all to you before this meeting, but I didn't dare to reveal the full plot before Mr. Tierney. No one can know what we are planning. Not a word of this must reach Gustavson."

He stared at her, looking as if he were on the edge of capitulation. Hope rose within her. Would he agree to their plot? Would he save Boritania?

"I need time, Stasia," he said, dashing those short-lived hopes.

"We haven't much," she warned him. "My betrothal to Maximilian will be announced in a fortnight, and you would need to travel to Boritania soon after. For our sisters' sakes and for the sake of our kingdom and our people, I pray you will make the right decision."

"I will send for you when I've decided," he said, his voice grim. "But know this. If I decide to return, *I* will be the one who kills him."

A chill traveled down her spine. In her heart, she knew what her brother's decision would be. For they had been born to fight for their kingdom. And Theodoric had been born to rule. There would be no better, no more merciful and courageous king, than he.

"For Boritania," she said, raising two fingers to her lips in a traditional salute before lifting them into the air.

"For Boritania," her brother echoed, returning the gesture solemnly.

She rapped on the carriage roof and then called in English to the coachman.

The man shouted down his response, and the carriage turned, lumbering back in the direction from which they had come.

∼

Archer was pacing in the mews, prepared to take a horse and set out after Stasia despite telling himself that he wouldn't, when his carriage finally returned. Relief washed over him at the nod from his coachman, reassuring him that nothing was amiss.

Allowing Stasia to meet with her brother on her own terms and entirely without him had been damned difficult to swallow, but he had done it for her. The fear eating him apart for the hours she had been gone had been punishment aplenty for keeping her locked in his bedchamber the night before.

One of his men leapt down and opened the door, laying out the stairs so that Stasia could descend. She wore a hat with a veil that he had managed to procure for the purpose of her jaunt, along with a purple pelisse he had purchased as well that was remarkably close in shade to the Boritanian royal colors. And although she was entirely covered from head to toe, Archer had never seen a more beautiful sight.

He strode forward, scattering his men as he offered Stasia his hand and helped her down.

"You're unharmed?" he asked, despite the reassurance from his coachman.

"I am well," she said.

Thank God. A blustery wind kicked up, and she shivered.

"You're cold." He tucked her hand into the crook of his elbow. "Let's go inside."

"Yes," she agreed, so quietly he almost couldn't hear her.

Archer led them into the town house, not stopping until they had reached the sanctity of his study. When they were within, he helped her with her pelisse, careful not to jostle her injured arm, and took her hat and veil as well, laying them over a chair. She watched him in silence, still wearing the blue gown that so complemented her eyes.

He wanted to take her in his arms, hold her there, never let go. Instead, he gripped the back of the chair over which he had draped her pelisse, so tightly that his knuckles turned white.

"How was it," he dared, breaking the silence, "with your brother?"

She remained where she was, just beyond his reach, a fitting metaphor for their future. "It went better than I expected. There is something I must tell you, however."

His gut twisted, every part of him tensing. "What has happened?"

"Nothing." She paused, shaking her head, worrying her lush lower lip. "It is something that I should have told you, I think, from the beginning. Only, I wasn't certain if I could trust you then."

A grim satisfaction settled over him. "But you know you can trust me now?"

She gave another small nod, her expression fraught. "I do."

"Go on, then," he urged, half terrified of what she might possibly reveal next. "Tell me whatever it is that is eating at you, Princess."

"There is another reason I must marry King Maximilian," she revealed.

Not that bastard's name again. Archer longed to heave up

the chair he was grasping and toss it out the damned window. The urge to watch something aside from his heart shatter into a hundred pieces was suddenly strong and burning in his chest.

He didn't want to think about Stasia marrying the behemoth who had threatened him in a carriage last night. Didn't want to think about her being anywhere else or with anyone else. And there was the true, brutal irony of love—a man could fall into it without any choice in the matter at all. He hadn't any control over whom he loved or why.

"Tell me," he bit out, bracing himself to hear what she had to say.

"Do I have your promise that what I am about to tell you goes no further than these four walls?"

He gave a jerky nod. "Of course, Princess."

"King Maximilian has been plotting to overthrow my uncle," she said, shocking him. "He has raised the army and power to do so, but because of Boritania's proximity to Varros, he fears lawlessness will reign if there is no suitable monarch to take Gustavson's place. He sought me because my brother is the rightful heir to the throne. It is a certainty that the people will not accept anyone who is not of the blood. We have been working together to find Theodoric so that he can aid in the uprising and become king when Gustavson is killed."

"Holy Christ," he muttered, reeling.

They were planning a bloody war.

He should have suspected it. Damn it, he had been one of the Crown's most-trusted spies. And yet, he had been too blinded by first lust and then love to see what was plainly before him. It was even more dangerous than he had suspected. So bloody reckless and foolish.

"If your uncle were to learn of your plan, Stasia…"

His words trailed off, for he couldn't bear to complete the

thought, to give voice to the violence and evil he believed her uncle capable of committing.

"He would do everything in his power to see me returned to Boritania and held in the dungeons," she finished for him, holding his stare. "I would receive the same sentence as my mother."

Death.

She would be executed.

He pushed away from the chair and went to her, taking her in his arms and holding her tight, burying his face in her hair and breathing deeply, so deeply of her scent.

"You cannot do this," he bit out. "You cannot believe that this mad plan is going to succeed. And when it fails, you could well be killed for your role in it."

"I have to do it. This is our only chance for Boritania and all the innocent men, women, and children within the kingdom. Gustavson will turn everything to dust with his greed before he is finished, and he will take my sisters Emmaline and Annalise with it."

He had thought her selfless before, but he had been wrong. He had called her the bravest woman he'd ever met. And it wasn't description sufficient enough. She was willing to sacrifice not just her future, but her very life for the good of her people and to save her sisters.

"Is there not some other way?" he asked, but even as the question left him, he knew it was futile.

"I wish that there were," she said with feeling, icy eyes glittering with tears that were welling over her lashes and spilling down her cheeks. "I'm promised to King Maximilian, and we need the help of his armies to overtake Gustavson's forces. And to win the revolutionaries in Boritania and see the rightful king on the throne, peace and prosperity restored, there must be Theodoric. I believe my brother will aid us, but he hasn't yet given me his final answer."

Archer had known she was lost to him, but some small, stupid part of him had believed that perhaps there would be some way she could throw King Maximilian over. Some way they could keep her uncle from hurting her sisters. He knew powerful men, after all. He possessed a fortune in his own right. He had scraped and clawed his way through the world so that he would never be helpless again.

And despite that, all these years later, he was every bit as helpless as the lad who had been sold to the abbess. It was a different sort of helplessness, to be sure, but he was powerless all the same. Because he couldn't have the woman he loved, and there wasn't a bloody thing he could do to change that—neither money, nor power would save him from having his heart ripped from his chest when she left.

There were so many things he wanted to say. So many words crowding on his tongue, demanding to be heard.

But in the end, all he uttered was two.

"I understand."

"Oh, Archer." She pressed her lips to his.

It wasn't a soft kiss. Not even a sensual one. There was no tenderness in it, and neither was there the promise of more. It was a final kiss, hard enough to bruise, a mashing of lips and teeth. The kiss told him without words how she felt. It told him that she loved him as he loved her. There could be no question. And he kissed her back with even greater force, cupping her nape to hold her still beneath the onslaught of his ravenous mouth. Kissed her and tasted the salt of her tears mingling with his own.

His cheeks were wet with emotion he hadn't thought he'd still possessed.

Had he wept since he'd been that boy in the darkened room with Lucky, his belly hungry, the greedy, grasping bawd coming to issue threats and coercions every hour? He didn't think he had.

It didn't matter.

Nothing mattered but that Stasia was still here for now. In his arms, making needy sounds low in her throat as she kissed and kissed him.

His conscience cried out that she wasn't his, that she was promised to another. That he shouldn't take her again, take the risk of planting his seed inside a woman who would be queen of a far-flung kingdom. A woman he'd likely never see again when she had left him.

But the rest of him roared with suppressed hunger. With the need to claim her again while he still could.

He tore his mouth away, panting and desperate, guilt warring with desire. "Tell me you don't want me."

Her kiss-swollen lips parted, and she said nothing.

"Tell me not to touch you." He buried his face in her throat, kissing and nipping and sucking until she made a breathy sound of surrender and her nails dug into his shoulder straight through his coat.

"Archer." His name was a whisper.

A sigh.

A plea for more.

He wanted her to deny him, and yet he couldn't stop. He found her waist with his hands, her curves melding to his touch. Backing her toward his rosewood desk, he kissed her ear, licked the hollow behind it. "Tell me to go to the devil, Princess."

A shudder racked her.

She grasped a handful of his hair and pulled his head back, holding his gaze with hers. "Never."

CHAPTER 21

In an instant, he had lifted her onto his desk, pulling her gown and underskirts to her waist so that she sat bare-bottomed upon the polished wood surface. The position was reminiscent of the day she had first propositioned him. When he had been determined to prove to her how wrong she was in thinking herself bold enough to take a lover. It seemed a lifetime ago now as his callused hands rasped over the sensitive skin of her upper thighs, parting them so that he could step between.

The rigid length of his cock pressed against the fall of his trousers as he ground himself against her aching flesh. She was wet for him already, wet from his nearness, his touch, longing for him, knowing each touch, each kiss, could be their last.

He stared down into her face intently, his green eyes searing her to her soul. "You'll always be mine, Princess."

No sense in arguing with the truth. Time and circumstance could tear them apart, but Archer Tierney had written his claim upon her heart, and there it would remain until the day she was no more.

"Yes," she said, needing him more than ever.

Wanting that hard flesh, grinding herself against his cock, seeking friction, relief, release. Her legs were locked around his waist, booted ankles crossed at his back. She rubbed herself over him again, feeling him grow harder, the groan that escaped him only serving to fuel her raging desire. And even though her wounded arm stung, she lifted it high enough to clutch his shoulder, the pain worth the pleasure of holding him tightly, keeping him anchored to herself. She needed it, the illusion that they were forever joined, that she could no more escape him than he could her.

"You'll hurt yourself, love," he protested instantly, concern for her furrowing his brow.

"I don't care." She rocked against him again. "All I want is you."

"God," he muttered, and then he took her lips.

She opened for his tongue, sucking on it, hungrier for him than she'd ever been. There was something about knowing she was about to lose him that heightened her frenzy. She suddenly hungered to feel him, to take all that male hardness nestled between her legs and touch.

Without breaking the kiss, she slammed her palm on the desk and leveraged herself backward, putting a small distance between their bodies. The moment it was there, she reached for him, her fingers flying over the buttons of his trousers. Plucking, pulling. She was trembling in her eagerness, fumbling. She'd never undressed a man before, and her desperation to have him inside her wasn't rendering the process any easier.

He nipped her lower lip with a growl, shifting to help her with the buttons on his fall. The last one came undone, and his cock sprang forth, jutting high and thick and proud into her waiting palm. Hot and sleek, the skin so soft and yet so undeniably masculine. She wrapped her fingers around his thick length.

He hissed into her mouth, kissing her harder.

But still, this wasn't enough. She wanted to see him. To see how much he wanted her. To know the effect she had on him was every bit as great as the effect he had on her. That they were equals in desire, perfectly matched.

She broke the kiss, staring up at his harshly handsome face. "I want to see you."

Archer straightened to his full height, giving her a perfect view of him, ruddy and beautiful, her fingers wrapped around the wide base of his cock, so much of him protruding from her small hand. She had known that he was large; she had seen him before, of course. But in the heated moments before he had made love to her, she had been too wild with need to truly examine this part of him. She meant to rectify that now.

Tentatively, she stroked him, not knowing what to do, how to please him.

A low sound loosed from his throat, and she glanced up to find him watching her hand on him.

He rocked into her touch, his cock seeming to thicken beneath her hand. "Look at what you do to me, Princess."

"I like touching you," she confessed, stroking him again, for she had sensed his pleasure in the motion.

"Touch me however you like. My cock is all yours."

His sinful words sent an answering flood of wetness between her thighs. Part of her wanted to bring his length to her entrance, feel him surge inside. And part of her wanted to take her time exploring him. To make him feel the way she had when they'd last made love and he had brought her to the edge of orgasm before backing away, only to take her there again.

"Your cock is beautiful," she said, her thumb circling the

blunt tip, where a pearl of seed had already seeped from a small slit.

She gave in to temptation and rubbed over the bead of his mettle, swirling the liquid over the head of his shaft until he groaned again.

"Ah fuck, Princess. Feel how hard you make me."

"I do," she said, stroking once more, enjoying the dichotomy, this man so powerful and yet hers to pleasure, utterly at her mercy in this moment. "I love the way your cock feels in my hand, so big."

His fingers laced over hers, guiding her motions now, increasing the pressure. "It would feel even better inside your sweet cunny."

She had no doubt it would, but she wasn't finished with him.

Stasia shook her head slowly, running her tongue over her lower lip and tasting him there. "Not yet."

Their entwined hands moved over him faster, drawing more moisture from that delicate indentation. She wanted to lick it. To taste him. But her position on the desk made that impossible. So she scooted forward on the desk, bringing him into contact with her intimate flesh again. His cock grazed over her clitoris, and she inhaled sharply at the frisson of sensation it sent through her.

"You're so wet and hot," he murmured, still looking down at himself, but now looking at her, too.

Watching their joined hands bring pleasure to them both as they handled his cock and teased her aching flesh at the same time. She imagined what she must look like to him, wanton and ready, all the evidence of her desire dripping onto his desk, bathing the head of his cock until it glistened with a combination of their desires. And then she grew wetter still at the thought. Wetter as they worked his tip over her swollen nub, then down through her folds, rubbing up and down until she was gasping and wriggling.

Until she had to have him inside her or she swore she would die from wanting him.

"So ready for me," he said, like a praise, glancing up at her, his face slack with passion, his green eyes darkened to the hue of a forest at sunset. "Do you want my cock inside you?"

An animal noise fled her, all the coherence she could manage with him between her legs, his length sliding through her slipperiness, teasing her clitoris with slow circles before gliding lower, to her entrance. Her cunny pulsed, flexing on emptiness, needing to be stretched and filled.

But just when she thought he would give her what she wanted, he stilled, the pressure at her opening almost too much to bear, so merciless was the taunt.

"Say it," he ground out, as if the words cost him gravely, as if he could scarcely form them.

She squirmed on the desk, her rump making a strange almost screeching sound as her bare skin slid over rosewood. But his cock was nestled deeper now. Almost hers for the taking. She didn't know why she didn't want to capitulate, to concede this small battle of theirs. Perhaps it was a desire to prolong their lovemaking. Perhaps it was merely that she craved some small semblance of control in a life that was increasingly becoming less her own.

Whatever the reason, she didn't give him the words.

With his free hand, he pulled her bodice down, yanking hard until one of her breasts sprang above the fabric and her stays. His head dipped, and he sucked hard on the pink peak of her nipple. Sucked and licked and sent another surge of moisture between her legs.

She surrendered.

"I need your cock inside me," she gasped out. "Now, please."

He entered her in a swift thrust, fully seated to the hilt. It was all suddenly too much. The pressure, the girth of him inside her, so wide and hard that she thought for a moment he might cleave her in two, and yet so good. The alignment of their bodies, her position on the desk, the hardness of wood beneath her, the scent of him curled around her, his mouth latched on her nipple, sucking harder.

And then he began to move. Fast, plunging strokes. In and out, his cock surging inside her to claim and then retreat. Each thrust set his pelvis against hers, the friction against her clitoris making her gasp for breath.

Close.

She was so close.

But there was more. He tore at her bodice until her other breast was freed, and then he greedily sucked the nipple harder than he had the first, using his teeth. They were frenzied. Frantic. He slammed into her, the sound of their bodies connecting and the little moans and gasps of pleasure torn from them the only noises in the chamber. She grabbed a handful of his hair, still grasping at his coat with her other hand, her entire body tensed and on the verge of flying apart. Her wound ached but even the pain would not dull her pleasure.

She was flying. Soaring. Reaching.

He flicked his tongue over her nipple, then bit the side of her breast. There was something crudely possessive about the action, as if he sought to mark her as forever his, and it made liquid pour from her center, sluicing over his cock.

"That's it, love," he grunted, fucking her with frantic motions, the cords of his neck standing in relief as he exerted himself. "I want you to come on my cock. Take what's yours."

Hers.

He was hers.

Not just now, but always.

Forever.

Another thrust, his body grinding against her clitoris, and she exploded. Her cunny convulsed and clenched on him, her release so potent and so strong that she almost feared she would expire beneath the force of it.

She cried out his name, burying her face in his shoulder as he continued to fuck her, his hips working faster than before.

"Just like that, Princess. God, you feel so good, so tight, so wet."

His words made her come again, a small wave crashing over after the first burst, this one every bit as intense. She moaned, the sound muffled by his coat, and rode out her second peak with breathless abandonment. Her muscles were still fluttering inside when he stiffened and withdrew from her.

"Your hand," he said, his voice strained. "Give me your hand."

He was stroking himself, she realized, about to reach his own pinnacle. She gave him her hand, and he wrapped it around his cock, sliding it up and down once, twice, before cupping her palm over the head. There was a sudden spurt of warm wetness filling her hand as he tipped his head back and closed his eyes, her name on his lips until he slumped against her, still standing, the two of them both fully clothed.

They remained that way, hearts pounding in unison.

And she couldn't keep the words to herself for another second more.

"I love you," she told him.

He had just fucked her on his desk like a ravening beast. Her hand was covered in his seed, and Stasia had said the three words he'd never thought to hear from her beautiful lips.

For a moment, Archer could do nothing more than try to catch his breath, his heart thundering in his bloody ears, and convince himself he must have imagined her telling him that she loved him. That it was a fanciful illusion wrought from the intensity of his orgasm.

His face was buried in the soft curls at her temple. He was sure he was panting into her ear.

"Stasia," he managed. "Say it again."

"I love you," she whispered, almost as if saying them too loudly would fracture the moment.

Or send fate intervening to instantly tear them apart.

She loved him. He closed his eyes, inhaling sharply of her sweet scent mingling with the musk of their lovemaking.

She loves me, he thought, his chest swelling with pride.

She loves me.

Saint's teeth, this glorious princess who was stubborn and brave and selfless and so damned strong she'd hefted a wardrobe halfway across the chamber alone with a wounded arm…loved him.

Impossible. Wonderful.

"I love you too," he breathed in her ear, eyes opening again as he withdrew enough to look down at her, to hold her gaze. "I love you, Princess."

He kissed her then. Kissed her because how could he not? His lips angled over hers gently this time instead of ravenously, showing her with words as well as deed. Relief welled up that he had told her at last, that she loved him as well. That they had this moment, if not the rest of their lives.

Belatedly, he recalled the state he had left her in. He had tupped her without a care for anything other than being inside her. Claiming her. Having her one more time. It didn't matter that she had been every bit as insatiable. He should have taken greater care.

He raised his head, breaking the kiss. "Forgive me for taking you so roughly, love. I shouldn't have—"

"Hush." Her injured hand moved from his shoulder, her finger pressing to his lips to stay further apology. She winced at the movement. "It was perfect. *You* were perfect."

He kissed her finger and reached into his coat to extract a handkerchief, using it to clean her other hand. "Far from perfect," he denied solemnly, taking in the full effect of his frantic desire.

Her breasts were spilling over the edge of her bodice and undergarments, her nipples hard pink buds that had his cock already twitching to life. He ignored the ever-persistent ache in his ballocks whenever she was near and tucked himself into his trousers, fastening his falls before attempting to tug her bodice back into place.

It was no use, her voluptuous breasts refusing to be subdued now that they were free.

"Even your bubbies are stubborn," he muttered, struggling with her stays and trying not to notice the absolutely mesmerizing way the soft globes swayed and bounced beneath his efforts, their hard pink nipples begging for his mouth again.

"Bubbies? Is this another of your curious English words I've never heard before?"

Blast.

"Like the other words you've learned from me, it's not one which ought to be repeated," he said.

"Like fuck?" she asked.

His stupid cock throbbed. How was it that a wicked word in her throaty voice could have such an effect on him after he'd just had one of the most powerful orgasms of his life?

"I've told you, love, I'm a terrible influence." He frowned, giving up on his effort to restore her toilette and grasping her waist to lift her from the desk instead. "Turn around. I'm afraid I'll have to undo your tapes if I'm to help you dress properly."

Apparently, his strength had been godlike when he'd been in the throes of passion. Either that, or tearing a bodice down was far easier than pulling it back up. He could honestly say this was the first time he'd ever bedded a woman whilst they were both fully clothed, so he couldn't begin to guess.

"Does it mean what I think it means?" she asked, presenting him with her back so that he could play lady's maid.

"I suspect it does." He made short work of the tapes, then loosened her stays. "Turn, love."

She did as he commanded, spinning slowly to face him, those gorgeous breasts still on full display like offerings. The distraction from what awaited them was welcome, but he knew it was only temporary. Every second that passed took them closer to their inevitable end and the day she would marry another.

With that thought firmly in mind, he tugged her stays and undergarments back into place, restoring her modesty, and taking care not to move her injured arm about more than necessary. All the while, he was keenly aware of her gaze on him. Watching silently, allowing him to repair the damage he had done.

God, how he would miss her. Would miss this closeness they'd shared, so unexpected. This love, so all-consuming and powerful.

"Thank you," she said softly.

He jerked his gaze up to hers, still tugging at her blue

gown. "I ruined your gown and undergarments. It is only fair that I repair the destruction."

"Not for helping me with my gown and stays. For putting yourself in peril to protect me. For loving me."

She was gazing up at him with so much tenderness that he almost couldn't bear it. The sight made something inside him seize so tightly that he feared it would break him.

"You needn't thank me for that either, Princess," he said, his voice thick and raw with restrained emotion. "Loving you is the easiest thing I've ever done."

Swallowing hard, he spun her about and resumed his work on the tapes of her gown.

CHAPTER 22

Like dawn when she was in the arms of the man she loved, Stasia's brother's answer came far too soon. A note hand-delivered by a lad the next day, summoning her to Hunt House. Some selfish part of her had hoped he would require more time to consider whether he would agree to King Maximilian's plot. An eternity. That she could remain happily ensconced in her idyll with Archer for a lifetime.

But that would have been far too perfect. Impossibilities always were.

She suspected she already knew what her brother's answer would be, but that didn't mean her palms weren't damp in her kidskin gloves or that her stomach wasn't tangled into a knot or that trepidation hadn't made her mouth go dry. Because this meeting meant far more than just an answer to whether Theodoric would agree to the plan to overthrow Gustavson.

It also meant the beginning of the end of her time with Archer, when and if Theodoric said yes.

She remained safely ensconced in the carriage, the same

three guards that Archer had insisted upon sending with her previously riding as outriders. They were situated not far from the mews behind the house where her brother was currently acting as a guard himself, Venetian blinds drawn tightly.

There was a knock at the carriage door, the voice of one of Archer's men signaling that her brother had arrived. One deep breath to prepare herself before the carriage door was wrenched open and Theodoric stepped inside.

"Brother," she greeted him in Boritanian, truly glad to see him despite the severity of the circumstances.

"Sister," he returned solemnly in the language of their homeland.

Switching to English, she raised her voice and gave the command for the coachman to begin. The carriage rocked into familiar motion, but the familiarity was of precious little comfort to Stasia. For, all too soon, she would be far from these roads, far from this place.

Far from the man who owned her heart, the man who had given her his heart in return.

She blinked furiously against a rush of tears she refused to shed. If she wept, her brother would ask questions. And Stasia couldn't bear to reveal the extent of her relationship with Archer to Theodoric. It was too painful, too personal.

She had to maintain her composure. Keep her mind focused upon her reason for meeting with her brother. On her reason for coming to London at all.

"You have made your decision?" she asked him, reverting to Boritanian again.

"You are familiar with Tierney's carriages," he said shrewdly, his gaze searching for an answer she had no wish to give.

Instead, she forced a smile to her lips. "He is a clever man."

"Too clever, perhaps," her brother countered, his tone steeped in caution.

Archer was also too handsome, too skillful at kissing her and making love. Too perceptive, too caring. Too much of everything she loved and yearned for. Quite unlike the man she would soon wed.

"I enjoy his company," she defended, the slight censure in her brother's voice, along with the tone of warning, nettling. "The opportunity to slip away from the guards and be free of our uncle's watchful eye is a liberty I'll not apologize for."

Her brother's face remained impassive, and she wondered what he had seen these last ten years, what manner of life he had lived as a man called Beast.

"I didn't mean to suggest you should," he said then.

She was grateful for his understanding in that regard. There were many in his position who would have judged her, who would have questioned her far more thoroughly than Theodoric had done. She had no doubt she would have a great deal to answer for when she was forced to face King Maximilian again.

Thinking of him brought bitterness rising anew.

"You needn't worry I'll not do my duty to the kingdom," she told her brother. "I know what I must do. The question is whether or not you do."

"You do not want the union between yourself and King Maximilian?" he asked, startling her with the question.

Only one other had ever asked it of her.

Archer.

You must not think of him now, she cautioned herself. *Think of anything and anyone but him.*

She answered her brother in the only way she could.

"Why should I wish it? But it is never a matter of what I want to do in this life. It is what I must do. It is what is best for Boritania."

Even if it wasn't what was best for herself.

"For that reason, I have made my decision," Theodoric said solemnly. "For many years, I was too angered over what had happened to me and what had happened to our mother to care about Boritania. But knowing that our people are suffering, and knowing how you and our sisters will suffer under Gustavson's evil rule, there is only one choice I can make. I'll return."

The tension that had held her in its relentless grip since her last meeting with Theodoric subsided, the feeling in her chest akin to sun shining from between parted clouds. She could breathe for a moment. Not every sacrifice she had made would be in vain.

"Praise Deus," she said, seeing for the first time the sadness in his eyes, which she thought must have reflected the desolation in her own. "You've made the right decision, Theodoric, although you don't look happy to have done so."

She couldn't blame him; leaving the life he had known for ten years to return to a kingdom filled with unrest, where the monster sitting on the throne wanted him dead, was more than any sane man would commit to doing. It was dangerous. Desperately so.

"It sits well in my soul," her brother said, "and yet it also sits heavy. There is a woman I've fallen in love with, and I very much hate to leave her here."

Her brother was in love. She would have laughed had she not thought doing so would also bring an accompanying rush of tears.

"Ah," she said simply, understanding all too well. "Who is she?"

"The widowed Marchioness of Deering."

A lady of the *ton*. That would complicate matters, should he assume the throne, she feared.

"Does she know who you are?" she asked softly.

Theodoric sighed heavily. "Not yet."

"She loves you, then?" she pressed.

He gave a jerky nod, and she knew what he was thinking, for her thoughts were the same—of what he was about to lose. "She does. How long are you to remain in London? It would please me if the two of you would meet."

Deus, she could see the determination in his eyes, hear it in his voice. Her brother meant to marry this marchioness of his.

"Perhaps it would be best for you to tell her who you are before we meet," she said gently. "She is trustworthy, yes?"

"I would trust her with my life."

"She can't know the details of our plan, regardless of your confidence in her," she cautioned. "Gustavson has trusted eyes and ears in London, waiting to carry the slightest hint of news back to him. If word reaches him of our plans, your return will be for naught, and she could be in danger as well."

He nodded again. "I'll not risk her for anything, and nor will I risk our plan. Gustavson has been allowed to live for far too long, free of repercussions. He killed our mother, he is stealing from our people, and he deserves to meet his end by my hand."

"How I hate him for all he's done and everything he has taken," she whispered. "I wish it were me going in your stead. I wish I were the one to rid the land of that merciless snake."

"We are doing it together," her brother said.

Together. To have their family reunited, to have her beloved brother on the throne where he belonged, to have their people free of tyranny and greed...it seemed an impossible dream. One at last within reach.

All she had to do was sell her soul to make it happen. Being torn away from the man she loved was its own kind of torture, emotional rather than physical. But what she'd had to endure was still nothing compared to what her brother had in the August Palace dungeons.

"Together," she agreed firmly, reaching out and taking her brother's hand in hers. "I am so sorry, Theodoric. Sorry for your suffering, for the years you've been exiled."

"It isn't your fault, Stasia. You were naught but a child."

"I should have done something to fight him." The guilt that was never far welled, uniting with her deep and abiding sadness, making the sting of tears return to her eyes. "If I had, then mayhap none of this would have happened."

"No," he denied, giving her hand a squeeze in return, a glimpse of the brother she'd known and loved. "You would have had the same fate as I did, or perhaps worse. I am glad it was me who went to the dungeon. I'm glad it was me who was tortured, who bears the scars. Did he ever hurt you? If he did, you must tell me now, so that I can revisit the same suffering upon him, only a hundred times worse. I'll not be merciful."

She thought of the lashes she had received. The scars on her back. She very much feared that if she revealed them to him, he would place himself in further danger, all to avenge her. The damage had been done. To tell him would be futile.

"The hurt was a different kind," Stasia said, a half-truth. "He was cruel and controlling, but he knew he could use us to his advantage. He wanted to see us married to increase his power and fortune, and he didn't dare ruin his chances by beating us or sending us to the dungeons." Except for that lone occasion, and she had the marks to prove it. But she forced a bitter smile for her brother's benefit. "Thank Deus for that."

"What of Reinald?" he asked. "Did Gustavson harm him?"

"I don't know for certain. We were never free to speak openly with Reinald. Over the years, I saw very little of him. He was forever meeting with the council or our uncle, and many times, he would remain in the king's chambers for weeks at a time." She paused, shaking her head. "Knowing what I do now, I suspect Gustavson was somehow making him ill. And then, there came a day when Reinald was gone and our uncle declared himself king."

"We will have vengeance," her brother vowed harshly. "That monster will be stopped, even if it requires my last breath to do it."

"I pray it won't be your last breath, brother," Stasia said. "Boritania needs you."

"I will do my utmost to see that it won't be. I've too much to live for. Now, tell me what must be done."

The carriage rocked through London, and their plotting began in truth.

~

ARCHER KNEW.

From the moment he saw Stasia's countenance when she returned from her meeting with her brother, he knew that the time he had been dreading had come. They were going to have to say their farewells.

His gut clenched as he moved toward her across his study, taking her in his arms and burying his face in her hair.

She wrapped her arms around him with a sob, holding him tightly despite her wound.

"It is done, then?" he asked, forcing out the words past the emotions threatening to choke him.

"Theodoric has agreed," she murmured into his coat.

"It is the right thing for your kingdom, for your people." His hands swept up and down her spine, absorbing the trembling shudders going through her as her tears gathered force. "For Theodoric, too. The rightful heir should be sitting on the throne. He is a good man, and I know he would make an excellent ruler, faithful and just."

This was all true. He'd spent the night before lying awake with Stasia pressed to his side, doing his best to make peace with what must happen. Stasia had suffered, her family had suffered, and her people had suffered. Theodoric had been wrongfully exiled, and their mother and brother had been wrongfully killed.

If only her brother's decision would be the right thing for Stasia as well.

"I know it is right for the people," she said. "Right for our sisters and to avenge our brother's and mother's deaths. Gustavson needs to be stopped before he destroys Boritania and everyone in it. I just wish…"

Her words trailed away, and he disengaged from her partially, tilting up her chin so that she had to meet his gaze, her face tear-soaked and ashen, bereft of its customary vibrant fire and ice. Instead, she was as gray and forlorn as the day was beyond the windows at her back.

"Is this what you truly want for yourself?" he asked. "This loveless marriage to a coldhearted king?"

More tears slipped down her cheeks as she shook her head. "You know it is not. But there is a vast difference between what I want for myself and what I *must* do."

"I know, love." He kissed her then, tasting the salt of her tears, wishing he could chase her sorrow.

Wishing he were not so damned helpless.

He'd never given a damn about being born a by-blow. He'd made his own way in the bloody world. But here and now, with Stasia weeping in his arms and the gaping maw of a life without her in it facing him, he wished to hell that he had been born a prince instead.

He ended the kiss and took out a handkerchief to

tenderly wipe the tears from her cheeks. "Don't cry, Princess. You're far too brave for that."

Her hands curled on his coat, grasping it as if she feared she would fall to her doom if she released him. "I'll always love you, Archer."

"And I'll always love you."

"There is something I want to give you," she said, lower lip trembling. "To remember me by. It isn't much, but it is one of my most-prized possessions."

A gift, when he had none for her?

He shook his head. "You needn't give me anything."

"I want to." She released his coat, her fingers tangling in the gold necklace at her throat, the heavy pendant hanging from its center nestled into that bewitching hollow at the base of her throat. "It is my mother's coat of arms. It's forbidden to wear in Boritania. King Gustavson outlawed it. One day soon, I hope it will no longer be outlawed. I wish for you to have it. Will you help me to take it off?"

He knew how much her mother meant to her, and the meaning of the gift was not lost on him.

"It's too precious," he protested. "I cannot accept it."

"It's yours," she insisted, blinking at the tears gathered on her dark, spiky lashes. "Like my heart." She spun about then, lowering her head and presenting him with the elegant, vulnerable swath of golden skin at her nape. "Please," she added when he hesitated.

"Very well," he relented, opening the necklace's clasp with clumsy fingers that refused to cooperate as they were thrown off by the warm, satiny skin beneath them.

At last, he had it open. "There."

She turned back to him, holding the pendant clutched in her fist, the twain ends of the necklace spilling through her fingers. "I'll never forget you, Archer Tierney."

She held her hand out to him, and he opened his, feeling

the gold warmed from her body spill against his waiting palm.

"Nor will I forget you, Princess." He raised the necklace to his lips, kissing the coat of arms as he blinked back the sting of his own tears.

CHAPTER 23

"When was the last time wot you slept?"

Archer glanced up from the reports he was poring over at his desk to find Lucky hovering at the threshold to his study.

The hour was—a consultation of his pocket watch revealed—half past five. In the morning? In the evening? Archer had forgotten. The curtains were drawn because he didn't care to see the outside world. Without Stasia, the days had become interchangeable and meaningless. Gray, rainy, and cold.

As gloomy as his bloody soul.

He hadn't an answer for his friend. He didn't remember when he'd last slept. It could have been two days. It could have been four. He'd thrown himself into his work with a vengeance in the wake of Stasia's return to her uncle's town house. Work was all he had left, and it had always stood him in good stead.

Pity, though, that even the business that had once filled him with meaning now felt as empty and hollow as his existence.

"Are you playing mother now, Luck?" he drawled to hide the pain that was his constant companion since bidding Stasia farewell and watching her slip inside the window in the night one last time. "How precious of you. I might remind you, however, that mine sold me to a brothel."

"You'll kill yourself carrying on as you've done, you will," Lucky warned, ignoring his jibe.

"Perhaps that would be a mercy," he muttered, glancing down again at his list of suspects for the attempted murder of the Duke of Ridgely.

Over the last few days, he had discovered the identity of the dead man who had attempted to stab the duke in his bed. An actor by the name of John Davenham. Now, he had to connect the dead actor to whoever had hired him for the grim task. The distraction was welcome, but not nearly sufficient.

Of course, nothing would be.

There was a princess-shaped hole in his goddamned black heart, and no one could fill it save her. And she would soon be announcing her betrothal to a bloody king.

"Saint's bones, you're a sorry sight, you are." Lucky was nearer now, hovering over him quite rudely, giving the air an indiscreet sniff. "When's the last time wot you bathed? Smell right foxy, you do."

Archer glared up at his friend. Strike that—his *former* friend. "Are you suggesting I stink?"

"Ain't suggesting it," Lucky growled. "Telling you square. I'll see a bath sent up for you."

"Fuck you," he said succinctly.

Why, he had bathed…

He didn't remember.

But it hardly mattered. He didn't want one. What he *did* want was more coffee, another cheroot, and to bury himself in his work. Anything to keep his mind from wandering to thoughts of *her*.

"And when's the last time wot you ate?" Lucky asked, as if he hadn't just been treated to a vile oath at all.

Despite himself, Archer pondered the question. Perhaps he'd have a better notion of when he'd eaten if he knew what day it was. Or whether it was morning or night.

He flipped open the case where he kept his cheroots and found it empty. "Damn it, I've no more cheroots. Send a lad to fetch me more, will you?"

"No."

Lucky had crossed his arms over his barrel-broad chest in a stubborn posture.

"No?" he repeated, incredulous.

"Not until you eat, bathe, and shave," his friend elaborated. "And bloody sleep."

He rose to his feet. "I'll rouse one of the lads from the stables myself."

Lucky blocked his path. "They've orders not to listen to you until I say."

"The hell they do." He made to skirt past his friend, but Lucky was unyielding and unmoving.

He'd have to force the man out of his way if he intended to go anywhere. Not an impossible feat, but Archer didn't particularly relish the notion of tussling with his friend. Because it was likely they would come to blows. He'd already had his nose broken once; he didn't care for a second.

"I know you're sad about the wench leaving you," Lucky began.

"She's not a goddamn wench," he bit out with more virulence than he'd intended. "And she didn't leave me. She's promised to marry another."

"She could cry off," Lucky pointed out. "It's been done before. Reckon it can be done again."

"She can't." He sighed heavily. "The circumstances are complicated. I'm not at liberty to explain."

"We can kill the other cove, then," Lucky suggested. "I've told you before. Bang-up way to win a wench's heart."

A bitter laugh fled him. "I'm not in the mood for your gruesome sallies, Luck."

"Still ain't joking," his friend said, his expression as hard as if it were set in granite, nary a hint of a smile.

"I can't kill him," he denied, shaking his head as he ran his fingers through his hair, which, admittedly, felt as if it were in need of a sound washing. "Believe me, I've thought about it."

But killing a king, albeit one of a tiny island kingdom in a far-flung sea, would only lead him to the gallows instead of back to Stasia's arms. No, he had to honor her wishes. Had to accept the fact that she was lost to him whilst he spent his every waking hour worrying about whether she was safe. King Maximilian had vowed he would protect her with his own guards—he had seen to it himself. Archer didn't trust the bastard, but he did trust the man's need to marry a living wife. And like so much where Stasia was concerned, it was out of his hands.

"We could set his house on fire," Lucky suggested conversationally. "Poison his soup…"

Damn it.

"No," he said firmly. "We cannot. It is over, Lucky. She's marrying another, and that is that."

"Aye, then," Lucky said, his tone gentling. "You need to carry on. This ain't like you."

No, it wasn't like him. Archer had prided himself on being impenetrable and cold. Harsh and ruthless. He was what the world had made him.

Until one stubborn princess of fire and ice had changed everything.

"I am carrying on, Lucky," he said. "Carrying on to find more cheroots and coffee, which is all I bloody well want at the moment. Now get out of my damned way."

Lucky glowered. "You're going to work yourself to death."

He held his friend's stare, unmoved. "So be it."

In a few days' time, he would aid Theodoric St. George in leaving England. Stasia's betrothal to the king would be officially announced. And perhaps then, he could begin the daunting task of living without her.

Until that day came and the final death knell was rung, all he wanted to do was forget.

~

"You should eat, Your Highness."

Stasia stood at the window she had climbed out so many times to meet in secret with Archer, staring down at the grim, gray landscape below, unseeing.

"I'm not hungry," she told Tansy.

The ache in her stomach had nothing to do with the need for sustenance and everything to do with the pain of having to walk away from the man she loved. Although she had told herself it was for the good of her people, her family, her brother, and for the future of Boritania itself, the days that had passed without Archer had been torturous. Painful as a blade sunk between her ribs, each breath reminding her of what she had lost.

"But you must eat, regardless," her lady-in-waiting urged. "You haven't taken a thing since supper last night, and it is afternoon. King Maximilian will be calling soon."

Yes, her future husband would be paying her the visit she dreaded at last. For while King Maximilian had sent the promised guards as a precaution against her uncle's further plotting, Stasia had yet to meet with her betrothed. She and

Tansy had managed to hold off Gustavson's men for another few days following her return. The wound on her arm was beginning to heal.

The wound in her heart never would.

"What does King Maximilian's visit have to do with eating?" she asked with a heavy sigh, watching a fat raindrop make its torpid path down the windowpane.

"It wouldn't do for you to swoon," Tansy said. "You must have at least a bit of tea and toast, Your Royal Highness."

"Call me Stasia," she bit out, whirling to face her lady-in-waiting. "I find the title is too heavy a mantle to carry on my shoulders at present, and you are like a sister to me. Let us cease with formality."

Tansy bowed her dark head in a show of humility. "I couldn't presume to do so."

"You can," she countered. "I consider you a sister, a friend. The only friend I have. And I am weary, so very weary, of being a princess."

"It is not wise of you to think me your friend, Your Royal Highness," Tansy said quietly, head still bowed.

"Because you're my lady-in-waiting?" she demanded. "Don't be silly. You have been at my side since before my mother's death, a lady in your own right."

"From a House that is impoverished," Tansy countered, glancing up to meet Stasia's gaze. "No better than an orphan."

It was true that Tansy had lost her parents and that the line had died with her father, who had squandered everything of value in his estate and household before his death. Stasia's father had taken Tansy into his care, and as she had been of similar age to Stasia, their pairing had been natural.

"The circumstances of our birth should not define us," Stasia said, meaning those words to her marrow.

For so much of her life, she had been a prisoner kept in a gilded cage. She had been confined to the August Palace, surrounded by courtiers, never permitted to mingle with any social strata deemed beneath her own. She was a princess, daughter of a king. Her life had been determined for her from the moment she had been born. Her lineage had proven itself more a curse more than a boon.

But Archer had been born a bastard son to a lord, betrayed by his own mother, and yet he had fashioned an empire with nothing save his own determination and cunning. He had shown her that the measure of a man was not in his title, nor his bloodlines. Rather, it was in his deeds, in his words. It was in the man himself.

"And yet, they must," Tansy said sadly. "I will never be your equal, Your Royal Highness. Nor would I presume to act as such."

"I am sick to death of my royal bloodlines," she snapped. "What have they dealt me, other than misery and despair? They have robbed every happiness from my life. Call me Stasia, or do not speak to me at all."

"Your Royal—"

"No!" she cried out, interrupting. "No more. I'll not have it." Tears were streaming furiously down her cheeks, and she dashed at them with the back of her hand. "I don't want to be a princess. I want to renounce my blood. To surrender the title and live the life I was meant to lead."

"You mustn't say such things." Tansy moved to her, offering a soothing pat on the shoulder, her voice calm. "You are overset."

Of course she was overset. She had lost the man she loved. She faced a future married to a man who was cold-hearted and ruthless. Her brother was about to attempt to overthrow her uncle. Her entire life as she knew it had been torn asunder.

And she wanted to hear her name, blast it all. She wanted to feel like a person instead of a princess.

"Call me Stasia," she demanded.

Tansy's stoic countenance cracked. "I cannot. I'm not worthy of the privilege. For I have betrayed you."

Everything inside her seized. "Betrayed me? How?"

Tears glistened in Tansy's eyes. "I've fallen in love with King Maximilian."

CHAPTER 24

It was dawn, and Archer was keeping company with his demons, coffee, and smoke. Rather a habit of late. But he wasn't fit company for anyone else. Indeed, he didn't know if he would ever be again.

A knock on his study door heralded the arrival of the man he'd been waiting for. The time had come to sever the final tie binding himself to Stasia.

"Come," he called, rising and abandoning the ledgers he'd been halfheartedly tallying.

The door opened to reveal Prince Theodoric St. George, the mercenary he'd spent the last few years knowing only as Beast.

"Your Royal Highness." He offered a bow, not bothering to extinguish his cheroot, even in the presence of royalty.

This was, after all, his domain.

The other man winced. "Deus. I haven't been called that in years. Not certain I like it."

Archer inclined his head. "When you take the throne, you'll be hearing it a great deal more, I reckon. May as well get yourself accustomed to it now."

Theodoric gave him a wry smile, his gaze alighting on a point over Archer's shoulder. "Stasia is here?"

Hearing her name spoken aloud was like a blow to the chest.

Archer struggled to keep his expression carefully blank at the mention of her, busying himself by taking a long puff of his cheroot. "Her Royal Highness? No. Why do you ask?"

He nodded toward the fireplace. "Her cloak is on your chair."

Shite.

He had forgotten to hide the cloak she had been wearing the night she had been wounded. She had left it behind, draped over one of the chairs by the hearth, and he hadn't had the heart to remove it. For *she* had placed it there. And seeing the garment there perpetuated the illusion she was still here. That at any moment, she would walk through the door, her eyes snapping sensual fire at him.

"That cloak doesn't belong to her," he said smoothly.

But Theodoric was undeterred.

"The color," he added. "It is Boritanian royal. Quite unique."

Fucking hell. Yes, it was.

He bared his teeth at Theodoric in what he hoped passed for a smile. "I'm afraid not. It belongs to a doxy I found at a house of ill repute."

The lie felt ugly as it left his lips, but he reminded himself that it was necessary to protect Stasia. Their relationship—such as it had been—was no one's concern, save their own. Moreover, it had already ended.

Her brother's eyes narrowed. "Tierney, if you are dallying with my sister, I'll carve your heart from your chest with my bare hands."

"I would never dally with your sister," Archer responded truthfully, for nothing that had happened between them had been a dalliance. He had loved her, he realized now, from the first, regardless of how unattainable she was. "I'm afraid that spoiled Boritanian princesses are not to my taste."

"She has suffered greatly beneath the dictates of my uncle," Theodoric warned, his tone grim. "She is sacrificing herself for the good of Boritania. She is far from spoiled."

No one knew just how selfless and good she was better than Archer. But he couldn't afford to allow her brother to see it. Didn't dare to show the depth of love and emotion he felt where she was concerned. Nor just how much it had torn him apart when she had left him.

Instead, he schooled his features into an impassive mask, puffing on his cheroot as if he hadn't a goddamn care in the world, when, in fact, it was quite the opposite. "The garment doesn't belong to her, St. George, and prince or no, you're overstepping your bounds. You've far more important matters to attend to, aside from a discarded cloak. The carriage has been prepared for you, and your time is limited."

Theodoric stared at him in silence for a heavy moment before nodding, seemingly accepting his word. "Tierney, promise me you'll look after Stasia whilst she is in London—and Lady Deering as well. Are you any closer to learning who was responsible for the attacks on Ridgely?"

It seemed a lifetime ago that the Duke of Ridgely had procured Archer's services in safeguarding his home after the attempt on his life. While Archer had been largely distracted by Stasia, his men had been hard at work, unearthing clues as to who was responsible for the attack. His recent investigations led him to suspect a former lover of the duke's was to blame, but the woman was also a widowed countess in her own right, complicating matters.

"We are," he confirmed simply, not bothering to elaborate, for the mystery was no longer Theodoric's to solve, much like Stasia was no longer Archer's to love. "And you needn't worry. Your womenfolk will be well looked after."

I would protect your sister with my life, he thought, but he kept those words to himself.

A muscle ticked in the other man's jaw. "Thank you."

Archer inclined his head and tossed his cheroot into the fireplace. "God go with you, St. George."

The poor bastard was going to need all the divine help he could get if he intended to overthrow his uncle and assume the throne.

But then, Archer was going to need all the divine help he could get as well if he hoped to live a life without the woman he loved in it.

CHAPTER 25

FOUR MONTHS LATER

Stasia took a deep breath, exhaling slowly, and then she lifted her fist to knock firmly.

A few seconds passed. Seconds that felt like an eternity. But after the last four painful months without Archer, what were a few more seconds?

And then the door opened to reveal a familiar, glowering face.

"You," Lucky said, as if the word itself were an epithet. "Wot you want?"

"I want to see Archer," she said.

"He ain't at 'ome."

The door snapped closed.

Stasia blinked at it, bemused. For all the long, painful months she had been far from London and the man she loved, she had dreamt of this moment, when she would return to Archer and he would be awaiting her with open arms.

Slammed doors had never been included in her fancies.

She knocked again.

"Go away," came Lucky's muffled voice from the other side. "You ain't wanted 'ere."

"Please, Lucky," she tried, not above begging. "It is of the utmost import that I see him at once."

The door opened to reveal one narrowed eye and half a snarling mouth. "You've done enough damage, marrying another cove."

Before he could close it once more, she wedged her booted foot into the gap. "I haven't married anyone else."

His eye narrowed even farther. "No?"

"No," she repeated, gathering her courage. "In fact, I hope that Archer will marry *me*."

A brave sentiment to utter. But a necessary one.

Supposing he hadn't forgotten her already. He had sworn that he wouldn't. Time had passed, however. Far too much without him. But they had needed it to journey to Varros to make sure they were beyond the reach of her uncle's minions. She had vowed she would bring no further danger to Archer, and she had upheld that promise.

And then had come the war. Now that victory had finally been achieved and Gustavson was dead, with Theodoric on the throne where he rightfully belonged, Stasia was free at long last.

As free as she had once dreamed of being.

She would forever be indebted to Tansy for that.

The door jerked open, and Lucky was still towering over her and glaring, but he had a new air of uncertainty about him. "You want to marry 'im?"

"If he will have me, yes."

"Reckon that's for 'imself to decide." He took a step in retreat. "Come in with you, then. You're getting rain on the marble, lingering out there as you are."

It was only misting, but Stasia didn't argue the point.

She stepped inside, grateful to be out of the damp. Far more grateful to be closer to Archer again.

He was here.

Beneath this roof.

Within reach at long last.

Lucky nodded to a wide-eyed footman. "Take the lady's pelisse, bonnet, and gloves."

She hastily handed off her garments, preparing to follow Lucky on the familiar path to Archer's study. But the butler stopped her with a splayed hand.

"You're to stay where you are until I say so," he growled.

It would seem that the tentative friendship they'd forged during her time here had faded. She supposed she ought not to be surprised. It had been four months, after all. Over one-quarter of a year. So much had changed.

What if Archer had changed as well?

Her stomach lurched.

What if he had found someone else during the time she had been gone?

A new knot of apprehension tightening in her belly, Stasia watched the mountainous butler stalking down the hall until he was out of sight. She twisted her fingers in the voluminous skirt of her gown, worrying the fine muslin until she was sure it was wrinkled.

Finally, footsteps sounded.

Harried ones, moving with undeniable haste.

Archer rounded a bend, striding into the marble-lined hall, tall, strong, and every bit as handsome as she remembered. He had a beard now, and his hair was even longer than it had been, held back at his nape with a queue. He stopped when he saw her, their eyes clashing, as if their enmeshed stares had a physical effect upon him.

Green eyes burned into hers.

"Your Royal Highness." His voice was hoarse as he offered her an eloquent bow.

"Just Stasia, if you please," she said, finding the courage to move toward him.

His brow furrowed. "I don't understand. You are a queen now, are you not? Why are you not in Varros where you belong?"

She stopped before Archer, near enough to touch. Was he leaner now than he had been? Were the angles of his face somehow harsher, as if he had found the last four months as punishing as she had?

"I'm not in Varros because that's not where I belong," she said simply.

She drank him in, realizing he was in his shirtsleeves and waistcoat, a flash of gold pinned over his heart that she recognized as her mother's coat of arms. The pendant from the necklace she had given him.

He hadn't forgotten, then.

His eyes were traveling over her too. Feasting on her, as if he were starved for the sight of her. "Why do you not belong in Varros?" he demanded. "That is where your husband the king is, is he not?"

"That is where the king of Varros is," she agreed, smiling. "With his queen."

Archer worked his jaw, as if searching for words. "I don't understand."

"King Maximilian married my lady-in-waiting," she explained. "I'm not in Varros because the war is over, my brother is the king of Boritania, and I'm free to be where I truly belong." She paused, summoning the rest of her courage. "At your side. That is, of course, supposing you still wish me there."

Shock washed over his features, his sensual lips falling open. "You didn't marry him."

She shook her head. "No. How could I, when he isn't the man I love?"

"But your sisters," he rasped, "your brother. The revolution."

"My sisters are safe, as is my brother, and the revolution is won. I returned to you as soon as I was able."

"Fucking hell." He shook his head, reaching for her, hauling her into his broad chest at last.

It felt like coming home. Because he was her home. Not Boritania, not Varros. This man she loved. Only, forever, always, *him*.

She wrapped her arms around his neck, staring up at his beloved face. "And I hope we might have a lifetime of you being a bad influence on me and teaching me more words in English that I shouldn't say, just like those."

"My God, Princess. You've come back to me." With a shaking hand, he cupped her face, his touch reverent, almost as if he couldn't believe she was standing before him. "I've dreamt of this so many nights, only to wake up alone, longing for you."

"How could I not come back to you? You have my heart, Archer Tierney." She turned her head, kissing his palm. "Will you marry me?"

He laughed then, a smile more beautiful than any she had ever seen transforming his face. "I believe I'm meant to ask you that, love."

"Ask me, then," she urged him, hope burgeoning inside her, bright and glorious, all her fears, all the time and distance that had separated them, falling instantly away.

They were Archer and Stasia again, man and woman, their love triumphing over everything and everyone that had stood in their way. Together again.

"Princess Anastasia Augustina St. George," he said, love for her shining in his eyes so potent and tender that she felt an answering prick of happy tears in her own, "will you pay me the honor of being my wife?"

Stasia didn't hesitate. "Yes."

"Yes?" he asked, still grinning.

"Yes," she repeated, falling into the emerald depths that had haunted her dreams so many nights. "Nothing would please me more."

He lifted her from the floor, spinning her around with a celebratory cry, before planting a long, lusty kiss on her lips.

A kiss that was interrupted by an indelicate snort.

Archer set her back on her feet, and they both returned to their surroundings to find Lucky watching them, a scowl on his face.

"Not in the mood to cast up my accounts all over the marble," he grumbled. "Off to a room with the two of you. I'd like to save my dinner."

It was Lucky's way of wishing them happy, Stasia knew.

"Forgive us, old chum," Archer said wryly, taking Stasia's hand and tangling his fingers in hers. "Come, love. I believe we've some reacquainting to do."

Indeed, they did.

Stasia followed him. As they ascended the stairs side by side, it occurred to her, just as it had once before, that she would follow this man to the gates of Hades and beyond. That was how right it felt to be at his side, in his care, their fingers entwined.

But this time, those discoveries were every bit as reassuring and welcomed as the future awaiting them both.

EPILOGUE

*A*rcher had a suspicion that, when the gossips wrote about the Duke and Duchess of Ridgely's ball on the morrow, every last one would feature an extravagant account of Princesses Emmaline and Annalise St. George dressed in gentlemen's trousers. The fête had already proven ample fodder for scandal broth.

Included on the guest list were an unusual number of foreign royals, one of whom was currently dancing in his arms for a waltz.

"Your sisters certainly made a stir this evening," he told Stasia as they linked hands and spun about the dance floor.

Both Emmaline and Annalise had recently made their debut in London, and they were setting the *ton* on its ear with their complete disregard for decorum. After ten years of being beneath their uncle's brutal thumb, the princesses were clearly savoring every moment of their newfound freedom. And good for them, he thought.

"The trousers, you mean?" Stasia asked with an approving grin. "In Boritania, it isn't such an uncommon sight, but I well understand the shock here in London. I did warn them, but you know how my sisters are."

"Every bit as stubborn as someone else I know," he teased.

He couldn't help but notice that his wife was looking astoundingly lovely this evening, wearing a purple evening gown trimmed with gold, her eyes gleaming in the glow of the chandeliers overhead, her summer-berry lips tempting him mightily, despite the fact that they were surrounded by a crush of guests.

Theodoric—King Theodoric, though the title still felt deuced odd to Archer—and his queen Pamela, the former Marchioness of Deering, had made the journey to London in anticipation of the princesses' first Season. While the king and his wife would be returning to Boritania soon, Archer and Stasia would be playing host. He didn't know a damned thing about launching two princesses into Society. Hell, he didn't know a damned thing about polite Society itself. Fortunately, his wife seemed more than prepared to take her wayward sisters in hand and act as guide.

"If I weren't so stubborn, I wouldn't have risked everything to find my way back to you," Stasia reminded him tartly.

"A fact which I am grateful for daily," he said, spinning them again and taking the opportunity to pull his beloved wife a bit closer than was proper.

But he didn't give a damn. He was hopelessly in love with the woman in his arms, and he didn't care who knew it. She was his, and he couldn't have been prouder of that fact.

"Do you think Emmaline and Annalise will be snubbed for their unusual ways?" she asked worriedly as one of the princesses whirled by them with an earl, followed by a smiling and clearly in love Duke of Ridgely and his duchess. "I should hate for my sisters to be unhappy here."

"They seem to have no shortage of dance partners," he observed, for it was true.

King Theodoric and Queen Pamela waltzed by, gazing at each other like a pair of lovesick pups. Beyond them, the other princess danced with a duke. It was a dazzling affair, and Ridgely and his duchess had spared no expense.

But all the gilt and sparkling jewels and gold paled in comparison to the true gem before him.

"I only hope that they can each find a husband to love them the way you love me," Stasia told him with a soft smile that he recognized all too well.

It was usually the one she wore just before she seduced him.

He felt an answering twitch in his cock and cleared his throat. "It is easy to love you, Princess. I've loved you from the moment we first met."

"The first moment?" She raised a brow. "Truly?"

He led them in another turn and leaned down so that his lips grazed her ear as he spoke. The soft swell of her belly, where their child grew, brushed tantalizingly against him. "It was either that moment or when you propositioned me. Both are equally memorable."

"You embarrass me," she said with a very undignified giggle.

"I love you," he said. "And I happen to know you haven't the capacity for embarrassment. It's quite Boritanian of you."

She gave him an arch look, catching her full lower lip in her teeth in the way that never failed to drive him mad with desire. "Guilty, my darling. And you know that I love you too."

"How soon until we can leave?" he muttered. "I want you desperately."

And he couldn't abide by balls. But he had come in a show of support for the princesses and his family and friends. Even his half sister Portia was in attendance, along with her husband, Wolf Sutton. It would have been desperately rude had he avoided the event, regardless of how much he hated to be respectable.

His wife's lips twitched as if she could read his thoughts. "Just a bit longer, or it will be terribly impolite of us, and no doubt remarked upon as well."

"What if I told you I had some more wicked English words to teach you?" he teased as the waltz drew to a close.

"How does an hour sound, my wicked rogue?" she asked, eyes sparkling.

"It sounds perfect, Princess." He winked. "As long as you agree to meet me in an accommodating alcove in ten minutes."

His bold and daring princess held his gaze, smiling back at him. "How about five?"

～

THANK you so much for reading Archer and Stasia's love story. I hope that you enjoyed their happily ever after and that you fell in love with my fairytale kingdom the way I did. In fact, I fell in love with it so much that I'm starting a new spinoff series, Royals and Renegades, with stories for Tansy and King Maximilian (*How to Love a Dangerous Rogue*) and the scandalous princesses Emmaline and Annalise. Read on for a sneak peek at Tansy and Maximilian's story!

Please stay in touch! The only way to be sure you'll know what's next from me is to sign up for my newsletter here: http://eepurl.com/dyJSar. Please join my reader group for early excerpts, cover reveals, and more here. And if you're in the mood to chat all things steamy historical romance and read a different book each month, join my book club, Dukes Do It Hotter right here: https://www.face

book.com/groups/hotdukes because we're having a whole lot of fun!

If you're starting the series here, you can find the Duke of Ridgely's story in *Her Ruthless Duke* and Beast/Theodoric's story in *Her Dangerous Beast*. Archer's half sister Portia's story appears in *Sutton's Scoundrel*, and Archer himself appears throughout *The Sinful Suttons* series.

∽

How to Love a Dangerous Rogue
Royals and Renegades
Book One

LADY TANSY FRANCIS has been a loyal lady-in-waiting for most of her life. In the eyes of the *ton*, she has come to London for the formal betrothal announcement of the princess who is like a sister to her. But secretly, Tansy has become caught up in the plans for a revolution in her homeland. She finds herself with no choice but to join forces with the last person she should ever trust, a coldhearted man who is feared by many: the king to whom the princess is about to announce her betrothal.

King Maximilian of Varros has a reputation that precedes him as a brutal, callous ruler who has stopped at nothing to claim his throne. After many long years of war, he has forged peace in his kingdom. But that peace is being threatened, and he'll burn everything and everyone to the ground to save it. There are only a few obstacles standing in his path, and one of them happens to be a fearless lady-in-waiting he can't stop wanting.

Tansy's allegiance is to the princess, but King Maximilian has no qualms about seizing whatever he desires, consequences be damned. With the fires of revolution lit and chaos swirling around them, their passion is forbidden and yet impossible to resist. Trapped between old loyalties and new longings, Tansy has to make the most difficult choice of all—risk her heart for a dangerous rogue, or watch as he marries her best friend.

Chapter One

THE KING of Varros had arrived.

The approach of the carriage in the streets below had warned her, along with the rustle of frantic movement in the hall beyond the chamber, the raised voices, the hastening footsteps. She hadn't expected him.

Not now. Not today. Not yet.

"Perdition," Tansy swore, then added another vicious Boritanian oath for good measure as she plumped the pillows beneath the counterpane on the princess's bed, a fine sheen of sweat on her brow.

She didn't want to see the king alone, without Princess Anastasia acting as a necessary barrier. But it would seem, like much of her life, Tansy didn't have a choice in the matter.

For in that moment, the door opened to admit *him*.

She moved away from the bed instantly, as if the empty piece of furniture had singed her hand, guilt warring with trepidation within her.

King Maximilian was obscenely tall and broad, seeming to take up half the chamber with his entrance. His size, in this instance, was fortuitous as it meant the guard in the hall couldn't spy the empty bed in which the princess was meant to be reclining as an invalid, nor the pillows which were a poor imitation of her feminine form.

The door clicked closed, and Tansy watched as the king

raised a massive paw to latch it in place, trapping her with him.

Alone.

He turned to her slowly, his brown eyes dark and unreadable, mouth grim and unsmiling. "You've a vicious tongue, Lady Tansy."

His English bore the traces of a Varrosian accent, but was otherwise flawless.

Sweet Deus above, had he heard her cursing? How? She had been muttering to herself, not shouting. Tansy felt lightheaded at the prospect, knowing full well that he could punish her for daring to utter such an oath in the presence of the king.

Belatedly, she remembered herself, dipping into a curtsy. "Your Royal Highness."

"Repeat it," he ordered curtly.

Tansy had just straightened to her full height, which wasn't considerable under any circumstances, and most certainly not when in the presence of the King of Varros, who towered over her as mightily as any mountain. But she dipped again, offering him a protracted curtsy, making extra effort.

"Your Royal Highness," she said.

"Not that." He flicked his hand in a dismissive gesture. "What came before it."

Curse the devil. He *had* heard. She didn't dare repeat the Boritanian oath. Literally translated to English, it meant *May God rot your cock.*

Decidedly not the sort of thing one said to a king, particularly one as menacing and imposing as the monarch before her.

"I beg your pardon, Your Royal Highness," she offered, bowing her head in a show of humility that she hoped would appease him. "I said nothing else."

He had drawn nearer. Soundlessly, which was impressive for a man so large in stature. With her head bowed, she saw the perfectly gleaming black boots—as immense as every other part of him—a mere foot away. The hair on the back of her neck rose.

"You dare to lie to me?" he demanded, his voice deceptively low.

It was the quietness that frightened her most. The stories of the horrors King Maximilian had visited upon his enemies were legion. He had battled for years to emerge the victor and assume the throne that was rightfully his, sparing no one.

Ruthless.
Pitiless.
Unfeeling.

Those were a scant few of the whispers Tansy had heard about him.

"I would never presume to lie to you, Your Royal Highness," she fibbed, head still bent, praying he would cease toying with her.

"Look at me, Lady Tansy."

She didn't want to. Particularly not given the king's troubling proximity. So near that she could detect his scent, spice and musk with a hint of leather and citrus. A pleasant scent. Altogether not one she would have expected of a man like him, but she had never previously been near enough to take note. She supposed it stood to reason that conscienceless murderers might smell as lovely as anyone else.

Tansy took a deep, shaky breath. "Forgive me, Your—"

"I said *look at me*," he interrupted, enunciating each of the words as sharply as if he wielded a whip.

She lifted her head and wished she hadn't. He was even closer than she had supposed, presiding over her like one of the old gods her ancestors had worshiped. Fierce and fearsome, his face a collection of angular blades—wide jaw, high cheekbones, a stern nose. A fine scar marred the skin above one of his slashing brows, a shocking hint of a past vulnerability. His black hair brushed over his broad shoulders, twin patches of silver at his temples. There were amber flecks in the dark-brown depths of his eyes, and his mouth was almost cruel to look upon, sensual and full lips so harsh and unyielding.

And then those lips moved. "Say it again, Lady Tansy."

She swallowed hard, her stomach knotting. Now she had done it. All these years of avoiding the wrath of the usurper Boritanian King Gustavson, and one foolish oath had ruined her.

In a quiet voice, she repeated the curse and then waited, shoulders tense, stomach swimming with agony, for a blow. For a cuff to the side of the head for her insolence. Everyone knew how brutal the King of Varros was.

"Are you a sorceress, madam?" he growled, the tone of his voice low and deep.

The question took her by surprise.

Confusion made her brow furrow. "Of course not, Your Royal Highness."

"Good, for I do not wish for my cock to rot off."

She stared at him, aghast. The King of Varros did not jest. Did he? No, it simply wasn't possible. And there was nary a hint of levity in his immovable countenance. Was there? The man could have been carved in marble, though she very much doubted he would be cool and smooth to the touch. Something told her he would be quite hot.

At the errant and most unwelcome thought, she nearly choked. The result was a strangled sound that was most unmannerly.

"Are you well?" he asked, his gaze narrowing.

No, she was not well. She was alone with a merciless

tyrant who would soon be marrying the princess who had become like a sister to her over the years she had spent as Princess Anastasia's lady-in-waiting. Tansy couldn't bear to hold his gaze. Her head dropped, her gaze falling to the carpet.

"I beg Your Royal Highness's forgiveness," she mumbled, still stricken by her lapse.

How could she have been so foolish as to exclaim the vile oath aloud?

She blamed the hours she had spent waiting for Princess Anastasia's return, fretting and fearing on her behalf.

"I asked if you are well," he reminded pointedly.

She was aware of him shifting; there was a rustle of fabric, his long arm stretching toward her slowly.

Would he strike her now, then?

"Very well, thank you, Your Royal Highness," she managed, scarcely moving her lips.

"Hmm," was all he said, his voice of steel and ice. And then his finger was on her chin, rough and firm and yet surprisingly gentle, urging it upward. Making her meet his gaze again. "I won't hurt you, if that is what you fear. Does King Gustavson strike the women in his court?"

The bloodied lashes she had tended on the princess's back rose in Tansy's mind, and she had to bite back the bile rising in her throat. She should lie, for the tale was not hers to tell. But with his fathomless gaze holding her in thrall, she couldn't seem to find the words. Still, she needed to say something. The king had spoken to her. Had asked her a question.

"I—" she began, only for his finger to settle in the bow of her upper lip, staying further explanation.

"You've answered me well enough," he interrupted.

As quickly as he had reached for her, he withdrew his touch, before spinning on his heel and stalking toward the door. He unlatched and wrenched it open. Then, he strode out, closing it smartly at his back, somehow taking the air from the room with him.

Tansy stared at the paneled door, holding her breath.

The only sounds were more muffled voices and booted footsteps disappearing down the hall, both finally supplanted by the rhythmic ticking of a mantel clock. The jangling of tack interrupted, rising from the street below. And still the door remained closed.

Tansy waited, lip tingling where King Maximilian had laid his finger.

Want more? Get *How to Love a Dangerous Rogue* now here!

DON'T MISS SCARLETT'S OTHER ROMANCES!

Complete Book List
HISTORICAL ROMANCE

Heart's Temptation
A Mad Passion (Book One)
Rebel Love (Book Two)
Reckless Need (Book Three)
Sweet Scandal (Book Four)
Restless Rake (Book Five)
Darling Duke (Book Six)
The Night Before Scandal (Book Seven)

Wicked Husbands
Her Errant Earl (Book One)
Her Lovestruck Lord (Book Two)
Her Reformed Rake (Book Three)
Her Deceptive Duke (Book Four)
Her Missing Marquess (Book Five)
Her Virtuous Viscount (Book Six)

DON'T MISS SCARLETT'S OTHER ROMANCES!

League of Dukes
Nobody's Duke (Book One)
Heartless Duke (Book Two)
Dangerous Duke (Book Three)
Shameless Duke (Book Four)
Scandalous Duke (Book Five)
Fearless Duke (Book Six)

Notorious Ladies of London
Lady Ruthless (Book One)
Lady Wallflower (Book Two)
Lady Reckless (Book Three)
Lady Wicked (Book Four)
Lady Lawless (Book Five)
Lady Brazen (Book 6)

Unexpected Lords
The Detective Duke (Book One)
The Playboy Peer (Book Two)
The Millionaire Marquess (Book Three)
The Goodbye Governess (Book Four)

The Wicked Winters
Wicked in Winter (Book One)
Wedded in Winter (Book Two)
Wanton in Winter (Book Three)
Wishes in Winter (Book 3.5)
Willful in Winter (Book Four)
Wagered in Winter (Book Five)
Wild in Winter (Book Six)
Wooed in Winter (Book Seven)
Winter's Wallflower (Book Eight)
Winter's Woman (Book Nine)
Winter's Whispers (Book Ten)

DON'T MISS SCARLETT'S OTHER ROMANCES!

Winter's Waltz (Book Eleven)
Winter's Widow (Book Twelve)
Winter's Warrior (Book Thirteen)
A Merry Wicked Winter (Book Fourteen)

The Sinful Suttons
Sutton's Spinster (Book One)
Sutton's Sins (Book Two)
Sutton's Surrender (Book Three)
Sutton's Seduction (Book Four)
Sutton's Scoundrel (Book Five)
Sutton's Scandal (Book Six)
Sutton's Secrets (Book Seven)

Rogue's Guild
Her Ruthless Duke (Book One)
Her Dangerous Beast (Book Two)
Her Wicked Rogue (Book 3)

Royals and Renegades
How to Love a Dangerous Rogue (Book One)

Sins and Scoundrels
Duke of Depravity
Prince of Persuasion
Marquess of Mayhem
Sarah
Earl of Every Sin
Duke of Debauchery
Viscount of Villainy

Sins and Scoundrels Box Set Collections
Volume 1
Volume 2

DON'T MISS SCARLETT'S OTHER ROMANCES!

The Wicked Winters Box Set Collections
Collection 1
Collection 2
Collection 3
Collection 4

Stand-alone Novella
Lord of Pirates

CONTEMPORARY ROMANCE
Love's Second Chance
Reprieve (Book One)
Perfect Persuasion (Book Two)
Win My Love (Book Three)

Coastal Heat
Loved Up (Book One)

ABOUT THE AUTHOR

USA Today and Amazon bestselling author Scarlett Scott writes steamy Victorian and Regency romance with strong, intelligent heroines and sexy alpha heroes. She lives in Pennsylvania and Maryland with her Canadian husband, adorable identical twins, and two dogs.

A self-professed literary junkie and nerd, she loves reading anything, but especially romance novels, poetry, and Middle English verse. Catch up with her on her website https://scarlettscottauthor.com. Hearing from readers never fails to make her day.

Scarlett's complete book list and information about upcoming releases can be found at https://scarlettscottauthor.com.

Connect with Scarlett! You can find her here:
 Join Scarlett Scott's reader group on Facebook for early excerpts, giveaways, and a whole lot of fun!
 Sign up for her newsletter here
 https://www.tiktok.com/@authorscarlettscott

- facebook.com/AuthorScarlettScott
- twitter.com/scarscoromance
- instagram.com/scarlettscottauthor
- bookbub.com/authors/scarlett-scott
- amazon.com/Scarlett-Scott/e/B004NW8N2I
- pinterest.com/scarlettscott

Made in the USA
Coppell, TX
17 April 2024